HEXMAKER

Other books from Jordan L. Hawk:

Hainted

Whyborne & Griffin:
Widdershins
Threshold
Stormhaven
Necropolis
Bloodline
Hoarfrost
Maelstrom
Fallow

Spirits:
Restless Spirits
Dangerous Spirits

Hexworld
The 13th Hex (prequel short story)
Hexbreaker
Hexmaker

SPECTR
Hunter of Demons
Master of Ghouls
Reaper of Souls
Eater of Lives
Destroyer of Worlds
Summoner of Storms
Mocker of Ravens
Dancer of Death

Short stories:
Heart of the Dragon
After the Fall (in the *Allegories of the Tarot* anthology)
Eidolon (A Whyborne & Griffin short story)
Remnant, written with KJ Charles (A Whyborne & Griffin / Secret Casebook of Simon Feximal story)
Carousel (A Whyborne & Griffin short story)

Hexmaker

Hexworld 2

Jordan L. Hawk

Hexmaker © 2016 Jordan L. Hawk
ISBN: 978-1537719757

All rights reserved.

Cover art © 2016 Jordan L. Hawk

This book is a work of fiction. Names, characters, places, and incidents are products of the author's imagination or are used fictitiously. Any resemblance to actual events or locales or persons, living or dead, is entirely coincidental.

Chapter 1

Malachi glanced casually back and forth along the alleyway, checking for any watching eyes. Earlier rain had left the pavement damp, and a brisk wind funneled down the narrow slot between mansions, biting through his threadbare coat. The electric lights of Fifth Avenue barely penetrated the shadows where he stood, but even in human form his night vision was better than the average person's. Not as good as when he put on his fur, of course, but he needed hands for tonight's work.

He stepped back and inspected the side of the gothic revival mansion in front of him. He'd already looked it over half a dozen times, slinking down the alley in fox form at night, or boldly strolling to the servants' entrance while disguised as an eyeglasses peddler during the day. The latter ruse had gotten him access to the kitchens, where he'd met a particular maid with a black eye and a grudge against her employer.

Still, he hadn't stayed out of the hands of the coppers by not being careful. The wall looming above him was clad in pale yellow marble, though no fancy carvings or fantastic gargoyles looked out over an alley that would only be seen by servants and tradesmen. The windows on this side mostly opened onto servants' passages and quarters, and all showed only darkness.

The sound of clopping hooves and the rumble of carriage wheels echoed even at this late hour, but distantly. There was some sort of dinner party going on further down Millionaires' Row, but no one stirred in any of the neighboring mansions so far as Mal could tell. Everyone either out or tucked safely into bed until morning.

Perfect.

Mal removed the shoes he'd worn on the trip over and pushed them against the downspout, which would hopefully help conceal them. A second pair of shoes waited in the small satchel he carried, and he slung them around his neck by their knotted laces. The satchel he placed in the deep shadows. Sophie stood lookout near the entrance to the alley, so it ought to be safe from any thief happening by.

Any other thief, that is.

He shimmied up the downspout with the ease of long practice, until he reached the second floor window. Even though the narrow window only provided light and air to a servants' passage, it still bore an alarm hex. *Guaranteed to stop any thief,* the ads claimed…so long as said thief didn't know the disarming phrase, at least.

Leaning close to the cold glass, Mal whispered, *"The robb'd that smiles, steals something from the thief; He robs himself that spends a bootless grief."*

The bit of Shakespeare didn't make any obvious difference, but unless the maid who'd given him the phrase had lied, the alarm hex ought to be disarmed now. A quick application of a jimmy, and he was in.

Mal paused, half over the sill, listening for any sounds of disturbance. Nothing came to his ears, so he slithered the rest of the way inside and pulled the window shut behind him. He removed the shoes from around his neck, unknotted the laces, and slipped them on. One of the witches in Madam Galpern's pay had drawn hexes on the soles, before he and Sophie made their way over here. The chalk would wear off with every step, so he needed to move quickly and directly as possible.

He counted himself lucky Madam Galpern had given him the job, let alone the hexes. She'd been introducing him to witches for the last three years, hoping he'd meet one he liked enough to bond with. She hadn't pressured him, but he knew she had her hopes up. More magic was always useful, both in her legitimate profession as a haberdasher and her less legitimate profession at the center of the East Side's largest ring of thieves.

But she'd come through for him, just as she always did. Other than Sophie, no one else had ever seen much use in him, and he was damned fortunate to work for her.

Sophie had done her own bit with the maid of a frequent guest of

Mrs. Jacobs, and passed along the second floor layout to Mal. He pictured the rough map he'd memorized earlier, then hurried down the passage to a discreet door. The hexed shoes made no sound against the wood, and the boards failed to creak beneath his weight.

According to Sophie, Jacobs was storing his new acquisitions in the library while sorting through them. Moving on his soundless shoes, Mal slipped out of the servants' passage into the main house. The door hinges were oiled to silence, no doubt to avoid an outburst of Jacobs's infamous temper, allowing Mal to pass like a ghost.

Even in the dim light leaking from the street, the room he found himself in took his breath away. Decorative woodwork covered the eggshell walls, all of it gilded. The furniture matched: spindly legged tables, carved to within an inch of their lives and covered in gold leaf, no less than two couches and a half dozen chairs of the same sort, a piano, and a sideboard. Luxurious carpets concealed most of the floor. Four huge bouquets of hothouse flowers perfumed the air.

Amazing to think anyone lived like this, when only a few blocks away thousands of people were packed into the tenements of the Tenderloin district. The tiny flat he shared with two others above a saloon would fit into this one room a dozen times over. According to the crude map Sophie had drawn, this was the "petite" salon. The grand salon was twice the size.

A small snuffbox, crusted with diamonds, sat on one of the delicate tables. Mal was here for one thing, and one thing only: a golden pendant wrested from some pharaoh's tomb. How Madam Galpern meant to sell such a recognizable object, he didn't know—that was her business, not his. Some other collector, probably, who just wanted the thing to look at.

Taking anything else, even something as portable as the snuffbox, might someday be used to link him to tonight's work. But it was sitting right there, diamonds winking in the faint light coming through the window panes. Even if he couldn't sell off the whole thing, prizing out the gems would buy more than a few drinks at Caballus.

He snatched it up and put it in his pocket. Madam Galpern would know how to sell it, and if she didn't, there were plenty of other fences in New York.

Mal let himself into the hall—lined with oil paintings probably worth enough to buy the whole block he lived on. The door to the library stood open a crack, and a thin beam of light fell through it. Mal froze at the sight.

Someone was awake after all. An under servant, hoping to get a look at his employer's new treasures? Jacobs himself, in search of a bit of late-night reading?

Either way, he had only two choices. The first was to go back the way he'd come, slip outside, collect Sophie, and try another night. Which meant their cut of the job would be even smaller, because they'd have to pay for new hexes on his shoes. Mal was already behind on his rent—though of course, the diamond snuffbox would help with that.

Or he could stay. See who was in there, and maybe wait for them to leave. Whoever they were, they'd probably just go back to bed once they were finished. He wouldn't get caught.

Holding his breath, Mal slunk to the door. Pressing his eye to the crack, he peered inside.

The steady blue glow of hexlights showed a room whose two-story-high walls were lined with books. Most of the desks and furniture inside had been pushed back to make room for a large number of packing crates. Some had already been opened and their contents piled on the floor or the desks. An entire mummy case, a bowl that looked cast from solid silver, a marble statue, and dozens of golden rings and arm bands—and that was just what Mal could see from the door.

He could also see the edge of what looked like a spreading pool of blood.

What the devil? Had someone been hurt? The servants hated Jacobs for good reason. Had he found one of them in here, admiring what they weren't entitled to, and flown into a rage?

Mal ought to turn around and go back the way he'd come. But it was the middle of the night. If the person in the room was badly hurt, they might die if no one found them before morning.

He had to at least check.

Holding his breath, Mal pushed the door open and slipped inside.

A man in a nightshirt lay sprawled across the marble floor, a dropped pistol not far from his hand. Blood spread from his head, which looked oddly misshapen. A heavy alabaster vase lay beside him, covered in red.

Mal's fingers turned to ice, and his heart knocked against his ribs. His feet seemed to move without his volition, carrying him across the floor to crouch beside the man. If the fellow was dead, Mal was leaving, Madam Galpern's pendant be damned. If not...Mal wasn't certain what he'd do. Sneak out and shout for help from the street, maybe. Find some way to rouse the house so the poor bugger could get assistance.

A flicker of movement out of the corner of his eye caught Mal's attention. He spun and found a man standing behind him.

Mal caught a confused impression of a narrow face and hair as red as his own, of hands holding something square and metal—maybe with the intent of bashing in Mal's skull just as the other fellow's had been.

He acted on instinct, exploding up from his crouch and ramming his head into the man's stomach. All the air left the man's lungs in a whoosh, and he fell backward, the object tumbling from his grip.

It hit the marble floor and burst apart. What looked like clockwork gears rolled in every direction, tracing trails through the pool of blood, and flat metal plates clattered hellishly loud over the inlaid floor.

The man snarled in fury. He started to reach for the parts, then stopped, perhaps realizing there was no point. Locking his eyes on Mal's, he backed up against the wall, to where a display case containing other treasures had been moved to make room for the new shipment.

Then he reached out and deliberately wrenched open the case.

The alarm hex went off instantly. An eerie voice rose in a disembodied wail: *"Thief! Thief! Thief!"*

Why the fellow had deliberately set off an alarm, Mal couldn't guess and wasn't going to wait to find out. He bolted out of the room and down the hall, all thought of concealment or subtlety banished. Other, more human, voices raised in alarm to join that of the hex. The sound of running feet in the service passage caused Mal to veer off, just in time for a maid to throw open the door and let out a scream at the sight of him.

Damn it.

He raced for the front of the house. Two men in nightshirts made their way down the hall leading to the foyer, blocking Mal's path.

"Stop!" one shouted. "Thief! He's here!"

Mal didn't slow, instead charging directly at them. Between one heartbeat and the next, he shifted into his fox shape. Instantly the hall became brighter, and the men loomed above him, their flailing arms high over his head. He slid between the legs of one, the hem of the nightshirt catching on his ears as he shot through the gap.

"A familiar!" the man bellowed. "He's a fox! Stop him!"

Mal raced full out for the balcony overlooking the foyer a story below. An enormous chandelier hung down from high above, and an elegant staircase curved along one wall of the oval room. A half-dressed footman crouched at the top of the stairs, blocking Mal's escape even in this form.

If he was caught, would they believe he wasn't in on it with the murderer? Or would the judge take one look at a redheaded Irishman and send him to the chair?

Best not to find out. Mal leapt for the balcony railing, shifting back to human form. One foot hit the rail, propelling him into the vast space of the foyer, its marble floor waiting twenty feet below.

He caught the edge of the chandelier in both hands. It swung beneath his weight: the iron hanger loop groaned, the crystals chimed, and plaster flaked down from the ceiling. For a moment, Mal feared he'd made a terrible mistake, and the whole thing would come crashing down on top of him.

It held. Mal swung with the chandelier, letting go as it reached the apex of its arc, momentum propelling him to the stairs. He slid down the polished oak bannister to the ground floor, even as the angry servants ran shouting down the stairs after him.

The huge front door lay before him. Sophie would have fled at the first sign of alarm within the house. All he had to do was get onto the street, shift into fox shape, and run until he reached the tenements a few blocks away. They'd never find him amidst the masses of humanity packed into the Tenderloin.

He flung back the bolt, ignoring the shrieking of yet another alarm hex as he hauled open the great door. Sprinting down the steps, he cast one last look over his shoulder—

And ran straight into a solid body. Hands closed on his arms, and he found himself staring directly at a broad, blue uniformed chest.

"Hold up there, boyo," the copper said.

"Let me go!" Mal cried, struggling to free himself.

An instant later, his back was pressed against the nearest lamppost, pinned there by the copper's larger bulk. "Running from a house with the alarm hexes shrieking fit to wake the dead?" Handcuffs snapped into place around Mal's wrists. "You're under arrest. Now, let's drag you inside and see just what it is I'm charging you with."

Owen Yates stepped onto the curb, checking his pocket watch. Nearly midnight—hours wasted at his mother's dinner party, when they would have been better spent in his laboratory at the Coven. He was so close to a breakthrough on a poison detection hex, which would indicate not just that a person had been poisoned, but identify the substance used. If he could only work out a reliable method for each of the common poisons, he might even be able to chain them together into a single hex. With such a hex, a doctor would have a chance to provide the right antidote in time, should the victim survive long enough.

Time was running out. If he wanted to make a positive contribution to the Metropolitan Witch Police—a *lasting* contribution—it had to be within the next six days.

One week from today, he would marry Edith Vandersee. It was one thing for the middle son of the Yates family to temporarily work at the MWP—after all, Roosevelt himself had been on the Police Board for a time. But after his elder brother, Peter, had his accident, Owen became the heir. His days at the Coven had been numbered, even before the engagement.

Once their brief honeymoon to Europe ended, Owen would join her father's business and spend his days working on industrial hexes. Or, more likely, looking over those produced by the hexmen the business employed, making sure they worked as needed, and patenting them before someone else could.

At least tonight's dinner party had been a small one, with less than a hundred guests in attendance. But then, the season wouldn't truly begin until after Thanksgiving. The wedding would be something of an opening event.

One week from today.

Edith was a kind woman. They were on good terms, having known each other since childhood. He'd gone to university at the same time as her older brother, Kirk. He would marry her and put aside his selfish dreams. Put aside the weaknesses that haunted him, the desires no one else must ever know about.

A carriage waited on the curb to take him to his apartment on the west side of town. As he stepped toward it, there came the clatter of hooves, the rumble of a conveyance traveling fast up Fifth Avenue. He paused to look, and was startled to see an MWP wagon rush past.

Frowning, he ignored the waiting carriage and walked to the corner. The house belonging to the Jacobs family was ablaze with light, as if someone had activated every hexlight in the place.

They hadn't been invited to Mother's little get together—Mr. Jacobs had tastelessly outbid Adam Vandersee, Owen's future father-in-law, for…Owen couldn't recall what. Both men were inveterate collectors of art and antiquities, and cycled through periods of enmity and friendship based on the outcome of various auctions. Perhaps Mrs. Jacobs had decided to host a competing party, even though doing so would risk complete social ostracism?

But no. The MWP wagon pulled to a stop outside, and a man in a blue uniform descended the stairs to meet it.

Owen ought to go home. Climb into the carriage and ask to be taken directly to the front door of his apartment building. He was a forensic hexman, not a detective. He'd never even been at a crime scene, unless one counted the horrible events of New Year's. Evidence came to him, not the other way around.

There was so little time left.

"I won't be needing your services after all," he told the carriage driver. Clutching his top hat to keep it from falling off, he jogged down the street to the Jacobs residence.

"Don't know if this is anything for your lot or not," the patrolman in the blue uniform was saying when Owen arrived. "There were hexes involved for sure, but it might just be a straightforward case of robbery gone wrong."

"What's the trouble?" Owen asked. "Dr. Owen Yates, MWP. I might—oh." To his surprise, he recognized the patrolman. "Bill Quigley, isn't it?"

Quigley looked equally startled, but nodded. "Aye, Dr. Yates. Wasn't expecting them to send a hexman over along with MacDougal here."

Ah, yes; MacDougal had returned from the recent war with Spain. Owen vaguely remembered hearing the news. "Oh, no; I was at a party." Owen waved at the Yates mansion. "At my parents' house. I saw the commotion and thought I might be of assistance."

MacDougal and Quigley exchanged a glance. MacDougal shrugged. "I'm just here for the body, sir."

"The body?" Owen asked.

"Aye." Quigley nodded. "Mr. Jacobs was murdered by an intruder less than an hour ago. The good news is, we already have the killer in custody."

God. Mr. Jacobs. Owen had known the man only socially, which meant he'd seen the fellow five or six times a year, then been expected to pretend that was enough to forge a lasting connection. He felt no particular sense of loss, but still…

The man was a millionaire. Not only a millionaire, but one with the requisite three generations separation from the original maker of the fortune, a distinction necessary to achieve real social status among the elite of New York. Men like Jacobs didn't get murdered in their homes.

There would be a panic. A scandal. The fate of the accused would be decided long before any trial.

"I see," Owen said. "May I view the scene?"

Chapter 2

"So," Quigley said as he led the way up the grand staircase to the second floor. Bits of plaster lay scattered across the marble foyer, and the chandelier appeared crooked, as if some weight had warped it. "That familiar we rescued New Year's Eve. Isaac."

"Yes?" Owen asked. He felt in his overcoat, patting the hexman's wallet inside. Carrying his tools with him so he could work on any idea which might come unexpectedly had become a bit of a habit.

"He's all right, then?" Quigley asked. "Doing well, I mean."

"Oh, yes," Owen said absently. "Quite recovered. Physically, that is. He's back with the MWP."

"Oh." Quigley frowned. "They're treating him right, though?"

"As far as I know." Owen shrugged. "You know how familiars are."

"Not really, sir."

The door to the library stood open. Just inside, two policemen loomed to either side of a handcuffed man seated in a chair. He was dressed in dark clothing, which made his absurdly bright red hair stand out even more. As Owen stepped inside, the man looked up.

Amber eyes fixed on Owen, piercing him to the core. He'd never seen a shade like that on anyone, at least not to his recollection. Combined with his brilliant red hair, a straight nose, and a mouth that seemed made to kiss…

All the air seemed to have drained from the room. His mouth went dry, and his cock swelled in reaction.

"This is the suspect," Quigley said. Mortified, Owen dragged his gaze away from the redhead in the chair.

"The suspect?" he repeated, like an idiot.

"Yes, sir. That's why he has the cuffs on."

"Oh. Quite." Owen glanced at the rest of the room and found his attention caught again, although this time for a far less pleasant reason.

Mr. Jacobs lay sprawled beside a pile of opened crates. The library reeked of blood, and Jacob's head was badly misshapen. An alabaster vase lay discarded on the floor beside the body. Blood and hair clung to its pale surface; clearly this had been the murder weapon.

Quigley cleared his throat. "Caught fleeing the scene, with this snuffbox in his pocket." He produced a silver snuffbox set with diamonds. Tiffany Company? Owen's mother would know. "It seems to be a simple case of theft gone wrong."

"Theft!" exclaimed the redhead in a broad Irish accent. "I ain't never heard such slander in my life! I want to talk to my lawyer."

"Shut it, you. You'll talk to your lawyer, assuming he even exists, once we've got you under lock and key." Quigley turned back to Owen. "His shoes are hexed to keep his steps quiet—old second-story man's trick, that. We figure Mr. Jacobs surprised him, so he grabbed the nearest weapon and walloped Jacobs over the head."

"It ain't true!" the redhead protested. "Maybe I was here for, ah, reasons of my own, but I ain't never hurt anyone. I don't hold with violence."

Owen wanted to believe the man. Which was foolish—just because he was good looking hardly meant he wasn't guilty. "What's your name?"

"Malachi," said the man—then looked surprised, as if he hadn't meant to answer. "I'm a familiar, so no last name to give." He hesitated, then cocked his head and flashed Owen a bright grin. "But you can call me Mal."

"Well then, Mal," Quigley began.

"It's Mr. Malachi to you," the familiar shot back.

Quigley heaved a sigh. "Mr. Malachi. If you didn't kill Mr. Jacobs, then who did?"

Owen turned his back on them both and bent down to inspect the body. Jacobs must have been standing with his back to his assailant—no defensive wounds.

"There was another man here." Mal sounded subdued. "Tall fellow. Redhead like me. I knocked that clock or whatever it was out of his hands."

"Clock?" Owen asked.

Quigley shrugged and gestured to a pile of gears, rods, and more esoteric pieces on one of the tables. All looked old, the bronze lightly pitted with age, and some were flecked with blood. "I had the men gather the pieces up, in case it's something valuable. I'd ask Mrs. Jacobs, but she ain't here. Servants don't seem quite sure where she is, other than she ain't expected back before morning."

A lover, most likely. Owen had heard no gossip about her at the party earlier. She must have been exceptionally discreet.

"I thought he was going to bash me over the head with it—murder me like Jacobs," Mal offered. "Fellow seemed pretty angry when I broke it, so I pulled foot. Can't blame me for that, can you?"

"You mean you killed Mr. Jacobs, then ran to save your own skin when you set the alarm hex off," Quigley said. Turning to Owen, he added, "We've got him dead to rights, sir. Take a look at this."

Quigley picked up the alabaster vase—Egyptian, it looked like, probably the bottom portion of a canopic jar. "That's Jacobs's hair." He pointed to the gray strands stuck to the jar with blood. "And this belongs to Mr. Malachi."

A single red hair clung to the jar, damningly out of place amidst the gray.

"I'm telling you, the murderer was a redhead, too!" Malachi exclaimed, rattling his handcuffs. "Ain't you listening?"

Owen frowned. Turning to Quigley, he said, "Are you certain Mr. Malachi—"

"Mal," the familiar piped up.

"Mal," Owen said, shooting an annoyed look at him. Mal offered him a cheeky grin in response. "Are you certain of his guilt?"

"Listen to the handsome detective," Mal said to Quigley. "He knows what he's about."

Handsome? Owen had been described as a great many things—scrawny, bookish, pompous—but this was the first time he recalled anyone ever calling him handsome.

And of course the man was a thief, who had most certainly not been in the Jacobs mansion for any innocent reason. Possibly he was an accomplice, even if he wasn't the actual murderer.

"I'm, ah, not a detective." Owen took off his spectacles and polished them; it gave his hands something to do, his gaze somewhere to rest besides the redheaded familiar who looked like he might snap Owen up whole, like a fox with a mouse. "I'm a forensic hexman with the MWP."

Quigley looked skeptical. "With all due respect, sir, it's the simplest answer. He's a thief—the snuffbox is proof of that. There's no evidence of any other intruder." He cast an unfriendly look at Mal. "Trust me, I deal with his type all the time. They'd lie to the Holy Familiar's face, and not think twice about it."

Owen shifted uncomfortably. He'd worked on the police force long enough to have become somewhat accustomed to the Irish Heresy, but he'd never entirely grow used to hearing it spoken so casually. "I'm sure you know your business," he agreed. "I can settle the matter now, if you wish."

Now both of them were looking at him skeptically. As were the two policemen standing watch over the prisoner. "That would be helpful," Quigley said cautiously. "How would that work, then?"

"I assume the housewitch is somewhere about? Good; have one of your men fetch her." Owen went to a table and spread out his wallet of hexman's tools. Selecting three squares of blank paper, he quickly drew up three hexes. Once the ink was dry, he beckoned Quigley over.

"It's quite simple," he said. "Perhaps you recall the unusual nature of the hexes used to disrupt the consolidation celebration on New Year's? They were chained together—the activation of one hex would change the effect of the second connected to it."

"Er," Quigley said. "If you say so, sir." The remaining patrolman looked equally blank. The familiar watched Owen with interest, however. His amber eyes gleamed in the hexlight, drawing Owen's gaze more firmly than the golden jewelry and glittering gemstones around them.

Owen brandished the hexes. Two of them were identical, both linked to the third. "We take the hair belonging to the presumed murderer and place it on one hex. A hair from Mr. Malachi—Mal—goes on the second. After we activate them both, we then activate the third hex. If the hairs are from the same person, the hex will turn black. If from different people, it will turn green."

Quigley looked impressed. "That is handy."

"And you created it yourself?" Mal asked.

"Yes," Owen said smugly.

"Well. I guess I'd better hope you know what you're doing."

Owen scowled. "I'm the MWP's first—and so far only—forensic hexman. I assure you, I achieved the position on my own merits." And not by buying his way to it, despite what some thought.

The other patrolman returned with the housewitch; a severe-looking older woman, her iron gray hair pulled up in a bun, the corners of her mouth turned down in disapproval. Her familiar, a small owl, rode on her shoulder.

At the sight of the corpse, she lost her disapproving look and turned a distinct shade of green. Still, she managed to say: "You s-sent for me, sir?"

"I simply need the hexes charged," Owen said, holding them out to her.

Focusing on the hexes rather than the body, she placed her hand on them one after the next. "If that's all…"

"It is. Thank you." Owen watched as she all but fled down the corridor. Her owl twisted its head about and stared back, though, until they were both gone.

Owen turned to the police. "Quigley, if you'd fetch a strand of the prisoner's hair."

It really was lovely hair: an intense, fiery orange-red that seemed brighter than anything else in the room. Combined with Mal's amber eyes, it made him look like something wild, the sort of being found beneath a fairy mound or in the depth of some untouched wood.

Owen shook his head at himself. What a bunch of nonsense. He needed to focus on the task at hand, not the familiar who inspired such absurd flights of fancy.

Quigley plucked a strand of hair free. "Ow!" Mal exclaimed. "That hurt. No need to be so rough, copper. I've got my rights."

The patrolman rolled his eyes. "You'll live." He handed the hair to Owen.

Owen carefully laid out the three hexes on the convenient surface of a display table. Placing Mal's hair on one of the hexes, he whispered the activation phrase. He took the hair from the alabaster jar and repeated the action with the second hex.

He hesitated, his gaze falling on the third hex, the one linked to both of the others. He shouldn't desire one outcome over another. If the hex turned black, it meant only that the charming familiar was a murderer as well as a thief. He shouldn't care one way or another about a man he'd met only a few minutes ago.

And yet, he couldn't help but hope…

"Reveal to me the truth," he said.

Green bloomed from the center of the hex.

Owen's shoulders sagged with unexpected relief. "Mr. Malachi is, if not precisely innocent, at least telling the truth. The hair belongs to someone else."

"I told you!" Mal held out his cuffed hands. "I'll thank you to be taking these off, then."

"I don't think so, thief," Quigley replied. Turning to Owen, he said, "So if there was another man here, where is he now? The staff didn't see anyone but Mr. Malachi, and with the whole house up in arms, it would have been hard for anyone else to sneak out. Where did he go?"

Owen slowly scanned the room. Other than the single door, the only ingress or egress seemed to be the windows. "Were any of the windows opened?"

Quigley shook his head. "The alarm hexes were still set on all of them."

"Which don't mean anything," Mal piped up, "if he had the phrases to disarm and set them."

"No one asked you," Quigley growled.

"Just trying to be helpful, patrolman." He grinned guilelessly at Quigley—then shot Owen a conspiratorial wink when Quigley turned his back in disgust.

Owen's face heated. Dear lord, the fellow was a menace. He looked away hurriedly. "The windows, then—is there any way to reach them from the outside? A convenient downspout or the like?"

"I've got the disarming phrase from the butler—hold up a minute," Quigley said. He went from window to window, speaking the phrase. Owen came after him and threw one open, leaning out. The room faced Fifth Avenue, and he could make out the familiar façade of the Yates mansion from here. It looked as though the last of the dinner party guests had left, and the lights were mostly out.

The street looked peaceful. Safe. No one in the surrounding mansions had the slightest idea that murder had come to Millionaires' Row, let alone that it had struck down one of their own.

"There are too many windows in this place," Quigley grumbled. "You two—give us a hand. Take the upper level."

The other two policemen left Mal handcuffed in the chair and hurried to the spiral stair leading to the library's second story. Owen went from the first window to the next, peering out, searching for any clue…

"Here," Quigley said abruptly. "See what you think of this, Dr. Yates."

He pointed to the carved sill outside the window. Something dark had recently stained the limestone. Owen leaned over and sniffed. "Blood. The killer must have gotten some on him, and brushed against the sill while opening the window."

Quigley scowled out. "Then where did he go from here? There's no downspout, and not enough carvings to climb down."

"No, but there are electrical wires." Owen pointed to the dark lines barely visible against the night. "A squirrel familiar, or something similar, could easily have jumped down to the wire and used it as a road."

"Blast." Quigley turned away from the window. "All right, Mr. Malachi, if you have any…"

The words trailed off. The chair where Mal had been seated was empty save for a pair of open handcuffs.

"For Christ's sake, I knew I should've taken the hexed shoes," Quigley groaned. "My captain's going to kill me for this."

Mal almost sobbed in relief when the saloon came into view. He'd run all the way from the Jacobs mansion, first in fox shape, then in human. His lungs burned, both from exertion and the cold air, and his heart thundered in his chest.

Except that no matter how far he ran, he kept seeing a lean form and silvery eyes surrounded by gold-rimmed glasses.

This couldn't be happening. This *wasn't* happening.

Thank heavens it was only a few blocks from Fifth Avenue to the heart of the Tenderloin. Even at this late hour, there were people out and about on the streets, every block packed with saloons, gambling rooms, coffee dives, and houses of assignation. A man and woman argued in Russian at the top of their lungs in the middle of the street as a night cart rattled past, trailing a foul stench behind.

The saloon occupied the first floor of the building where Mal rented an apartment. *Caballus* was painted on the window, the sign flaking and badly in need of repair. Beneath the saloon's name, a small hand-written placard declared: Familiars Only. The sign served as both a warning and a challenge to any witches who might happen by.

Light showed from between the saloon's drawn curtains. Shaking with exhaustion and gratitude, Mal stumbled through the door.

Caballus was shabby but cleaner than the average dive. At least, in this neighborhood; probably the silver-eyed man—Dr. Yates—did his drinking in some fancy joint like Hoffman House, with crystal glasses and velvet seats.

Fur and feathers, Mal had to stop thinking about him. Had to.

The bar was nothing more than a long board at one end of the room, balanced on barrels. A few men and women sat slumped around the scattering of mismatched tables. Most of them seemed to be asleep, which the owner Nick usually allowed for the price of a five-cent beer. The air smelled like vile whiskey and sweat, combined with the faint animal musk that accompanied ferals living together.

Thank Mary, Nick himself was behind the bar. Mal made his way through the tables and sprawled bodies, grabbed a chair, and planted his elbows on the bar. "Nick—thank the Good Lord you're here."

Nick continued his task of wiping down empty glasses with a mostly clean rag. He was a big man, brown skinned and black haired, with full lips and a broad nose. "What do you want, Mal?"

"I need your help." Mal licked his lips. "I'm in bad trouble, Nick."

Nick set the rag aside and filled the glass. Depositing it in front of Mal, he said, "Calm down. Is there a witch after you?"

Some of the tension between Mal's shoulders loosened. Nick kept a cudgel and a shotgun behind the bar, and he wouldn't hesitate to use either if a witch should come around, looking to force bond one of the ferals under his protection.

"Not exactly." Mal swallowed down the whiskey. It burned his throat like kerosene, but loosened the tight muscles at the back of his neck.

There were only a few people Mal would trust with the truth of what had happened, and Nick was near the top of the list. Even though his brother was an MWP detective, Nick had no patience with the law, or witches, or anything but the ferals no one else cared enough to look out for.

When Mal finished, Nick tossed his head, sending his long black hair flying like a mane. "I won't have you bringing trouble down on the rest of the colony, Mal. If the coppers are after you—"

"They know I'm innocent," Mal protested. "I mean, aye, they had me on the snuffbox, but they know I didn't kill anybody. I ain't looking to bring trouble down, Nick, I swear. It's just that…"

He could see those pewter eyes again, so clearly. Soft lips that parted in surprise. The pink flush staining high cheekbones, tinting otherwise ivory skin that looked to seldom see the sun.

"One of the MWP men there—Dr. Yates." Mal swallowed. "You ever heard of him?"

"What the devil do I care about some witch?" Nick asked. "Let alone one with the MWP."

"Come on, Nick. He was dressed like a nob. Said he was a forensic hexman. Your brother ain't said anything to you about him?"

Nick sighed. "Yeah, I suppose. He's one of *those* Yates. The ones who live on Millionaires' Row in their fancy mansion, with another mansion up in Newport or some such. Dr. Yates is the middle son, bunks over in one of those fancy apartment buildings by Central Park. The Folly, I think it's called. He's slumming with the MWP, though why I've no idea. Fucking useless parasite, even for a witch. What do you care?"

This was getting worse and worse. "He's...Dr. Yates...he's my witch."

Mal had never spent a great deal of time thinking about what he'd do if he encountered the witch whose ability to channel a familiar's magic was most compatible with his. And even if he had, he surely wouldn't have imagined some rich nob who blushed so prettily when Mal winked at him.

Nick snorted and stamped a foot. "Please say you didn't tell him."

"Of course not!" Mal shoved his empty glass away, leaving a wet streak across the rough plank of the bar. "He's a copper. A rich copper." And Mal was just a thief.

"He's a *witch*." Nick refilled the whiskey without being asked. "Fur and feathers, what more reason do you need? The MWP would love to get their filthy paws on you. On any of us."

Mal chewed his lip. "Your brother..."

"Don't bring my idiot brother into this." Nick scowled ferociously. "Rook couldn't wait to hand over his freedom in exchange for a full belly. He's some witch's tame crow, fat and happy. And to hell with the rest of us who want to live our own lives, without some *witch* telling us what to do."

"Aye," Mal said, subdued. "This one—Yates—has got money, though." Handsome, too, though Mal didn't say that part aloud.

Nick snorted again. "Rich nobs are *worse* than coppers, when it comes to treating their familiars like possessions. I hear they don't even let them take human form, except in front of the servants. You don't want to get involved with that sort, Mal. Trust me."

Nick was right. Still, Yates hadn't just jumped to conclusions like everyone else. Hadn't just assumed Mal was guilty.

If he hadn't been there, Mal would be sitting in the Tombs right now. Eventually gone to the electric chair for Jacobs's murder, if no one else thought to try the new hexes on the evidence.

Nick clapped him on the shoulder with a big hand. "Go upstairs to your bed, Mal," he said. "Get some rest. Everything will seem better in the morning."

Mal downed the second shot. "Aye," he said, subdued. "I'm sure you're right, Nick." He just had to lay low and forget about Yates. Forget about his silver-eyed witch.

With any luck, their paths would never cross again.

Chapter 3

Owen's morning was not going well.

He'd slept restlessly, and upon arising, found every newspaper in New York vying for the most lurid headline concerning the murder. THE MILLIONAIRE MURDER blared one, while another shrieked MILLIONAIRE SLAIN IN OWN HOME—IS ANYONE SAFE?

Breakfast had been interrupted no less than five times. His neighbors at The Folly Apartments knew he worked for the MWP, and Jacobs's murder frightened them in a way an ordinary violent death wouldn't have. Murder was viewed as something that occurred amongst the lower classes. For a man of Jacobs's wealth and status to be struck down in his own mansion, amidst all his hexes and servants and diamond crusted snuffboxes, hit rather too close to home.

Money made no man invincible. His older brother Peter had certainly proved that. But most of Owen's neighbors had escaped the brutal reality of such a lesson. Now, they flocked to his door like frightened chicks looking for a hen to protect them.

Giving up on breakfast, he took one of the elevators down from the seventh floor. It provided no escape.

"No, Mrs. Singer," he said as he exited into the lobby. "There is no truth to the rumor that a madman is going about killing the elite of this or any other city."

The middle aged woman clutched at his arm. The plumes of her hat bobbed into his face, and he resisted the urge to knock them away. "Are you certain?"

"Quite certain. Now, if you'll excuse me, I must get to work."

Her eyes widened. "On a Sunday morning?"

He smiled thinly. "Alas, those in my line of work must often break the Sabbath."

It wasn't strictly true—the business of the police went on seven days a week, but his efforts in the lab didn't have the same urgency as arresting criminals. Still, given the short duration of his remaining employment, it seemed a waste not to go in today.

Besides, if he went to church with his family, he'd be swarmed by terrified society matrons certain they were about to be murdered in their beds. A quiet morning in the lab seemed far preferable.

Soon, he was lost amidst the anonymous crowds on the Ninth Avenue El. As the train rattled and jerked along the track, he stared out alternately over the city and into the second floor apartments passing by.

Malachi was out there, somewhere.

Owen took a deep breath. He was just angry the familiar had made a fool of him and Quigley, that was all. That was the only reason he couldn't seem to stop thinking about the slender red-haired man, with the amber eyes and sly, vulpine grin.

Why had none of the men he'd been with looked like that? Clever and insolent. Not at all overawed by Owen. Mal would order Owen to his knees, snap the handcuffs around Owen's wrists for a change, and…

Owen shook himself sharply. What was wrong with him? He couldn't indulge this weakness, not even in fantasies. Not even when the subject of such a fantasy was a thief, a mere criminal whom Owen would never see again.

Reporters crowded the steps leading up to the Metropolitan Witch Police Headquarters—more casually known as the Coven. "Dr. Yates!" one shouted upon spotting him. "Do you have any comment to make on the murder of Mr. Jacobs?"

"Er, no." Why hadn't he realized reporters would be thronging every police building this morning, hungry for any scrap of news? "Please, let me through."

"Dr. Yates, is it true you were attending a party nearby, at your parents' mansion?"

"Dr. Yates, you were the MWP officer responding to the call—was Mr. Jacobs a personal friend?"

"Is it true you were brought to the scene to avoid word of a scandal getting out?"

"I have nothing to say!" he exclaimed. "Please, let me through!"

A large, imposing shape loomed up suddenly at Owen's side. "That's enough, you lot," said Tom Halloran, aiming a glare at the reporters. The black cat draped around his shoulders cracked open one eye, then shut it again. "Get back. Back, I said, if you value your toes."

Thankfully, the reporters gave way to Tom's imposing presence. Owen adjusted his spectacles as they stepped through the doors and into the Coven proper, leaving the newspapermen rushing away to file whatever reports they could fabricate from the brief exchange.

"Thank you, Tom," he said, brushing a flake of ash from his jacket. "Bunch of jackals."

The black cat leapt gracefully from Tom's shoulders, shifting on the way down. "What an awful racket," Cicero complained. "I hope they've cleared off by nap time."

"It's always nap time to you, cat," Tom retorted affectionately.

Owen looked away. He wasn't envious, precisely. Certainly not over a silly creature like Cicero. And of course, even if he found his familiar, they couldn't have the sort of relationship Cicero and Tom had. No one expected a simple policeman like Tom to marry out of duty. No one cared what he did in his spare time; no one expected him to always represent the height of propriety, even when alone.

It was churlish to envy that freedom. Owen's position in society gave him all the advantages of wealth; marriage to Edith was simply the price he was required to pay. Most people would envy his life, not Tom's.

"Dr. Yates?" called the witch at the front desk. "Chief Ferguson left word for you. You're to report straight to his office."

"Chief Ferguson is in today?" Owen asked in surprise.

"Uh oh," Cicero said with a smirk. "It sounds like someone's going to get a spanking."

Owen's mind flashed involuntarily to the redheaded feral, and his cheeks heated. "Don't be crude," he snapped.

Cicero arched a brow. "My, darling, you did wake up on the wrong side of the bed."

"I'm sure it's nothing to worry about, Owen," Tom said. "Ferguson probably wants to talk to you about last night, that's all."

Owen considered detouring to his laboratory long enough to take off his overcoat and hat. But Ferguson didn't ordinarily spend much time at the Coven on Sunday, which meant Tom was likely right, and it had something to do with Jacobs's murder. He squared his shoulders and set off through the maze of the Coven's halls.

The chief's office lay on the other side of a huge room filled with the desks of the witch and familiar detective teams. A crow drifted past, narrowly avoiding Owen's hat. Several cats milled about, and a frog shifted into a young man in the midst of a hop. Unbonded familiars wove through the crowd, gathering and delivering paperwork, and generally making themselves useful.

He rapped on the chief's door and received a muffled grunt in reply, which he took as permission to enter. As usual, Ferguson sat at his desk. His familiar Athene stood beside him, arms folded over her chest, her golden eyes unblinking.

"You wanted to see me?" Owen said warily. Athene preferred to spend time in owl form on her perch; he didn't know if the fact she greeted him in human shape was a bad sign.

Ferguson fixed him with a ferocious glower. He'd never been particularly awed or impressed by Owen's family ties. Owen had thought that a good thing, but now he wasn't so certain. "Want to see you? What I *want,* Yates, is to send you out the door with my boot in your arse."

Owen's throat tightened, threatening to cut off his air. "Sir?" he managed through the constriction.

"Why the devil didn't you leave well enough alone last night?" Ferguson ground his teeth together. "MacDougal and the patrolman, Quigley, had the matter in hand. You're a hexman—why did you find the need to go sticking your nose into a crime scene?"

Owen's shoulders hunched. "I-I thought I could be of help. The familiar—Malachi—he wasn't responsible."

Ferguson leaned forward. "Which you didn't know until after you'd already intruded."

Owen fixed his gaze on the inkwell sitting on Ferguson's desk. "No, but I still kept an innocent man from being charged with a crime he didn't commit. Without my new hexes, Mal would be heading to the electric chair, and the real killer walking free."

"Mal, is it?" Ferguson shifted back, arms crossed. "You know this feral, Yates?"

"No!" Owen struggled to keep his cheeks from heating. "I never met him before last night. With all due respect, sir, I don't know why you're upset. I did nothing wrong."

"Tell that to the Police Board," Athene said, her teeth clacking as though she bit off every word. "You and the patrolmen lost the only witness to the murder of a prominent man. In fact, looking at the reports, it appears that your desire to play detective is what distracted the regular police long enough for him to escape."

"Quigley was destined for a promotion," Ferguson added. "After last night, I imagine he'll never get off the beat."

Owen winced. Quigley had struck him as a good man. "I'm sorry. If it would help, I could speak to his captain—"

"It wouldn't." Ferguson shook his head. "Thanks to you, I spent an hour in front of the Police Board this morning, while they took turns biting chunks out of my arse. They wanted to know why a hexman was involved at all, when it was a matter of murder and theft."

"What was the murderer trying to steal?" Owen asked. "Malachi mentioned some sort of clock, but the pieces looked far too old."

"Interesting that you should bring it up." Ferguson leaned back and regarded Owen. "The ordinary police took the pieces in as evidence, but they've already sent it over to us. Looks like it might have some sort of hexwork on it. I had them leave the box of parts in your office—take a look at it, see what it's meant to be."

Owen frowned. "Surely Mrs. Jacobs or another family member could tell you."

"It seems Mrs. Jacobs wasn't much interested in her husband's mania for collecting," Ferguson said. "She did allow the police to take a listing of everything he acquired at the last auction. Take a look and see if you can figure out why a thief would take this clock, or whatever it is, instead of the gold and gems that would be a lot easier to sell."

Owen clasped his hands behind his back and nodded. "Yes, sir." At least he'd have a chance to redeem himself for letting Mal slip away. "I'll get right to it."

"And Yates?" Ferguson called after him. "You only have six days left here. Up until now, you've been a credit to the MWP. Quiet, hardworking, and—most importantly—you haven't caused me any trouble. Let's keep it that way the rest of your time with us, shall we?"

Mal made his way to Madam Galpern's haberdashery on Clinton Street, his hands thrust deep into his pockets as he wove through the Sunday morning crowds. The wind chilled his ears, but the day itself was warm and sunny, and families thronged the streets. He slipped between them, trying not to meet anyone's eyes, his hat pulled low over his red hair.

Weariness made his bones ache. It had taken forever to fall asleep, curled up in fox shape since the apartment wasn't large enough for beds. When he had, his dreams had been filled with the witch from last night.

His witch.

He couldn't stop thinking about how intense Yates had seemed, intelligent gaze raking the room for clues. How he hadn't just dismissed Mal's protests of innocence, but used hexes of his own devising to separate the innocent from the guilty. Like he actually cared about justice, even if Mal was just a thief.

And that blush, staining his cheeks…

Mal shifted uncomfortably, his prick swelling at the memory. Fur and feathers, he had to stop thinking about the man. Yates was a rich nob as well as a copper. Not the sort of man who would bond with a lowlife thief like Mal, even if it would make for stronger hexes. Probably he'd have Mal arrested on principal, if Mal dared tell him.

The haberdashery was closed on Sunday, which meant he had to use the back entrance. Madam Galpern was inside, serenely applying feathers to one of her hats. She looked up when Mal entered. Her elegantly cut yellow dress contrasted with her brown skin, and she wore one of her own hats pinned to her elaborate curls.

"Mal, darling," she exclaimed at the sight of him. "Come in; come in. Are you all right? You look dreadful."

"Didn't sleep well," he admitted. "I suppose you heard about last night?" Not that she could have avoided it, with newsboys shouting about Jacobs's death from every damned corner.

"Not here, dear," she said, patting his arm. "Let's go upstairs to the parlor, shall we?"

Mal followed her up to the second floor. Neither the shabby exterior of the building, nor the shop downstairs, gave any hint of the wealth which transformed the upper two floors. All courtesy of Madam Galpern's second, more lucrative business as the biggest fence in New York state, if not the entire east coast. Draperies stolen from Fifth Avenue mansions covered the parlor windows, and the walls displayed a number of oil paintings currently being sought by Scotland Yard, the Pinkerton Detective Agency, and the Metropolitan Police. All gifts from grateful friends and former students, along with the lavish furnishings and crystal decanters of expensive liquors.

The secret to her success was that she did more than just pass stolen goods from one set of hands to another. Her true talent lay in organizing. She introduced those working on the shadow side of the law to each other, set up jobs, and even ran an informal school in the art of pickpocketing, which Mal had graduated from with the highest of marks.

"Mal!" Sophie rose from her seat on a velvet covered couch. Before he could answer, she was on him, her arms wrapped tight around his waist. "I've been so worried! I thought the coppers might have caught up with you."

"Nay." He patted her shoulder, and she drew back to study him with big blue eyes that had beguiled many a mark. "Well, aye, but I slipped away when they weren't looking."

"You poor thing," Madam said. "Sophie, won't you pour us drinks?"

While Sophie hurried to the sideboard, Mal settled into a chair across from Madam Galpern. She held herself very straight, with a bearing that would put any of the nobs to shame. If she'd been born to a Knickerbocker family, or hell, even one of the nouveau riches, she'd have ruled New York society. As it was, she merely ruled its underworld.

"Now, darling," she said, accepting a brandy from Sophie, "you must tell me what happened. The papers are full of the most dreadful news, and all of them contradict one another as to the details. Did Mr. Jacobs discover you?"

"Nay!" Mal sat up straight, almost spilling his drink. "I didn't kill him!"

Madam's dark eyes watched him coolly. "Malachi, you're one of my best second-story men. We've been together since you stood no higher than my elbow. You can tell me the truth."

"It wasn't me, I swear." Hand shaking, he downed the brandy without savoring it. "I can't stand violence, you know that. Better to go to Sing Sing for robbery and escape later, than go to the chair for killing a millionaire." His stomach turned sour at the thought of how close he'd come to that very fate. "Even the coppers think I'm innocent."

"Speaking of which, my dear." She sipped her brandy, watching him over the cut glass of her tumbler. "The papers said the police are searching for a witness to the crime. A red-haired man with yellow eyes, five and a half feet tall, slender build. That sounds rather like you."

"Aye." He swallowed hard. "I found Jacobs already dead on the floor. Ended up scrapping with the murderer, but he set off an alarm, and I ran for my life. Right into a blasted copper."

"I see." She put down her brandy. "Did you recognize the murderer?"

"Nay!" A shudder ran through him. "A redhead like me, about my height. Sod almost got me charged with murder, leaving one of his hairs behind. But one of the coppers used a hex to prove it belonged to someone else."

"How fortunate," she murmured. "Less fortunate is that I have no jewelry to pass on to my client."

"That ain't Mal's fault!" Sophie exclaimed. Coming to his defense like always.

"Of course not." Madam Galpern offered them both a reassuring smile. "Well, then, is there anything else you want to talk about, Mal darling? If not, I should really get back to work. You know I do my best planning while I make my hats."

Mal clasped his fingers together. "I thought…another job? If you have anything."

Nick wouldn't throw him out into the street because rent was due. But Mal might find himself sleeping on the floor of the saloon instead of in one of the rooms above. And Nick's charity could only go so far; there were too many ferals in too much need. Mal might at least have a roof between him and the weather, but that didn't mean he'd have food for his belly.

He'd spent too many nights as a child, unable to sleep due to the gnawing in his empty stomach. He didn't want to go back to that if he could help it.

But Madam Galpern shook her head. "It's too dangerous. The police are looking for you."

"Aye, ma'am." Knowing he'd been dismissed, he rose to his feet. "Thank you for your help."

He took the back stairs down, Sophie on his heels. "Don't look so glum," she said when they reached the alleyway behind the shop. She hooked her arm through his, steering him away from Madam Galpern's. "She's disappointed because we didn't get the jewelry her buyer wanted. Give it a few days." Sophie squeezed his arm. "Let's go pickpocket the swells showing off their fancy clothes at the park. That will cheer you up."

He forced a smile onto his face. "Good idea. Then I'll buy us both dinner someplace nice."

Sophie laughed and kissed his cheek. "That's why I love you. Come on."

They crossed out of the alley's shadow and back into the weak sunlight of a late November day. Even so, a chill clung to Mal that owed nothing to the weather.

Because the murderer was still out there…and Mal was the only witness who could identify him.

Chapter 4

Owen sat in his lab, frowning at the scattering of parts in front of him. There were precisely sixty gears of all sizes; twenty bronze plates of varying shapes, engraved with parts of ancient hex signs; and forty-two different gemstones, some carved and some not, which fit into slots on the plates. A series of rods, a hand crank, and various levers completed the pile.

And he had no idea what any of it was for.

There came a rap on the door. "Come in," Owen called. He swiveled about in his chair, expecting to see one of the witch detectives.

"Owen!" exclaimed his future brother-in-law with a grin. "Hard at work, I see."

"Kirk?" Owen rose to his feet and shook his old friend's hand. Kirk wore a heavy wool coat against the November chill, and a hat worked with hexes to keep off rain and snow. "What on earth are you doing here?"

"You must know." Kirk took off his coat and hat, and hung them beside Owen's. "Everyone is going mad over the Jacobs murder. I suspect there were more earnest prayers uttered in service this morning than on any other day since the cathedral was built. Your mother is practically hysterical, along with every other society lady. And gentleman, for that matter. Well, except Edith, of course."

Owen sat down at the table where he'd been working and gestured for Kirk to take the other chair. "Oh?"

"You know Edith," Kirk said wryly. "Sensible to a fault."

Thank heavens. If Owen did have to marry, at least they would be well matched in that. "I'm glad to hear it."

"If only everyone took after my sister." Kirk sighed. "Father is convinced we'll all be slain in our beds tonight. He's to spend the afternoon meeting with the mayor and the Police Board, before giving interviews to the *Times* and the *Herald*. I understand your mother intends to send outraged letters to every respectable newspaper, demanding something be done about the lawlessness infecting the city."

Of course they cared about crime now, when it affected them. Owen suppressed a sigh of his own. "And they sent you to question me, because they're convinced the police aren't telling them everything."

"I volunteered, actually." Kirk sat back in his chair and glanced around the laboratory. "It occurred to me this might be my last chance to get a look at your laboratory."

Kirk's casual statement summoned up a sour feeling in Owen's belly. Most of the time, hard work concentrated his mind, and he could forget this room would soon belong to someone else. He'd spend the rest of his days in an office somewhere, looking over hexes drawn up by other people. A respectable employment for the heir to the Yates fortune.

"I can show you around, if you'd like," Owen offered. He and Kirk had both studied hexology at university, though of course Kirk had been some years ahead of him. Owen had taken up the study because of personal interest, and Kirk because the founder of the Vandersee fortune had invented a hex still used in factories today to keep canning lines sanitary.

"I don't want to take up too much of your time." Kirk gestured to the parts lying on the table. "I am curious as to what that is, though."

"As am I," Owen replied dryly. "We think the man who murdered Mr. Jacobs was trying to steal it, when Jacobs interrupted him. It was dropped during a struggle and brought in for evidence."

Kirk frowned, brows drawing down over his aquiline nose. "You don't know what it is?"

Owen picked up the file Mrs. Jacobs had surrendered to the police. "It was part of a lot bought at auction. All of it stolen for the collector's market from a tomb in Egypt, without any sort of official eye or proper archaeology."

Kirk winced. "A shame."

"Indeed. Even worse, these pages are supposed to list everything in the lot. But some of them are missing, including the ones describing this device, whatever it is. Shoddy record keeping on the part of the auction house, I suspect."

"So there's no way of discovering what it is? What it does?"

"On the contrary." Owen picked up a plate and passed it to Kirk. "The tomb this came from was from the Ptolemaic period—you can see the hexes are Greek in origin, not Egyptian at all. Or parts of hexes, that is—none of the plates has a complete hex on it."

Kirk examined the plate closely. "I don't understand."

"Neither do I. Yet." Owen accepted the plate back from Kirk. "I'm just going to have to put it back together."

Eagerness bubbled up in his blood. Yes, it meant setting aside his hopes for the poison detection hex—but this could be an even greater discovery. So much ancient hexwork had been lost to time and destructive hands. If he could reassemble the device in the next few days, he might yet have a chance at making a lasting contribution to hexology and the MWP.

"Something to keep you out of trouble, at least." Kirk grinned and slapped him on the shoulder. "I was going to ask you to dinner, but I can see you're eager to sink your teeth into the puzzle. I'll give your regards to Edith, shall I?"

"Oh, yes. Of course." Owen started to stand, but Kirk waved him back and let himself out.

Alone again, Owen turned back to the bewildering piles of gears, plates, and gemstones. "Well, then," he said aloud to the assorted parts. "Let's see what we can make of you."

Mal's feet dragged as he made his way up to his room above Caballus. The weather had remained fair, and he and Sophie had worked the crowds at the park. They'd come back a little richer, at least. Enough to eat for a few days.

Still, it was damned depressing, to be back to picking pockets at this point in his life. He'd worked hard to become Madam Galpern's best second-story man. He owed her, for seeing that he wasn't completely worthless, for taking him out of the orphanage and teaching him a skill. Even though there wasn't anything he could have done differently last night, he couldn't help but feel he'd let her down.

Mal unlocked the door. With any luck, both roommates would be out, and he could catch a few hours of sleep before heading back out and trying his luck at the gambling tables. Cheating at cards wasn't the safest way of raising funds, but there was no way to know how long it would be before Madam Galpern had another job for him. Given the headlines about the Jacobs murder, it would be a while before the police lost interest.

He stepped into the room and was struck by a wall of freezing air. The window opposite stood wide open, an icy breeze pouring through, whisper-thin curtains billowing toward him like ghostly hands.

Had one of his roommates left it open? "Stupid bastards," he muttered, and started across the tiny room to close it.

A flicker of movement in the corner of his eye was all the warning he got. An arm went around his throat, yanking him back against a hard body.

A lifetime of scrapping, first on the streets, then in the orphanage, had Mal acting even before he was fully aware of the danger. He twisted his head to the side, tucking his chin into the crease of his attacker's elbow and buying space to breathe. His left hand shot behind him, found the man's thigh, and went higher to his crotch.

Mal squeezed with all his strength, digging his fingers in behind the man's balls and twisting as hard as he could.

His attacker yelped, and pain flared across Mal's right side. The man's hold loosened. Mal tore free and spun to face him.

And found himself face-to-face with the killer from the night before. He held a knife in his hand, its edge dark with blood.

The pain in Mal's side seemed to flare. Christ, if he hadn't grabbed the fellow's balls at just the right moment, he would have ended up with the knife hilt-deep in his lung instead. Hot blood trickled over his ribs, and his mouth tasted of metal.

"Wait," he said, holding up his hands, though he didn't know what good it would do.

The murderer ignored him, instead lunging with his knife. Mal leapt aside, fetching up against the wall beside the open window.

The window.

Not letting himself think, he slithered out the opening. Balancing on the ledge, he slammed the window down behind him, just in time for the knife blade to strike the glass instead of his legs.

It would only buy him seconds. Just long enough for his attacker to open the window and shove him off the ledge.

So he'd just have to get off the ledge on his own terms.

He jumped, shifting into fox form. For a moment, he was falling, and an involuntary bark of terror escaped him.

Then he struck the awning above the saloon below. A man's weight would have ripped through the cloth, but in fox form, he merely slid down it, then dropped safely onto the sidewalk.

He landed on all four feet. Several pedestrians cried out in surprise, but he ignored them in favor of running for his life.

Mal didn't slow until he was several blocks away. Stumbling into an alleyway reeking of garbage, he crouched behind a pile of broken pallets. Blood stained his ruddy fur, and his legs trembled, whether from exhaustion or the aftershock of the fight, he didn't know.

He was supposed to be safe at Caballus, and in the apartments above. That was Nick's promise to them all.

But Nick couldn't be everywhere at once, protect every feral. Could Mal go to Madam Galpern for refuge? The coppers were still looking for him, though; she couldn't risk her whole organization just for him.

Fur and feathers.

He licked gingerly at the wound on his side and was rewarded with a sharp stab of pain. He needed aid. Needed protection.

Would his witch help?

Mal held himself very still. Dr. Yates: copper, nob, lived on the west side according to Nick. Did Mal dare go to him?

Probably he'd just call his fellow coppers and have them haul Mal off to jail. But he hadn't seemed cruel last night. He'd taken the time to examine the situation, not assumed Mal was guilty. Maybe he'd at least hear Mal out.

And if he wanted to bond?

Nick's tirade came back to him. *"...live our own lives, without some witch telling us what to do."*

Which was all very well, except Nick's fantasy of freedom wasn't going to do Mal a damned bit of good if he was dead.

Flicking his tail, Mal trotted down the alley and made for the west side.

Owen descended the stairs from the Ninth Avenue El well after dark that night. His back ached, and he'd developed a crick in his neck from hours bent over the device's gears and rods, trying to fit them together. He'd regain Ferguson's confidence, complete the device, and prove himself once and for all.

As he strode along 72nd Street, a dark figure lurched from the shadows. Owen jumped away, hands coming up into fists. "Get back!"

"Hold up!" The man held out his palms. "It's me."

Owen blinked. Instead of the drunken beggar or armed robber he'd expected, the electric lamps revealed the fiery hair and handsome features of the thief from last night.

The thief every policeman in New York was searching for.

"Mal?" he asked dumbly. "What are you doing here?"

"Aye." The smaller man gave him a toothy grin, but it faded into a grimace as he lowered his arms. "I could, ah, use a bit of help." He turned to display a rent in his clothing, revealing bloodied flesh beneath.

"Dear Lord! You're injured."

"Noticed that, I did." Mal leaned against the lamp post. "Seems like the man who killed Jacobs last night didn't want any witnesses to testify against him in court."

"Here—let me help you." Owen slid an arm around Mal's shoulders for support. "We'll go straight to the police."

"Nay." Mal's lips pressed into a tight line.

"Why ever not?"

"I'll explain everything. Just not here." Mal shifted slightly and winced. "You have a place nearby, don't you?"

"I...yes?" Owen started down the street, Mal leaning against him. "How did you know that?"

"A friend told me about you." Mal glanced up. His face was very close; Owen could make out each individual lash framing those extraordinary amber eyes. He smelled like musk and moss, like something from the deep reaches of a wild forest brought incongruously into the midst of the city.

The security guard emerged from his nook as Owen approached the entrance into the inner courtyard. "Good evening, Mr.—gracious! Is everything all right?"

Owen suppressed a sigh. Dragging a bleeding man—particularly one so obviously from the lower classes—into The Folly was exactly the sort of thing that would result in his lease being prematurely cancelled. True, after the wedding Edith and he would move in with the Vandersees while their mansion—a wedding present from her father—was being built. But even a small scandal so close to the nuptials wouldn't be looked upon kindly by either family.

Owen thrust his hand into his pocket and pulled out a wad of bills. "Just a friend who had a bit too much to drink," he said blandly.

The bills vanished quickly into the guard's pocket. "Yes, sir. Have a good evening."

At least Mal had the sense to remain silent. Owen hurried him through the courtyard to the lobby in the southeast corner. The elevator attendant also gave them a startled look, but it smoothed away after the application of yet more dollars. "Good evening, sir," he said, as though Mal didn't even exist.

Mal let out a startled gasp as the cage began to move. When Owen cast him a questioning look, he shrugged. "Ain't never been in one of these before."

"Ah, yes," Owen said. "I'd forgotten—you prefer to reach the upper floors via window."

Mal let out a bark of laughter. The elevator operator glanced at them both in alarm.

Thankfully, the door to Owen's apartment was immediately off the elevator. He urged Mal inside, then locked the door. When he turned back, it was to find Mal staring around at the ante room, mouth open. Not that there was much to see—dark wood, a velvet-covered chair for removing one's shoes, a table where the servants left his mail, and a hall tree carved with the Yates family crest. The parlor opened directly across from the elevator, and to the right lay the door leading to the hallway running the length of the apartment.

"You live here by yourself?" Mal asked, sounding stunned.

"Yes, but it's one of the smaller apartments," Owen replied. "Now, let's see to your wound. I have some bandages in the bedroom."

Mal continued to look around as Owen led him down the hall. "How many rooms?"

"The dining room is here," Owen gestured to the right, "and the library here. The two bed chambers are beside each other at the end; each has a private bath. And of course there's the pantry and kitchen."

"Oh, of course," Mal said.

Owen frowned. "Don't get any ideas about the silverware."

"I'm shocked at the very notion!" Mal put a hand to his chest. "You've done me a great injustice, you have."

"The snuffbox Quigley found in your pocket suggests otherwise," Owen said as they entered his bedroom. The walls were covered in gold cloth, which contrasted nicely with the scarlet bedclothes and upholstery, and the dark wood of the furniture. Mal craned his head back and gaped at the scene of clouds and angels painted on the ceiling.

"Sit down," Owen said, steering Mal into the heavy chair. "Remove your shirt; I'll fetch some water to clean up the wound." Taking the basin from the wash stand, he went to the bathroom and filled it with warm water.

Mal awaited his return, having stripped to the waist. Owen's step hitched slightly at the sight. The feral was slim but wiry, muscles showing beneath the pale skin of his shoulders and arms. A dusting of red hair covered his chest, and a thicker trail traced a path from his navel, vanishing beneath his worn trousers.

The strict propriety of The Folly had formed a welcome cage, more than capable of containing Owen's desires. The thought of bringing a man back to his apartment for anything improper, of facing the scrutiny of guard, elevator attendant, and possibly neighbors, had been more than enough to keep him chaste. True, he might yet have gone to the poorer parts of town in search of company, but as he doubted his ability to avoid being robbed and beaten, he'd never done so. There had been no real possibility of indulging in any sort of desire. Certainly not in the weakness that most haunted his dreams.

And now a half-naked thief sat in his very bedroom.

Owen took a deep breath and put down the basin. Wetting a towel, he turned to Mal, forcing himself to focus only on the blood staining the man's side. "Let me know if I hurt you," he said, kneeling beside the chair.

"I appreciate this. I do," Mal said. He let out a little hiss of pain as the towel touched the wound.

Owen carefully wiped away the blood. "Why don't you tell me exactly what happened?"

While Mal told his tale, Owen finished cleaning the injury. Though blood had been smeared all around it, the cut itself was shallow, and had already sealed. Setting aside the towel, he picked up the roll of bandages.

"They're hexed to prevent infection," he explained, as he wrapped the soft cloth around Mal's slender torso. His fingers couldn't help but brush against Mal's skin, warm and hinting of hard muscle beneath.

"What money can't buy, eh?" Mal said, sounding impressed.

His scent, of musk and something earthy, like the green shadows in the deep woods on a hot summer day, filled Owen's nostrils with every breath. To Owen's dismay, his prick started to harden. He'd removed his coat so as to avoid staining it, and could only hope Mal didn't happen to glance down.

"There," he said, struggling to keep his voice level. Unaffected. "How is the pain? I have hexes to ease any discomfort, if you'd like."

For a long moment, Mal didn't reply. Owen still knelt beside him; he'd have to crane his head back to see Mal's face. Or stand, but that didn't seem wise at the moment.

Then Mal shifted forward. Closer. Fingers trailed across the front of

Owen's trousers, drawing an involuntary gasp from him.

Mal had noticed, all right.

"No pain," Mal murmured. "But maybe there's something I can do for you? Want to switch places, have me on my knees in front of you?"

Shocked by the feral's bold speech, Owen looked up. Their eyes met, Mal's amber gaze seeming to strip him raw with its heat. Then a slow, vulpine smile curved Mal's lips.

"Oh no," he murmured. "I see how it is. You're right where you want to be, ain't you? You belong on your knees. On your knees, sucking my cock."

All the air seemed to leave the room. How could Mal possibly have seen, have guessed, when no one else ever had? It was as though something in Mal recognized something in Owen; a connection that defied all logic.

Owen knew he should object to such effrontery, no matter its allure. He should grab the feral by the scruff and throw him out. Summon the police to take him away. Regain mastery of the situation.

But his prick had gone fully hard at Mal's words. A shuddering hunger went through him; a base longing he had to resist.

The mere thought of giving in was madness. He couldn't do this. It was too dangerous—what if Mal decided to blackmail him? Not that anyone would take the word of a criminal feral over that of a Yates, but could he risk the hint of a scandal so close to the wedding?

Mal leaned insolently back in the chair, deliberately spreading his legs wide. Displaying the erection tenting his trousers. "You've got your orders, copper. Now get to it."

God, Owen wanted to. Every buried fantasy emerged to clamor in his brain, begging him to indulge just this once. Mal's red hair and amber eyes seemed to glow, everything else reduced to colorless shadows, as though he were the only real thing in the room.

Just once. No one else would ever know.

Half-dazed with lust, Owen reached out with trembling hands and unbuttoned Mal's trousers. The familiar lifted his backside from the chair in silent command, and Owen pulled them down, along with Mal's drawers. Mal's cock sprang free, the slit already beaded with clear fluid.

God.

With a groan, Owen leaned forward and lapped at the slit, tasting bitterness and salt. Mal's hand cupped the back of his head, urging him forward, and he went. Swirling his tongue around the head, tracing the veins, then swallowing it all down at once.

"Fuck!" Mal swore, hips lifting from the chair again, involuntarily this time. The head of his prick hit the back of Owen's throat, drawing tears from his eyes and nearly gagging him. He sucked harder, was rewarded with a string of curses and fingers tight in his hair.

"Fur and feathers, you're good at this, ain't you?" Mal gasped. "Good at taking a cock." He tugged on Owen's hair. "Leave off a minute and suck my balls."

Owen pulled back uncertainly. He'd sucked pricks before, as Mal had guessed. But nothing so vulgar as what Mal was suggesting. "I…"

Mal's hold tightened in his hair. "Do as you're told."

The rough order sent a shock of pure lust through Owen. He leaned in, lifted Mal's cock out of the way to get better access. Mal's musky scent surrounded him, making his mouth water and his own prick leak. He sucked one ball into his mouth, tongue laving the surface of the wrinkled sack.

Mal moaned encouragement. "Aye. Just like that. You'll do anything, won't you? Anything I tell you."

No, Owen wanted to say. He shouldn't even be doing this; shouldn't be on his knees, pleasuring the balls of a two-bit thief. He was a Yates. He had the dignity of his position in society to uphold, he shouldn't…he couldn't…

Unable to stand it any longer, he reached for the buttons of his trousers. "Nay," Mal growled. "Take yourself out, but no touching beyond that. The only hand that's going to toss you off tonight is mine."

Almost sobbing with need, Owen nonetheless obeyed. Mal pulled away, grabbed his cock, and aimed it at Owen's lips in a silent demand. Owen could taste how close he was; two thrusts, and Mal let out a shout as he came down Owen's throat.

Owen swallowed convulsively, gave a last, desperate suck as Mal drew free. His heart pounded, unattended prick bobbing in time. He wanted more, needed more, though what he didn't even know.

Mal slid from the chair, straddling Owen's thigh. Gripping Owen's hair, he tilted his head back—and kissed him.

Owen hadn't expected the thief to want that. For a kiss, it was hard, almost savage. Mal bit at his lips, then slid his tongue into Owen's mouth at the same time his hand wrapped around Owen's cock.

Owen groaned, the sound muffled by Mal's mouth on his own. A long firm stroke, followed by another, and—

He pulled free of the kiss, crying out helplessly as he came. Lights flashed behind his eyes, and he bucked under Mal, jets of semen spattering white against the parquet floor of his bedroom.

It seemed a long moment before his lungs remembered how to breathe. Mal's fingers slipped from his hair, curling around the back of his neck. "Mmm." Mal nuzzled his ear, bringing an involuntary shiver from Owen. "Seems like it's been a while."

Owen pulled away sharply. How had he allowed this to happen? Bad enough he'd let his control slip enough to give into the feral's charms, but to have done it in such a way? To have eagerly followed orders like some cheap whore, utterly forgetting his place in the world?

Just as he had always secretly wanted.

Shame burned his face, and he stood hastily, tucking himself back in. "That's none of your business," he said brusquely.

Mal arched an impertinent brow. He sprawled on the floor still, making no attempt to cover his flaccid cock. "Ain't it?"

"No." Owen scowled, though disapproval seemed to have no effect on Mal. "Tomorrow morning, we'll go to the Coven. Chief Ferguson will make sure you get real protection. I work in a laboratory, so likely you and I will never set eyes on each other again."

A sly grin slid onto Mal's face, and his eyes lit up with mischief. "Oh, didn't I say?" he drawled. "Dr. Owen Yates…you're my witch."

CHAPTER 5

OWEN CRADLED HIS head in his hands as his coffee slowly cooled in front of him. When he'd waked this morning, he'd half hoped the events from the night before would prove to have been a terrible dream. But the damp towel and empty basin in the bathroom dashed that wan bit of optimism.

This was a disaster. An unmitigated disaster.

He'd spent most of his life devoted to the art of making hexes. Yes, he'd scored high on the witch tests, but there were always far more witches than familiars. He'd never built his future around the assumption he'd bond; although there was naturally some overlap, most hexmen weren't witches. Not to say the thought hadn't occurred to him at all. In his idle imaginings, his familiar had been regal. Cultured. Commanding.

Mal had certainly been commanding last night…

No. He lifted his head and took a deep breath. That had been a terrible mistake. If he'd known Mal was his familiar, he'd have never displayed such weakness. How could he expect Mal to respect him now?

If only that had been the worst of his problems. Admittedly, having a familiar would be useful…if he'd intended to stay with the MWP, at any rate. He could test new hexes himself, without having to wait for a bonded pair of detectives to find the time to make the journey down to his lab.

But the fact remained that Mal was a thief. A *thief*, for God's sake. An uneducated criminal who couldn't even speak proper English. The scandal if anyone found out…

He could only imagine his parents' disapproving eyes. He'd spent his entire life trying to live up to their standards. His only excuse, that it wasn't his fault, that he hadn't chosen Mal, would fall on deaf ears.

There were no excuses in the Yates household. Only success or failure. And this was undeniably in the latter category.

A slender figure appeared in the doorway to the dining room. Owen glanced up and found himself glad he'd dismissed the servants after they laid out breakfast. Mal's red hair was damp from washing, and he wore nothing but a silk dressing gown, which did little to hide his lithe form.

Something of Owen's thoughts must have shown on his face, or perhaps Mal simply read him as easily now as he had last night. "Well. Good morning to you, too," he said with the arch of a brow.

Owen flushed. "Forgive me. Did you sleep well? How is your wound?"

"Feels better than I've any right to expect," Mal said, opening the dressing gown to display his naked body. Had he no sense of propriety whatsoever? "Even managed to re-bandage it myself, see?"

Mal's nipples were hard, perhaps from the cool air—all the rooms in The Folly were provided with steam heat, but winter still made its presence known. Owen tore his gaze away with effort. "I…see."

"Something wrong?" Mal asked warily.

"No. Not at all." Owen cleared his throat. "Please, help yourself to breakfast."

"Don't mind if I do." Mal sat down and began to grab whatever was in reach, piling the food on his plate all at once. He popped an entire boiled egg into his mouth, then used his thumbs to tear open one of the soft biscuits.

Dear God, the man had no manners whatsoever.

"I sent the servants away so we can speak freely," Owen said.

Mal's ravenous chewing barely slowed. "So talk."

It was a slim hope, but Owen forced himself to voice it. "Are you certain I'm your witch?"

"Aye. Knew it the moment I clapped eyes on you."

"So why didn't you say anything at the Jacobs house?" Owen countered.

Mal's brows climbed toward his hairline. "Oh aye, just blurt it out to some rich nob I've never even set eyes on before?" He shook his head. "What a kick in the balls, eh? A copper as my witch."

Owen gaped at him. "I hardly see that *you* have any place to complain, considering you're a-a thief! My familiar, robber of widows and orphans."

Mal straightened in his chair. Any trace of playfulness vanished, and his look grew serious. A minute ago, Owen would have thought it an improvement, but he found himself preferring Mal's impertinent grins.

"You listen here, copper," Mal said, brandishing the remains of the biscuit at him. "I ain't never stolen from a poor man. I ain't never taken bread out of the mouth of any woman or child, neither. Maybe I ain't lived the most honest life, but I've only ever taken from rich nobs like you, or the swells throwing away their money on cards."

Owen frowned. "I hardly think I, or men like me, deserve to be robbed."

Mal snorted. "You'd never miss it. Jacobs wouldn't have, neither. He'd have been angry, but he'd still live in a fancy house, drinking fancy wines and abusing the servants whenever he felt like it."

"What do you mean?" Owen asked.

Mal looked at him a long moment...then helped himself to another biscuit. "How do you think I got past all those expensive hexes on the windows?"

"I don't know. Honestly, that's one of the things that has high society beside itself in terror, that you and the murderer managed to get inside."

"I don't know how the killer got in," Mal said, washing down his breakfast with a swallow of strong coffee. "As for me, I noticed the maid with the bruised face. A little bit of charm, a few glasses of whiskey, and a sympathetic ear was all it took. Jacobs had a temper, and everyone from the lowliest kitchen girl to the butler himself bore the brunt of it."

Owen sat back. He'd *met* the man, many times. "I had no idea. He never seemed...that is, he seemed an upstanding sort."

"They always do," Mal said, a trace of bitterness in his voice. "At any rate, everyone hated the fellow, only stayed on for the pay or because they didn't have anywhere else to go. He threatened to withhold a recommendation from anyone who left before he was done with them, you see."

"Still, I don't understand what any of this has to do with how you broke into the house."

"I'm getting there, ain't I? Don't rush a fellow." Mal lounged back, looking rather as if he enjoyed being the center of Owen's attention. The silk robe slipped open, revealing one nipple, and Owen had to force himself to remain focused on Mal's face. "The alarm companies tell people they need a different deactivation phrase for every window and door, don't they? And change it every month or two? But that makes a lot of work in a house that big. Easier for the butler if he just uses the one. Less to remember, and makes the work go quicker in the morning. And of course people are going to overhear him, ain't they?"

"I see," Owen murmured.

Mal's look sharpened. "Don't you go making trouble for the servants. If Jacobs didn't want someone stealing his things, he should've treated them better. Ain't no one to blame but himself."

Owen rather doubted most people would agree. Certainly none of the so-called Four Hundred who formed the pinnacle of New York society. But if Jacobs had been abusing the servants...

"I don't wish to cause trouble for anyone," Owen replied. "But as you're my familiar, I feel I need to understand what happened that night. You truly don't know who the killer was? You weren't his...well, his accomplice?"

Mal's mouth tightened. "Nay. I don't hold with violence. I got to the door, saw Jacobs lying there. I came inside to see if he was still breathing, and when I turned around, there was the killer holding the clock, or whatever it was. At the time I thought he was going to kill me, but now I'm wondering if he was trying to sneak off behind my back, without me noticing."

Was Mal telling the truth? He seemed sincere...but he was a thief, and probably a liar as well. Still, one detail seemed worth pursuing. "Why did you come into the room? Why not run when you saw Jacobs on the floor with his head bashed in?"

"Well I couldn't tell if he was dead, could I?" Mal looked at Owen as if he'd lost his mind. "What was I supposed to do, let him lie there until someone found him in the morning? If he was just badly hurt, that would've been the end of him, wouldn't it? I wasn't going to be responsible for some poor bastard dying in his own blood. I figured if he was still alive, I'd slip outside, around the front, and do something to wake up the house. Then I'd run, let them find him."

"Oh." It wasn't what Owen had expected. He'd assumed Mal's first thought would be for his own skin. The man was a criminal, after all.

A thief, but not a killer. At least there was that. How Owen would tell his family, he couldn't imagine. But that was a worry for another day.

"All right," Owen said heavily. "Get dressed."

Mal's expression turned wary again. "Where are we going?"

"The Coven, of course." Owen finished off his own coffee and rose to his feet. "If we're to keep you safe from this killer, you'll have to talk to the MWP, at least."

"Lovely," Mal said, making a face. "Saint Mary, I hope none of my friends find out about this."

Mal shifted back into human shape as soon as they passed inside the doors of the Coven. A couple of blocks away, Owen had warned him to take on fox form, so the reporters camped on the Coven's steps wouldn't recognize Mal as the missing witness.

"Your coat's very bright," Owen said, once Mal put on his fur. He sounded as though he wasn't certain he liked it or not.

Well, that was one thing they had in common at the moment. Not uncertainty about Mal's coat—he was a very handsome fox, thank you very much, and so what if he stood out on the drab winter streets? More about, well, *everything*.

Last night had been like some sort of fantasy—and that was even apart from the sex. Not to suggest that hadn't been an unexpected delight. Bossing around a rich nob was satisfying in and of itself, but the way Owen responded, with such yearning to please…that was the sort of thing a fellow could get used to, no two ways about it.

After, he'd slept in Owen's guest room, all alone in a big bed with a soft mattress and warm sheets. He could sprawl all he liked, even in human form, and not have to worry about rolling off onto the floor. The room even had a private bathroom, complete with a huge, claw-footed tub and all the hot water he could wish for. Actually bathing, without a lot of hauling and heating of buckets, able to submerse himself entirely beneath the surface if he wanted…

It was like something from a dream. But Owen…well, it was clear he didn't have much of an opinion of Mal. Rich nob like him, he just looked at Mal and saw some unwashed thief, not even high enough in society to scrub the toilets at a place like The Folly.

Not to mention, Owen was tighter than an over-wound watch. Last night, he'd seemed to relax for a few moments, when he'd been on his knees in front of Mal and following every order. But that fellow had disappeared the second he'd come, and he'd been right back to tight-lipped disapproval this morning.

Well, it wasn't as if they had to *like* each other, right? Mal had something Owen wanted—his magic. He'd give Owen what he wanted, and get what he needed in return. Namely, some sort of protection to keep him from dying in an alley.

Mal peered around the inside of the Coven warily. He'd been hauled into a few precinct houses over the years, but never in MWP custody. Now he was completely surrounded by witches and coppers. It made the skin between his shoulders itch.

The witch sitting at the desk near the door stared curiously. Owen ignored him, instead beckoning Mal after him as he set off into the building. "We'll need to speak to Chief Ferguson," he said, a singular lack of enthusiasm in his voice.

Mal nodded, trying to keep his nervousness from his face. He was used to being surrounded by familiars at Caballus and the tenement rooms above, but it was different here. A hedgehog perched alertly on her witch's shoulder, ducking instinctively when an owl swooped past. A babble of voices intermingled with barks, meows, and hoots. The silver familiar's badge flashed from the vests of those who were in human form. And of course, there were the witches. So many witches; his nerves drew tight.

At least if he bonded with Owen, he wouldn't have to worry about any other witches grabbing him. The next time he felt the sting of a hex on the street, meant to check whether or not he was bonded, he'd be able to ignore it instead of running for his very life. Not that Owen had said he wanted to bond, exactly. But he hadn't rejected the possibility outright, either.

"This is the detectives' area," Owen said as they emerged into an enormous room crammed with desks.

"You said you ain't a detective," Mal replied.

"I'm not. I have my own laboratory downstairs."

The room was crowded with witches and familiars, all of them milling about before settling in to work. The scent of coffee spiked the air, and newspapers rustled as detectives frowned at the morning headlines.

Then the crowd parted, and Mal glimpsed a figure he recognized.

"Nick?" he exclaimed. "What the devil? Nick!"

Nick loomed up beside one of the desks, hands on his hips, glaring down at someone. On hearing Mal's voice, he turned sharply. His scowl softened, but only by a degree. "Well, at least you're alive."

"See?" said a familiar who was a shorter, slimmer version of Nick. This must be the brother, Rook. "He's fine."

Nick ignored him, stomping over to Mal instead. "What the devil happened? Your roommates came home to find blood on the floor and you missing." He shifted his glare to Owen. "And who the fuck are you?"

Owen's silvery eyes turned frosty. "Dr. Owen Yates."

Nick snorted. "Of course you are." Turning his back on Owen, he said, "Malachi? You all right?"

"I'm fine." Mal said. "It was the killer from the other night. Somehow he knew where I lived."

Their conversation attracted the attention of others around them. A familiar whose yellow-green eyes were outlined in kohl sashayed over. "I can't imagine how that could possibly have happened with Nicholas here looking out after you."

"Shut it, Cicero." Nick's brows drew down sharply. "I do my best, which is more than *you* lot can say."

"If you'd told the truth yesterday, when I asked if you knew the feral, he wouldn't have been in danger," Rook said exasperatedly.

"You shut it, too." Nick folded his thickly muscled arms over his chest. "Like I'd ever tell someone who works with witches the whereabouts of a feral."

"Well, someone obviously did." Rook mimicked his brother's posture, and they both glared at each other.

"And I'm going to find out who," Nick said ominously.

"Do bring them in to us in one piece, darling," Cicero drawled. "Since chances are they know who wants to kill poor Malachi here." His peridot eyes found Mal again. "And you went to dear Owen for help? That *is* interesting."

"And none of your business," Nick snapped. "Come on, Mal. You can stay in my apartment until we get to the bottom of this."

Mal ran a hand down the lapel of the overcoat he'd borrowed from Owen, since his own had been ruined by blood. The wool outer layer had hexes worked into it to repel both stains and damp—expensive, since they were part of the weave itself, and thus had to be worked by hand. The inner liner was of emerald silk, the buttons silver. It was probably worth more than every scrap of clothing he'd ever owned put together.

The idea of going back to the tenement, the rooms so small he slept in fox form so as not to need a bed, didn't seem particularly appealing after last night. Owen might not have the best opinion of him, but he'd done right by Mal so far. Might as well stick with it and see how far he could go.

"I almost got killed yesterday," he said aloud. "I'm sorry, Nick, but I'm leaving the colony. I'm going to stay here." He glanced at Owen. It seemed the right time to find out how Owen felt about the situation.

"With my witch."

There came a moment of stunned silence. Then Cicero threw his head back and laughed. "Oh, darling," he said. "Ferguson is going to *love* this!"

"The witness every member of the regular police is looking for," Chief Ferguson said slowly. "The second-story man who broke into Jacobs's mansion." He looked from Owen to Mal and back again. "Is your familiar?"

Mal held himself still and tried to look as respectable as possible. The chief of the MWP didn't strike him as the sort to be easily charmed, and the enormous owl familiar on her perch was eyeing Mal like she might just add some fox to her dinner.

"That's right," Owen said. He didn't exactly sound thrilled about the situation, but he met Ferguson's gaze calmly.

Ferguson rubbed at his face. "Listen, Yates. This is your last week with us."

Mal perked up. It was? Owen hadn't bothered to mention this tidbit to him. So his witch wouldn't be a copper much longer. That had to be good news.

"If you don't want to go through with bonding, I'll support you," Ferguson went on.

"The devil?" Mal exclaimed. "I thought you lot couldn't wait to get your hands on familiars."

"We have standards, here at the MWP," Ferguson said, glaring at him. "A lot more relaxed than the regular police, especially when it comes to familiars, I'll grant you. But you're a thief and a liar, and Yates is a good man. I'd not see him bound to the likes of you."

Mal's throat tightened, and he felt as if he'd been slapped. Of course Owen, with his luxury apartment and fine manners and breakfast table laden with more food than Mal had ever seen, could find a familiar with more class. But he couldn't find one with better magic. "There's no one whose magic is more compatible."

Owen placed a light hand on Mal's shoulder. "Chief Ferguson, I think you're selling Mal short," he said. "He risked his own life to see if Mr. Jacobs was still able to be helped."

The owl clacked her beak loudly. "So he says," Ferguson said.

Mal's cheeks grew hot, and his hands clenched. "I do say it." How could he convince the chief to let him go with Owen, and not just toss him in a jail cell?

"Mal is reformed," Owen said. "Or going to reform. No more thieving." He glanced at Mal for confirmation.

Mal nodded rapidly. "Aye. I swear on my mother's grave." As far as he knew, she was still alive and well, but surely it was the thought that counted.

"It's your choice, Yates," Ferguson said at last, though his tone made it clear he thought Owen had lost his senses. "There is one thing, though. Mr. Malachi is a valuable witness to a highly publicized murder, who's had one attempt made on his life already. I trust your apartment building is secure against ordinary intrusion, and that you'll make it even more so. But if he sets foot anywhere else outside of the Coven, I'd prefer to have someone to keep an eye on him. One of the unbonded familiars, I think."

Mal stiffened. Curse Ferguson. He needed to talk to Sophie, let her know he was still alive—and warn her. The killer had learned where Mal lived; what else might he have discovered? Sophie might be in danger, if the killer thought she knew where he was hiding.

But he couldn't risk bringing her to the attention of the coppers. "If you think I'm going to run off again, I ain't," he said. "Be right stupid of me. Besides, once we bond, Owen will be able to find me again easy enough."

"Don't talk to me like I'm an idiot, boyo." Ferguson fixed him with hard eyes. "I know your type. You think you're damned clever. For the next five days, though, you're going to do as I say. After that, you're Yates's problem."

Owen's hand tightened on Mal's shoulder. "Thank you, sir. I'm sure there won't be any trouble."

Ferguson snorted. "Well," he said, waving them in the direction of the door, "that makes one of us."

Chapter 6

"**And here is** the lab," Owen said, pushing open the door gratefully. "At last."

Mal slipped past him, eyes darting here and there, absorbing the sight of tables loaded with the tools of Owen's chosen trade. Draftsman equipment for the creation of hexes cluttered a desk: rulers, protractors, and bottles of inks made from exotic compounds. A long table held the alchemical necessities that went into formulating new inks and testing new hexes: distillers, beakers, burners, and more. A second table held the pieces of the device.

While Mal inspected the room, Owen shut the door. "Don't mind Chief Ferguson," he said. "Or the other witches and familiars, for that matter." Word had clearly spread while they were in Ferguson's office, and a host of eyes both curious and hostile had followed them out.

Mal shrugged, as though it didn't matter. "Not like I expected otherwise. Can't ask a bunch of coppers to be happy they've got a thief among them, after all."

"Former thief," Owen said. And hoped it was true.

"Aye." Mal paused. "Are you sure about this, witch?"

Was he? Owen hesitated. Having magic to charge hexes would be useful—more than useful. And Mal *was* his familiar, like it or not. It meant Owen had a certain responsibility to him, a duty, just as he did to his family.

If he refused the bond, Mal would go straight to jail on whatever charges were needed to hold him until Jacobs's killer was found and put on trial. A wild thing like Mal surely wouldn't do well in a cage. That his bright grin might lose its spark felt unendurable.

Owen straightened his shoulders. This week seemed all about doing his duty, no matter how personally distasteful. "I'm sure. You'll have to give your statement about the attempt on your life yesterday, but you can do that here. We'll send it over to the regular police. There's no reason to subject a bonded MWP familiar to their questioning."

"Well, that's surely a relief." Mal hesitated, then nodded to himself, once. "Guess we'd best get about the bonding, then."

A little flutter went through Owen's gut. Bonding was an irrevocable step. Once done, he'd be tied to this man for life.

In theory, at least. In practice, Cicero's witch, Tom Halloran, was a hexbreaker. He could destroy almost any magic, including the bond between witch and familiar. The two of them had spent the last ten months on special assignment, investigating cases of alleged forced bonding, freeing the victims and sending the perpetrators to jail when possible. It wasn't something widely spoken of, but surely word had spread through the feral colonies. Owen was under the impression Nick had quietly sent several cases their way, despite his usual disdain for the police.

"If you're ready," he said. "I believe I know what is required."

Mal ended his circuit of the room in front of Owen. "Do you now?" he asked with a sly smile.

The smile sent Owen's pulse to racing. "Y-Yes."

Mal pointed casually to the stool sitting in front of the worktable. "Then sit down."

Owen knew the request—the order—was simply because he was too tall for Mal to reach him otherwise. But his mouth went uncomfortably dry. At least Mal hadn't told him to get on his knees.

Once he was settled, Mal pressed in—too close, their thighs threading together. The heat of Mal's body radiated through the cloth of their trousers. Mal's pupils widened, narrowing his irises to amber rings, and his hungry grin revealed very white, very sharp, teeth. "Close your eyes."

Part of the bonding process. That was all. Still, Owen trembled as he obeyed.

For a long moment, nothing happened, and Owen's nerves drew even tighter. Then Mal's fingers brushed his jaw, making him jump. They slid down further, caressing the vulnerable skin of his throat. He tipped his head back, a little moan escaping him.

Mal's lips feathered across the back of his left eyelid, then the right. "Let me in, Owen," he breathed.

This was old, old magic, evidenced by the taste of blood in Owen's mouth. Mal's lips slid down from his eyes, and the familiar gave him a rough, punishing kiss.

That wasn't part of the ritual. He ought to object, ought to pull away, tell Mal to stay to the script…

"Now keep your eyes shut," Mal growled when he was done plundering Owen's mouth.

Owen obeyed—but light bloomed behind his eyelids anyway. He found himself staring up from a position low to the floor. The lab looked strange from this angle, the colors washed away. Through Mal's eyes, he stared at his own face: teeth white against his lower lip, cheeks flushed darker, fists balled on his thighs.

"Handsome lad," said a voice in his head. Mal's voice.

"We can't do this," Owen thought. His blood thundered in his ears.

Mal backed away, leaving him with the disorienting view of his own body receding. Owen opened his eyes, blinking wildly.

Mal shifted to human form, crouching on the floor. "You don't want to bond?"

Owen couldn't read his tone. Whether it was fearful, or hopeful, or something else. "Not that. This." He swallowed. "Whatever this is between us. I'm to be married."

"That's why you're leaving the MWP, ain't it?" Mal cocked his head. "I'm guessing it's not a love match."

"No." Owen let out a long breath. "But Edith is a good woman. And even if she wasn't, I couldn't break my wedding vows and bear to look at myself in the mirror each morning."

There came a soft rustle of cloth as Mal rose to his feet. "Why not do as you wish, and let her do the same?"

"Because a vow is a vow," Owen snapped. "If a gentleman goes back on his word, then what does he have?"

"A fucking lot of money?" Mal hazarded. "Everyone knows what Mr. Astor was doing on his yacht, and it wasn't his wife."

"Another man's dishonorable conduct is no excuse for my own." Owen crossed his arms over his chest. "I'm sorry, Mal. I will be your witch, but I cannot be your lover."

Mal's lips pressed into a thin line. Owen had the wild desire to say something, anything, to bring back his smile. "And me? Am I supposed to live like a monk, then?"

"Of course not." Owen tried not to imagine his future, duty bound to provide Edith whatever she required in bed, with nothing to ease the ache deep inside his own soul. Tried not to picture Mal ordering some other man to his knees, then bringing him off with such savage pleasure. "I wouldn't expect you to abide by such restrictions."

"Oh right. Because I ain't a nob like you." Malachi rose to his feet and snatched up a piece of paper. "Draw a hex and finish the damned bond."

Everything was going wrong, and Owen wasn't certain how to make it right again. "Mal…"

The familiar turned away from him. "Do it, Yates."

He wanted to take back the last few minutes, although what he would have done differently, he didn't know. He had a duty to Edith; couldn't Mal see that? He and Mal had sex once, nothing more. Mal certainly had no reasonable claim to be upset by Owen's choices.

"Very well," he said. He turned to his drafting tools. In the back of his mind, he'd imagined drawing up some beautiful, elaborate hex, something to honor the bond between himself and his familiar. Something special.

As it was, he sketched the first that came to mind. A simple fire hex.

Mal drifted near to watch over his shoulder. "You're good," he said grudgingly. "Steady hand."

"Thank you." Owen laid the hex carefully in front of him. "I suppose this is it, then."

"Suppose it is."

Owen waited, but Mal made no further objection. Taking a deep breath, he laid his palm on the hex.

And the magic flowed.

There came a soft knock on the laboratory door. Yates had retreated to the table with the device and turned all his concentration on it. Mal perched on the desk, the new bond like a warm coal nestled in his chest, just behind his heart. If he closed his eyes, he could sense Owen's presence, the same way a blind man could feel the direction of the sun from its heat on his face.

Owen. His witch.

Owen, who acted like what they'd done last night was wrong. Like he was ashamed he'd let himself be tossed off by a *thief*.

Mal's throat tightened. Which was stupid—he didn't have any claim on Yates. Owen had saved his life, probably, with that clever bit of hexwork back at Jacobs's mansion, and given him shelter last night. And sure, they'd had a little fun in the bedroom, but it was only the one time. It would've been nice to do more, but if Owen wanted to act all morally superior, that was his problem.

He didn't have to make Mal feel like a whore about it, though. Like he was some lowlife who couldn't be held to a standard.

Not that Mal wanted to be held to a stupid standard like that one. But still.

At least their stay at the MWP was only temporary—and that was something Owen could've seen fit to mention over breakfast, if he hadn't been so busy interrogating Mal. Maybe he didn't feel like he needed to explain anything to Mal, just expected him to accept whatever came his way.

"Like a pet," Nick would say.

So he was almost glad when the knock sounded, and a man stuck his head in the door. He looked to be a few years older than Owen and Mal, with soft brown hair and eyes whose deep, chocolate color made them seem hollow next to his pale skin. "Dr. Yates," he said, then nodded to Mal. "Mr. Malachi."

"Yes…er, Bertie?" Owen asked, clearly uncertain of the name.

The fellow nodded, so he must've gotten it right. He pushed the door open, his large frame filling most of the doorway. "Letter for you, sir," he said to Owen. "And Chief Ferguson said one of us unbondeds was needed to play bodyguard for the fox, so I thought I might as well volunteer."

Curse it—Ferguson hadn't wasted any time, had he?

Mal gave Bertie a broad smile and stuck out his hand. "I'm certainly glad to have a big, strong fellow like you looking out for me," he said.

Out of the corner of his eye, he saw Owen's head come up sharply. A little flash of jealousy, maybe?

Bertie only looked confused. "I'm a bear," he explained, as if he thought Mal might have been joking.

"Excellent." Owen folded the letter and rose to his feet. "I just received a note to meet my sis—brother," he corrected quickly, "for dinner. I haven't seen him in a while, so I may be gone for a few hours. I'll return once we're finished, however. Bertie, if you could look after Mal while I'm gone? Find him some food?"

Mal ground his teeth together. He wasn't a child, or a pet, and he didn't appreciate Owen treating him like one.

But he swallowed it back for now. He couldn't raise suspicion with an argument, not if he was to warn Sophie. At least the timing of the letter was in his favor. Would Owen tell his brother about Mal—and if so, what would he say?

Once Owen was gone, an uncomfortable silence descended over the lab. Bertie watched Mal with a speculative look on his face. Probably waiting for Mal to steal something.

"You don't have to actually stand there and watch me," Mal said. "Ought to be safe enough here in the Coven, oughtn't I?"

"I'd expect so," Bertie agreed. Still, he kept looking at Mal. Maybe he *did* think Mal was going to start stuffing things in his pockets. "What about dinner, then? We could step out and get a sandwich. I know a good place not far from here—quiet."

Mal patted his belly. "No need. Had one for lunch, and that was after eating myself silly at breakfast. You wouldn't believe the spread Yates put out. Eggs, biscuits, bacon, *and* jam."

"Quite the feast," Bertie said. Mal couldn't tell if he meant it or not. "Suit yourself, then. I'm going back to my office. But if you want to leave the Coven, come find me first. You're not to wander the streets alone."

"Of course not." Mal smiled sunnily at him. Bertie let out a soft huff, but turned and left.

Finally.

Mal waited for several minutes, giving the bear plenty of time to lumber back to his office. Then he slipped off the desk and out the door.

A half hour later, Mal strode down Broome Street, hands shoved in his pockets, shoulders hunched. Sophie ought to be at their usual saloon this time of day; the barkeep was one of Madam Galpern's, and fenced pocket watches and smaller items. Mal had mostly left behind pickpocketing except when he had to, but Sophie liked to work the morning and noon crowds on the El, when everyone was packed in tight, and the men too distracted by the feel of her breasts to notice the touch of her hand relieving them of their valuables.

He'd barely stepped through the saloon door, before Sophie let out a squeal and ran to him.

"Mal! Saint Mary, we thought you was dead!"

Her thin arms wrapped around him in a tight hug. Then her hold loosened, and she stepped back, frowning up at him. "What's this, then? I was worried half to death after Nick came stampeding through here looking for you. And now you show up, barely a speck of dirt on you, dressed in a fancy coat, and smelling like you rolled around in a bunch of flowers?"

"Aye." He glanced around. It was too early for the factories to have let off work, so there weren't many other faces in the saloon at the moment. "Let me buy you a drink, and I'll explain everything."

She cocked one sandy brow at him. "I'm still mad at you for scaring me, but I ain't going to say no to a drink. Come on, then."

They ordered drinks and sandwiches—actual sandwiches, not the sad excuse of dry bread and wilted lettuce some saloons kept on hand, passed from customer to customer with no one taking a bite, to satisfy the technicalities of the liquor laws. Careful to keep his voice low, Mal told her everything that had happened over the last day.

"Saint Mary," she breathed, when he was done. "You found your witch?"

"Aye," he said cautiously.

It wasn't something they'd spoken of often. He and Sophie had met at the orphanage, when both of them were but wee slips of things. They'd come up together through Madam Galpern's "school," and formed a good team. Sophie would distract the mark, while Mal picked his pockets clean. And when he graduated to doing second-story work, it was only natural she came along as his lookout, to distract the coppers or sound the warning as needed.

They'd shared a lot over the years. Money and booze; laughter and tears. Slept together even, the one time, then agreed after they didn't suit that way. Far better off as friends than lovers.

But talking about his witch, or the possibility of finding his witch… that was hard even with other familiars. As much as he cared about Sophie, she'd never quite understood the mix of hope and terror the prospect carried with it.

Now she leaned across the table, her eyes going round and her voice dropping into a hoarse whisper. "And he's a *Yates?* One of them as lives on Fifth Avenue?"

Mal grinned, absurdly pleased by her surprise. "Aye. And set to marry one of the Vandersees, he is."

"Holy Familiar of Christ!" Her eyes shone. "You going to be living with them, then? In some mansion?"

"I guess." The notion didn't sit well with him, somehow. It was the usual arrangement, of course, witches and familiars moving in together. Hopefully the wife-to-be—Edith, that was her name—wouldn't hate Mal on sight.

Or demand he stay in fox shape all the damned time. Nick had said rich folk did that, but what did he know? Between the bribes to the police and taking care of half the ferals in the city, Nick didn't have two pennies to rub together.

Sophie nodded slowly, but the excitement ebbed from her face. "That's good, then. I'm real glad for you, Mal."

"So am I." He shifted awkwardly. "You got to be careful, though. One of the reasons I came looking for you was to warn you. If the man who killed Jacobs knows where I lived, he might also know we're friends. Come around asking where I am."

"I won't tell him," she said loyally.

"Nay, you don't understand." He leaned over and gripped her arm. "I've got protection, now. My own bodyguard—well, I slipped away so as to talk to you without the coppers, but from now on."

She drew back. "I can't…"

"You ain't turning on me," he said. "Just tell them I'm Yates's familiar now, and let us worry about it. I want to know you're safe."

Her expression shifted, lips parting with realization. "Right. I guess this is it, then. I won't be seeing you again."

He'd been so focused on surviving the next few days, few weeks, he hadn't even thought that far into the future. He'd agreed when Owen said he was reformed, but he'd never thought about what that really meant.

"Nay," he said. "I can't…I mean, I ain't going to forget about you. We'll…"

"What? Have lunch?" she asked. "Drinks of an evening?"

"I don't belong with those rich nobs," he said. That was one thing he knew, for sure. "I need you, Sophie. You're my only friend. Maybe we can't work jobs together any more, but…"

"But I still got a living to make." She sat back, and he could feel her slipping away, the distance forming between them like a wall. "Don't suppose you'll have to worry about that again."

"Take this." He pulled out a handful of the bills Owen had given him that morning. "For all I know, Owen might toss me out on my ear, or the new wife send me packing. We've been together too long, you and me. I'll see you again soon, all right?"

She took the money with alacrity. "Thanks, Mal. You're one of the good ones, you know?"

"Aye." He didn't feel like one, though. Abandoning her so he could go live in the sumptuous apartment on the west side…it felt like a betrayal.

She saluted him with her drink. "See you, Mal."

He left the saloon with his hands stuffed in his pockets and his head bowed. What else was he supposed to do? He'd gone to Owen to save his own skin, not thinking a moment about Sophie or anyone else.

Nick wouldn't have done it. Wouldn't have traded his freedom for anything. Not even his life. Certainly not for a soft bed and big breakfast.

Well, that was Nick's problem, wasn't it? Besides, Nick was a horse, and a damned big one at that. The sort knights rode into battle back in the day, seventeen hands high and solid muscle. Maybe when he was a colt he would have been vulnerable, but now no one was going to be forcing him to do anything.

It was different when you were a fox, or a cat, or a bird; something small that could be held in a cage and starved until you broke.

Mal shook his head. What was done was done. He'd made his choice. Even if the rumors were true, that the MWP had a means of breaking the bond, he still needed their protection.

One of the new hexed advertisements caught his attention in a shop window. A soap advertisement, meant to appeal to the viewer's sexual preferences, but it couldn't decide whether to show him a man or a woman in the tub. Mal smirked at it and started to glance away…but the reflection of two men behind him caught his attention.

They'd both been in the saloon.

Which meant nothing. He was getting paranoid.

Still, Mal increased his pace. When he reached the next window clean enough to show a reflection, the men were still with him, having sped up as well.

Fur and feathers.

Mal broke into a run.

Chapter 7

"I apologize for the surroundings," Owen said, as he settled across from his brother. The twenty-four hour restaurant was a far cry from Delmonico's or the Metropolitan Club. The tables were jammed close together, their checked tablecloths stained from a hundred previous diners. "It's convenient to the Coven and police headquarters, both. Roosevelt used to eat here often."

"You don't have to invoke Roosevelt's name to me," Nathan said, leaning back in his chair and casting a curious eye around the place. Corned beef and cabbage scented the air, and police in blue uniforms sat next to lawyers, tradesmen, and criminals alike. "I'm not our parents, Owen. You don't have to justify doing what makes you happy."

A server appeared with a carafe of coffee. Owen ordered a sandwich, and Nathan the brisket. Once the server left, Owen asked, "How was France?"

"Quite different from here." Nathan grinned and stretched his arms to either side, deliberately pulling his shirt and vest tight across his chest. No trace of feminine curves remained. His collar tugged down slightly, revealing the edge of one of the hexes now tattooed at strategic places on his body. "But look. You'd never know anything was there."

"The surgeons did fine work," Owen agreed. Nathan's smile had been absent for so much of their childhood; it was good to see it returned.

"And as soon as I healed, I let the tailors work their own magic."

Nathan admired the sleeve of his handsome suit. "I wish you'd come with me. You would have loved Paris."

Their food arrived. "Too much work here," Owen said regretfully as he picked up his sandwich.

Nathan snorted. "There will always be too much work and never enough time. When was the last time you did anything just for yourself? Just for the joy of it?"

Owen suppressed a sigh. Nathan simply didn't understand. Peter had been the apple of their parents' eye, the heir on which they'd placed all their hopes for the future. Owen had been a distant second, and Nathan an afterthought. But when Peter had his accident, everything had changed for Owen. His duty was no longer to be the best in his class at university, then the best hexman in the MWP. His duty was to be the Yates heir, and everything that entailed.

"I have news," Owen said, before his courage could fail him. "I'm bonded. To a familiar."

He could feel the bond as a sort of warmth in his chest, curled up behind his heart. The sensation was disconcerting, and he did his best to ignore it.

Nathan's eyes widened. "When did this happen?"

"Earlier today, actually."

"What? Today?" Nathan put down his fork. "And you didn't bring him? Her?"

"Him," Owen admitted. "Malachi. A fox. And no, because…he's not exactly…"

Nathan leaned forward. "Malachi. He's Irish, then?"

"Yes." Owen plucked at his napkin, all of his appetite gone. "But there's more. He's…well. A thief."

"Dear heavens!" Nathan sat back again. "I don't know whether to laugh or offer my sympathies."

"Sympathies. But I had no real choice. He was a witness to the Jacobs murder, and in danger, and…well."

"You couldn't pass up the opportunity to be the best witch possible, even if the fellow is entirely unsuitable?" Nathan guessed.

Owen forced himself to take another small bite of his sandwich. "I have responsibilities."

"Hmm." Nathan stirred more sugar into his coffee, but didn't drink any. "And what did Mother and Father have to say?"

"They don't know yet. No one does outside of the MWP, except for you." Owen gave up on the sandwich and set it aside. "I'll have to tell them before the wedding."

They would be horrified, of course. Even if he hadn't been the heir, the very idea of a Yates associating with someone of Mal's lowly class would appall them.

"Then I have the perfect opportunity," Nathan said. "Mother wanted me to…invite is the wrong word. Command you to appear at a dinner party Wednesday night."

"Wednesday?" Owen frowned. "Not Thanksgiving?"

Nathan heaved a sigh. "Thanksgiving is dinner at Delmonico's, as usual. But as I'm…well, no longer entirely respectable, shall we say, I won't be attending."

Nathan made it sound so simple. As though there hadn't been shouts and recriminations, and bitter arguments. For a while, Owen had feared their parents would disown him altogether.

"Wednesday night is intended as a compromise," Nathan went on. "Only Mother's closest friends and their families are invited. I suppose she hopes that, if there must be gossip concerning my transformation, she can at least keep it to a minimum."

"I'll be there," Owen said. "But you've reminded me of another reason I was glad you asked me to dinner today. Will you stand as my best man at the wedding?"

Nathan arched a brow. "You've missed the part where I'm no longer respectable, have you?"

"Don't be absurd." Owen took a swig from his coffee. "The Four Hundred resist any modern ideas—that's the whole point of having a select society, isn't it? But I'm already meeting their expectations by marrying Edith. I won't let them tell me I can't have my own brother beside me while I do it."

Nathan stared at him for a long moment…then sagged back against his chair. "Why are you marrying Edith?" he asked. "You're throwing away the life you want to have for the one our parents think you should live. And now you're asking me to stand by you, as if I approve. I won't give you an answer, until I have one of my own."

Owen ground his teeth silently. Why did Nathan refuse to understand what should have been obvious? "I have a duty to our family," he grated out.

"And their duty to you? To see you happy? What of that?"

"That is a child's selfish logic." He lowered his voice, conscious of the newspaper reporters who sometimes dined here. "Our finances aren't what they once were, Nathan. Surely even you are aware of that.

Commodities grow ever more expensive, yet the rent on the land we own in lower Manhattan continues to fall as the city expands to the north and west. We lost too much on investments in the Panic of '93, and while some of the stocks have recovered, many have not. If something isn't done, we'll have to sell the mansion in Newport."

"Then sell the bloody house!" Nathan exclaimed. "And Mother will have to learn to live without throwing parties that each run to the tens of thousands of dollars. None of that is worth your life!"

"Keep your voice down!" Owen snapped. "This isn't about the mansion, Nathan, or the parties. It's about our entire family, even you, facing social ruin."

"Social ruin, because we can no longer afford to keep up the Newport house," Nathan said with a twist of his lips. "Oh yes, what a wonderful society to belong to, that cares about nothing except one's bank account. In Europe—"

"This isn't Europe," Owen cut him off. "Mother has spent her entire life ensuring our place in society. I won't be the one to doom our family to ruin, either financial or social. Certainly not when the solution is as simple as marrying Edith Vandersee. Her father is prepared to bestow a very generous yearly sum on us, some of which, yes, will go to keep the house in Newport and make certain both Edith and Mother are able to entertain on the necessary scale."

Nathan shook his head in disgust. "If Peter could talk—"

"But he can't." Owen flung down his napkin. How could Nathan invoke their older brother's name so casually, especially after what had happened to him? "Which means the responsibility falls to me."

"Peter would never have wanted—"

"You don't know what Peter would want!"

Nathan's mouth pressed into a line. "I disagree. I think we both very well know what our brother wanted."

Owen felt all the blood drain from his face. "How dare you," he said, his voice shaking with the effort to keep from shouting the words.

"Yates! Can you hear me?"

Mal's voice, right in his hear. Owen started and looked around, but there was no sign of his familiar.

"Blast it, can't you hear me? Ain't this how it's supposed to work?"

"Mal?" Owen asked aloud. The bond. Right—Mal must be speaking to him through it.

"Thank Mary." Relief, mingled with fear, curled through the words, almost as though the bond carried some of Mal's emotion with it. *"I need*

help. I'm being followed. I think they mean to kill me."

Heavy footsteps thudded down the street after Mal. He fled, darting and weaving through the crowd. Surely the men following him wouldn't dare anything in sight of so many—

"Thief!" one of them bellowed. "Stop him!"

Fur and feathers.

Angry cries sounded, and a vendor standing beside his pushcart on the sidewalk made a grab for Mal. Mal dodged, the man's fingernails snagging in his coat, and kept running. It was a stroke of brilliance on the part of his pursuers, really—get bystanders to do their work for them, catch Mal, and then drag him off into an alley for what anyone else would assume to be private justice.

Unless the coppers heard them first. But for once, there was no blue uniform anywhere in sight. Of course the damned coppers wouldn't be there the one time Mal actually wanted them.

"Get him! Thief!"

A girl sweeping off a stoop swung her broom at his head. Mal ducked, then jumped back to avoid a fist from a man dressed like a laborer.

Enough—he couldn't escape in human form. He shifted, darting between the man's legs and down the road, while shouts of surprise rang out. Feet kicked at him, but he was too fast, shooting through the crowd and into the street.

The wheel of a cab nearly took off his nose, and he skidded to a halt. A shout sounded from the sidewalk, and he glanced back to see one of his pursuers shift into a foxhound.

Of all the damned luck.

Mal fled blindly, the hound baying behind him. If he could just make it to the Coven...but that was blocks away, through traffic and across streets. If only...

Saint Mary preserve him, he was an idiot. He had a way of summoning help now, didn't he?

"Yates! Can you hear me?"

He concentrated on the bond with Owen, the warm spot manifesting right behind his heart. He was in animal form, so his witch should be able to hear him, to look through his eyes.

No response. *"Blast it, can't you hear me? Ain't this how it's supposed to work?"*

"Mal?"

"Thank Mary." Mal risked a look back, caught sight of the foxhound's brown and white coat behind him. *"I need help. I'm being followed. I think they mean to kill me."*

"Where are you? What happened to Bertie?"

Mal's heart thudded in his chest, and he gasped for breath through an open mouth, tongue lolling into the freezing air. *"Broome and Allen Street. I'm making for the Coven, but one of them turned into a foxhound, and I can't run much farther."*

He sensed a wash of fear from Yates, catching him unexpectedly. *"I'm coming. I'm on the Bowery now. Just keep going, and I'll meet you."*

Mal dodged under a row of carts heaped with potatoes. He slid out from under them, shifted form, and snatched a pumpkin from a passing cart. He hurled it at the foxhound, forcing him to dodge, then clambered over the cart itself. The driver twisted around with an angry yell and snapped his whip in Mal's direction. Mal launched himself from the cart, took on fox form again, and sped through the crowd. A vicious kick caught him in the ribs, right where the knife had cut him the day before, and he staggered.

A glance over his shoulder showed the foxhound almost on him. Ignoring the pain, he took off running again.

There—the wide expanse of the Bowery, bisected by the scaffolding of the El, lay just ahead. Owen had said he'd be there—he'd promised—

A cab careened to a halt at the corner, and the door flew open. "Mal!" Owen shouted frantically. "Come on—hurry!"

Mal rushed for the cab. Owen's eyes widened, and he held his hand out. There came a tremendous growl from just behind Mal—

The door slammed shut the moment he cleared it. An instant later, the whole cab rocked as the body of the foxhound crashed into the door. The horse shied, and the driver let out a furious curse.

"Go!" shouted Owen. "Just go!"

The cab lurched into motion. Mal crouched on the floor, every limb trembling. Safe. He was safe.

His eyes drooped. Maybe he could just curl up on the floor…

Owen's arms scooped him up. Startled, Mal opened his eyes, to find himself cradled against Owen's chest.

"Thank God you're all right," Owen said. He stroked the fur between Mal's ears soothingly. "What happened to Bertie?"

Mal cringed. *"I snuck out. I didn't think…"*

Owen let out a sigh. "Mal…"

"It's a busy street! I didn't imagine I'd need a bodyguard. I figured the killer

was working alone—I never thought he'd have accomplices out looking for me."

"True." Owen hugged him tighter. And despite everything, there was a comfort in being held by his witch. "They must be desperate... which makes them dangerous." He pulled away his hand a let out a gasp. "You're bleeding."

"The wound opened again."

Owen sighed once more. Clearly, he thought Mal was an idiot. Given he'd almost been killed, Owen might even be right. "Let's get you home to The Folly, and I'll bandage you up. Again."

"Does this happen to you often?" Owen called through the half-closed door to Mal's bathroom. "Injuries, I mean. Because this is the second time in two days, and I'd like to know if I need to stock up on bandages and salve."

There came the splashing of water, followed by the sound of the drain. "Only since I've met you, copper," Mal called back. "And you know, you can come in. You've already seen the goods up close and personal."

Which was the problem. Owen had abandoned Mal for a long soak in the tub as soon as they returned to The Folly and spent the intervening time trying very hard not to picture his familiar bathing. Sprawled in the claw-footed tub, the ends of his fiery hair trailing in the water. Little wavelets lapping against his pale thighs, the nest of red curls around his cock...

Owen shifted uncomfortably, trying to will his erection away.

The door swung open all the way, and Mal stepped out, once again wearing nothing but that silk dressing gown. The edge of a bandage peeked out from under it. The scent of soap rose from skin flushed pink by the hot water. Amber eyes glanced up at Owen; they were the same color as in fox form, though his human pupils were round instead of slitted.

"You came for me," Mal said quietly.

God, he was standing too close. Owen could so easily reach out and brush aside the thin layer of silk, lay his palm on Mal's flank.

"Of course I did," Owen said. "You're my familiar. Did you think I'd just calmly finish my dinner while someone murdered you in the street?" The uncertainty that flashed through Mal's eyes bit deep. "Dear Lord, what did I do to give you such a low opinion of myself?"

"Nothing," Mal said with a shrug that sent the robe slipping lower on his shoulder. "But I know you ain't happy with me. I'm just a thief, after all."

Owen couldn't help himself; he caught Mal's chin in his fingers, tipped his head back slightly. "You're my familiar," he repeated. "Not anyone else. You."

"Aye," Mal said softly.

Then they were kissing, and there was nothing soft about it. Mal seized his lapels, as if seeking to haul him even closer. Their tongues slid together, and Owen's lips were pressed hard against his teeth. And oh God, it was so good, he'd wanted this so badly, and he couldn't have it. He couldn't.

Mal drew back, staring at him, eyes wild as if he wore his fox form. "Owen…"

"I c-can't." Owen closed his own eyes and willed his hands to let go of Mal. He had to put distance between them, but his cock begged him to rub against Mal instead.

Mal's chest slid softly against his as the familiar breathed. "Owen," Mal said, but this time with authority. "Open your eyes. Look at me."

He did so, telling himself all the while it was only out of politeness. Mal looked exquisite, his pale skin pink from the bath and from desire, his lips swollen from kisses. "You say you won't break your wedding vows," Mal said, his voice husky with need. "But you ain't made them yet."

"N-no." The words rasped coming out. Owen swallowed. "But what difference does it make?"

"You're like a watch, wound too tight," Mal murmured. His hands stroked Owen's chest, and Owen couldn't help but wish he wasn't wearing quite so many layers of clothing. "You don't do this sort of thing often, do you? Fuck?"

God. "No," Owen whispered. "I want…"

Too many things society would look down on. At the end of last year, he'd briefly visited several neighborhoods he ordinarily would never have set foot in, as part of the investigation into the plot to disrupt the Greater New York consolidation ceremony. He'd seen men there, brazen men on the streets, dressed to indicate they were available for hire by other men.

All of which was fine for the lower classes; no one expected them to be discreet. But he was a Yates. Even if he did give into desire, he had to maintain control. It was expected. Necessary.

And the last thing he wanted.

Mal considered him. "Why not find some Fifth Avenue swell and bring him back here? Get what you need?"

Owen shook his head, denying the possibility. "Word might get around if someone found out I like…this sort of thing."

"Being ordered around like a five-cent whore?"

Owen flushed. "Yes. I might have to face some of these men in a board room someday. If they knew the truth, they'd lose all respect for me. They'd see me as…weak."

Mal snorted. "Well, that's damned stupid of them. You ain't weak just because you like somebody telling you what to do in the bedroom. Probably none of them would've known how to treat you right anyway."

Mal's plain speech caught Owen off guard. It sounded as if he believed it—really believed it, and wasn't just saying something to make Owen feel better about his desires.

"On the other hand…" A slow, vulpine grin made its way across Mal's face, sending a delicious shiver down Owen's spine. "Their loss is my gain, ain't it? Got an offer for you, Owen Yates. Once you say your wedding vows, you belong to your blushing bride. But until that day, you're mine. To do with as I will, at least when it comes to the bedroom. That's what you want, ain't it? For somebody else to take control and make you *feel.*"

Owen's mouth was dry and his cock hard. He couldn't speak the humiliating words aloud, so he nodded instead.

Mal's eyes burned like yellow flames. "Say it."

"Y-yes."

Fingers curled around his wrist, tight enough to ride the edge of discomfort. "Yes what?"

Oh God. "Yes, sir."

That hungry grin again. Like Owen was a mouse about to be snapped up in the fox's jaws. "Then what do you say? Do we have an agreement?"

He had to tell Mal no. To stop this madness before it could begin.

Except…this was his chance. What Mal offered, a few days of hedonism, of indulging in his most secret, shameful desires, might be enough to satiate him. If he took this opportunity, if he satisfied these strange urges that gripped him, they'd surely cease to trouble him. He could enter into marriage with Edith, if not with joy, at least with equanimity.

"What do you get out of this?" he managed to ask.

A startled look flashed over Mal's features, followed by a short bark of laughter. "I'd think that part would be obvious. Do we have an agreement, Yates?"

"We do," he said, and was shocked his voice didn't shake.

"Well, then." Mal stepped back. "Let's go to bed."

Chapter 8

Mal's pulse throbbed at the base of his throat, echoed in his groin. His prick tented the thin silk of the robe, and the soft slide of the material over the head as he followed Owen sent shocks of pleasure through him. His hands trembled with desire, and he took a deep breath. It was up to him to make sure this wasn't over before it started, after all. He was the one who had to be in control.

Owen. God.

Owen had come for him, like he'd said he would. But he'd done a hell of a lot more. Held Mal the whole ride back to The Folly. Carried him upstairs in fox form, refusing to let him change and risk hurting aching muscles. Drawn the bath and laid out an array of hexes to ease any strained muscles, along with the bandages and salve.

Taken care of Mal. So now it was Mal's turn to take care of him.

Owen stepped into his bedroom, then turned to Mal, hands folded in front of him. Lips parted, eyes dilated. Just waiting for Mal's command.

Mal took a deep breath, sternly reining in his own excitement. He needed to show Owen he'd made the right choice. Which meant more than just a quick suck.

"I want you naked," Mal said. "Bare as the day you were born. Take off your coat."

Owen moved to comply, letting it fall heedlessly to the floor, the expensive fabric crumpled against the parquet.

"Now your vest."

It followed, though Owen paused to set his pocket watch aside. Gold, of course, and studded with sapphires. A good thing Owen hadn't gone to a disorderly house, looking for satisfaction. He'd have been robbed blind.

Bracers came after, then shoes. Socks.

"Take your shirt off," Mal ordered.

Owen's fingers trembled visibly as he undid each button, revealing pale skin beneath. And more.

"Fur and feathers, that must've cost a pretty penny!" Mal stepped closer to inspect Owen's skin. "Turn around. Let me get a good look."

Owen turned obligingly. Hex tattoos covered a good portion of his back, the ink bright against his ivory skin. Mal ran his hand over them, and Owen's flesh pebbled beneath his touch. "What are they for, then?"

"Health." Owen's voice came out rough. "To keep the lungs strong. To ward off infection, heal injuries more quickly. That sort of thing."

The sort of thing only the richest nobs and swells could afford. Not only the original work by the hexman tattooer, but the regular recharging of the hexes by a witch and familiar team to keep them working. "Who's been recharging them?" Mal asked, tracing the lines with a finger. "Who's been touching you?"

Owen swallowed convulsively. "Dominic and Rook, actually. But it's all very professional."

"Is it?" Mal let his hand slip around the front of Owen's trousers, and gave his stiff prick a hard squeeze.

A hiss and a buck of the hips rewarded him. "Yes, of course," Owen managed to say. "I swear."

Mal let go of him and stepped back. "The rest of it off. Now."

Owen hastened to obey. Soon he stood completely bare, without even his spectacles, his prick flushed red with desire, his nipples tight from either want or the chill air, or some combination thereof. "Ain't you a sight," Mal murmured. "Pinch your nipple."

A little gasp escaped Owen. "You like that," Mal said. "Good. Do it again. Harder."

Fur and feathers, but Owen looked edible. He followed Mal's commands like he was born for it, like he couldn't wait for someone to tell him what to do. Mal let the silk robe slide to the floor, so the only thing separating them was air. "Maybe I ought to fuck you," he mused. "Bend you over the bed right here and have my way with you."

Owen's lips parted, his silvery eyes gone dark pewter with lust. He trembled visibly, either from nervousness or anticipation. Mal cast about the room and spotted Owen's silk handkerchief, fallen out of his pocket onto the floor while he stripped.

Mal picked it up, an idea forming. "Get on the bed. Where are the rest of your handkerchiefs?"

"In the dresser."

Mal removed several and tied them together, before turning back to the bed. Owen had climbed on it, as ordered, and lay flat, watching him avidly. At the sight of the handkerchiefs, the color rose to his cheeks. "What are you going to do with those?"

Mal grinned. "Whatever I please. Stretch out your arms."

The bed posts were nice and sturdy. Had Owen chosen his furniture with this in mind? He bound Owen's wrists to the posts, then stepped back to observe. The muscles in Owen's arms tensed as he tested the restrictions, and a whimper escaped him. He looked wild, desperate, his prick leaking clear fluid onto his belly.

"All mine," Mal mused. "What should I do with you, eh?" He climbed onto the bed beside Owen. "I could fuck you." He let his hand drift across Owen's chest, pausing to give one nipple a hard pinch. Owen gasped in response and arched half off the bed. "You're so worked up, I bet you'd come just from having my cock in your arse, wouldn't you?"

Owen licked his lips. "I…"

"And we can't have that," Mal went on. "Can't have you spending until I tell you to." He moved down the bed and gave Owen's prick a very deliberate lick. "So don't come."

He slid his mouth down Owen's cock, all the way to the base. Owen cried out frantically. "Stop, please!"

Mal sat back, grinning. "Good boy." He gave Owen a few moments to calm down, then repeated the action.

Soon he had Owen thrashing, whimpering, and begging. Each time Owen got too close to the edge, he stopped.

And there was something damned arousing about having this sort of control over someone. About taking Owen right to the verge of coming, then backing off, again and again. The way Owen was struggling against his bonds, he'd have bruises on his wrists in the morning. His teeth showed white against his pink lip as he fought not to come, because Mal had told him not to.

"Well done," Mal murmured, shifting farther up the bed again. He ran his fingers down Owen's face, over his lips. Owen sucked on them, and Mal's prick ached with need. "I think you're going to suck my cock until I'm almost off. Then I'm going to finish on your face."

A moan of desire escaped Owen. His eyes were fixed on Mal's, pleading. Needy.

"Like that, do you?" Mal asked. "Beg me to do it. Say: Please come all over my face, sir."

The words were almost a whimper. "Pl-please come all over my face, sir."

"Good boy." Mal leaned in and gave him a swift kiss. The he slid onto Owen, straddling his chest. Owen's breathing was harsh, chest heaving under Mal's thighs, and he licked his lips at the sight of Mal's cock pointed at his mouth.

Which posed a potential problem, if Owen didn't like the way things were going. Fortunately, the solution was easy enough. Mal ran a finger along Owen's face, tracing the line of his jaw. "You feel it, don't you? The connection between us."

Owen nodded. "Something in you recognized something in me."

As poetic a way of putting it as Mal had ever heard. "I ain't interested in hurting you, understand? So if anything starts feeling wrong, concentrate on the bond. We can't talk through it while I'm in human form, but this close, I'll still know. Agreed?"

"Yes." Owen swallowed. "I mean, yes, sir."

Mal braced one hand against the headboard, then switched when the cut on his side pulled painfully. With his other hand, he grasped the base of his cock, dragging the head across Owen's cheek, then down to his lips. Owen opened his mouth eagerly, tongue flicking out and catching the underside of Mal's prick.

Mal thrust in. The head of his prick hit the back of Owen's throat, and Owen made a choked sound. His body jerked under Mal, bindings going tight as he struggled. Owen sucked hard, using his tongue, his lips, and whimpered when Mal pulled back, before shoving in again.

"Fuck," Mal swore. "You look so good, sucking on my cock."

Owen stared up at him, those gorgeous silver eyes vulnerable without the protective glass lenses. Hungry and wanting, and so very desperate. It was almost enough to make Mal come, so he pulled free, grabbed his shaft, and tugged.

It only took a few strokes. The first jet of spend hit Owen on the corner of his mouth, and the next decorated his cheek. Owen moaned, wriggling beneath Mal.

"Fur and feathers, you look amazing, with my spunk all over your face." Mal reached behind and grasped Owen's cock, stroking him.

"Come for me. Now."

Owen shouted, back arching off the bed. Warm spend coated Mal's hand. He gave Owen a few extra strokes, until he whimpered, then let go and licked it off his palm.

"Mmm." He untied the silk handkerchiefs from around Owen's wrists. The red marks beneath would definitely leave traces on Owen's skin tomorrow. When he'd freed Owen, he flopped beside him. "Good?"

Owen's breathing had just begun to even out. "I...yes. God, yes."

"Good." Mal dropped a kiss onto Owen's shoulder. "You might want to clean up."

He watched Owen cross to the bathroom. A moment later, water rattled in the pipes. Mal shook his head, still hardly able to believe it. Water, right there whenever you wanted, cold or hot. No hauling buckets or heating it over the stove.

Sophie would be amazed.

Owen returned, hesitated by the bed for an instant, then slid beneath the covers. Mal snuggled against him, idly tracing patterns over his pale chest. Owen caught his hand, but gently. "How are you feeling?"

Mal grinned lazily. "Pretty damned good."

A smile tugged at the corner of Owen's mouth, but it vanished quickly. "I meant your injury. I have some pain hexes if you need them."

"Nay, I'm fine."

"Good." Owen rolled onto his side to face Mal. "Then I shan't feel guilty about demanding to know what the devil you thought you were doing."

Mal sat up, the blankets sliding to pool around his waist. Now that his blood had cooled, the chill air raised gooseflesh on his bare skin. "I already told you. I didn't think anything would happen. I was walking down a crowded street in the daylight. I certainly didn't think the killer would have accomplices watching for me."

"That was foolish," Owen shot back. "You should have been careful and taken Bertie with you."

"I didn't think—"

"Obviously." Owen glared up at him. "You've almost been killed twice now—once in your own apartment and again today. Whoever murdered Mr. Jacobs will get the electric chair if he's caught, no question about it. If he's part of a larger criminal gang, as seems likely, they'd be looking at life in prison as accessories. Until they're all in jail, you're in danger. Why on earth did you take such a risk?"

Mal hunched his shoulders. He hadn't wanted to tell Owen, but if he didn't, Owen would think him a fool. "I went to visit a friend of mine, who I didn't want to bring to the coppers' attention, all right?"

Owen sat up as well. "Are you saying you went to visit some of your—your criminal colleagues?"

To Mal's surprise, he sounded more hurt than anything else. "I'm going to reform, like I promised," he replied defensively. "But I had to see Sophie. She didn't know if I was dead or alive, or rotting in Sing Sing. I at least had to warn her some dangerous types might be coming around looking for me, didn't I?"

Owen's eyes narrowed fractionally. "A friend."

"Aye, a friend. You have those, don't you?" Mal returned Owen's glare without flinching. "Sophie and I've been together since we were both guttersnipes."

Uncertainty flickered in Owen's argentine eyes. "Together?"

"As friends. And business partners, from time to time." Mal arched a brow. "And if you're asking if I've got a lover, the answer is nay. I ain't going behind anyone else's back by fucking you."

A light flush crossed Owen's cheeks. "I wasn't—that is—good. But my point is—"

"Your point is, I have to give up a friend I've known my whole life? Just abandon her, because she ain't convenient to know anymore? Let her be surprised when a killer turns up looking for me?" Mal shook his head. "Nay. I ain't doing that."

Owen sighed. "Very well. You've made your point. But the men who followed you clearly knew you'd be there."

"Not necessarily," Mal said. "It's a saloon we go to often enough. They were probably there looking for me, or for Sophie to ask her if she knew where I was." It was probably sheer luck no one had beset him after leaving Madam Galpern's yesterday. "And before you ask, Sophie didn't tell them anything. I'd trust her with my life."

"Honor among thieves?"

"Fuck you, Yates." Mal started to slide out of bed, but Owen grabbed his wrist.

"I'm sorry," Owen said. "That was uncalled for. I just…I don't understand."

Mal frowned. "Don't understand what?"

"Your life. Why you'd choose to be a thief, rather than find honest work." Owen's pale brows drew together. "You seem clever enough to have done any number of things."

"I suppose I could have been a copper," Mal said. "Oh no, you said *honest* work."

"Very funny." Owen released him. "But not much of an answer."

Mal sighed. "It seems easy for you, don't it?" He picked up the silk robe and pulled it on. "I'll bet you've never been locked out in the freezing cold, with no food in your belly and no shoes on your feet."

Owen's expression turned uncertain. "I can't say that I have, no."

"Didn't think so." Mal shrugged, as if it didn't matter. "I ended up in an orphanage. There's a person, whose name I ain't going to mention to you, who…well, she has a couple of nuns who look for talented youngsters, one might say. They brought me to her attention, and she taught me a trade."

"To steal," Owen said flatly.

"Aye, to steal." Mal slid from the bed and went to the door. "But you know what? She was the only one who ever looked at me and saw something worthwhile. So maybe the only thing I was ever good for was being a thief, but at least I was good for something."

The next morning, Owen unlocked the door to the lab and ushered Mal inside. They'd risen early, and had a light breakfast of coffee and biscuits bought from a pushcart on the way to the Coven. Mal then spent a half hour filing a report on the attack yesterday, with Bertie's assistance.

Needless to say, Bertie hadn't been pleased. At least Mal had the grace to apologize to the other familiar.

"Someone will come soon and show you the rogues gallery," Owen said as he shut the door behind them.

Mal stripped off his overcoat and hung it on the coatrack. "Why can't you go with me now?"

Owen crossed the room to the table where the device lay in its many pieces. He took off his suit coat, placed it over the back of a chair, and unbuttoned his cuffs. He started to roll them up, then realized doing so would expose the bruises on his wrists.

The reminder sent a rush of blood to his cock. God, last night had been good. The feel of the silk around his wrists, of being bound and helpless. Of Mal's weight on his chest, pressing him into the mattress while he fucked Owen's mouth…

He'd always heard rumors that sex between witch and familiar could be amazing, thanks to the bond. Certainly his experience seemed to confirm it.

"Because I have other work to do," he said, endeavoring to focus on something other than his memories.

"Figuring out what the clock that ain't a clock does," Mal said.

"Exactly." Owen seated himself and picked up a magnifying glass. Fitting the gears and cogs together would go quicker if he had some idea of what the device was meant for. Some of the pieces seemed to have various elements of hexes on them, though what good only part of a hex would do, Owen couldn't guess.

But he had to. If he couldn't solve this puzzle within the next four days, likely no one could.

Oh, a hexman like Dominic might try to pick up where he left off. But Dominic, as competent as he was, merely studied existing hexes. Known quantities. Owen's gut told him that reassembling the device would take the instincts of an inventor.

"Those are some fancy degrees," Mal said. He stood at one end of the lab, staring up at the framed parchments. "Doctorate of Hexology from Harvard, eh?"

"Indeed." Owen studied the parts of the device, laying them out as they seemed to relate to one another. "I studied the theory of hexology, as well as its history. What remains of it, anyway, after the Inquisition tried to stamp out magic across half the world. Many of the hex principles we use today weren't developed until the Enlightenment, in an attempt to replace what had been lost."

"Huh." Mal drifted over and perched on a stool close to Owen. "And this device has some of those old hexes on it?"

"It does. The Hellenistic methods weren't entirely lost, fortunately, and the remains provided a foundation for our current system." He held out one of the bronze plates for Mal to examine. "You can see the components of a hex on this. These don't do anything on their own, however; they have to be combined with others. Which makes the purpose of the device a bit hard to discern."

"So how did it all start, anyway?" Mal asked. "Hexing, I mean."

"No one knows, exactly." Owen paused, wondering how much Mal actually wanted to know. He seemed genuinely interested, though. "Archaeologists recently discovered depictions of familiars in the Cave of Altamira. And there is evidence of hexed amulets from what seems to be ancient times. Most of those are primitive—they rely on the native power of the object they're carved on, enhanced only by a few lines carved into them."

Mal frowned. "Native power?"

Owen cast his mind back to his earliest lessons, trying to recall a simple way to explain it. "In the end, a hex is like…like a pudding mold. It both contains and shapes the magic put into it."

Mal chuckled, but nodded. "Aye, I understand that much."

"Some objects—certain gemstones, bones, rocks worn into specific shapes by the action of wind and water—are natural containers for magic. Probably the first hexes were cast using such objects. As time went on, someone realized altering them further made the magic more focused, or changed the nature of the spell." Owen shrugged. "We'll never know for sure, of course."

"You know a lot," Mal said. "Your family must be proud."

Owen ducked his head. "I suppose. They would have preferred I study something more practical. Law, perhaps, or finance." Mal passed him back the plate, and he put it with the others. "Something useful."

"And this ain't useful?" Mal asked, looking around. "No offense to your parents, but you saved my life the other night. Seems damned useful to me."

"Hexology is a respectable enough study for a second son," Owen said. "So long as I wasn't the heir. But when Peter…"

Owen caught himself. He hadn't meant to talk about Peter. Not yet.

"Peter?" Mal asked, cocking his head.

"You don't follow the society columns, do you?" Owen asked, as lightly as he could. "My older brother. He was the heir, meant to follow in Father's footsteps and ensure the Yates fortune continued to prosper for another generation."

And he might yet have, if Owen hadn't been so selfish. If he'd answered Peter's invitation to lunch that awful day, everything might have been different. Owen would have realized something was wrong. Peter would have told him his intentions, and Owen would have insisted on watching over him until an alienist could be summoned. Peter would be whole today, strong and healthy and joyful. He wouldn't require a wheelchair, or a nurse to attend to his every need. He'd be able to talk and laugh, and Owen would know Peter understood when he spoke to him.

Mal's hand came down on his shoulder, fingers warm through the fabric of Owen's shirt. "What happened?"

Owen pulled away and returned his attention to the device. He'd start with the rods and try to determine which gears fit them. "There was an accident," he said. "Peter's gun discharged when he was cleaning it."

A lie, of course. But one meant to protect Peter's reputation.

And the family's. Always that.

"Ah, hell," Mal said. "I'm sorry."

Owen shook his head, though he didn't know what he denied. "Peter survived, but his injuries were severe. He lives in a small house off Broadway, where he must be cared for at all times." Owen fit a gear and a rod together and set them aside. "With Peter incapacitated, everything falls to me as the next in line. So far I've avoided my responsibilities, but once I wed Edith, it will be time to assume my proper role. Even if my parents approved of me remaining with the MWP, the Vandersees certainly wouldn't."

Mal snorted. "Oh right. Wouldn't want anyone thinking their new son-in-law actually did something useful for a living."

"That isn't so," Owen objected. "I'll be working with Mr. Vandersee, my father-in-law. Mostly likely I'll be in charge of approving any newly developed hexes. I won't be the one creating them, of course, but it will still be useful work."

The words sounded hollow, even to him. Mal's lips parted, but before he could say anything, Owen added, "You'll meet them tomorrow night. If you'd like, that is. Mother is having a small dinner party. I thought it would be a good opportunity to introduce you."

A look of surprise flickered over Mal's face, but he nodded cautiously. "All right. I'll go."

There came a sharp rap on the door. Bertie stuck his head inside. "I've got all the paperwork turned in," he said. "Mal, are you ready to take a look at the rogues gallery?"

Mal nodded. "Aye." He started for the door, then paused and glanced back at Owen. "I can't say I was exactly thrilled to find out my witch was a copper," he said quietly. "Or that I want to stay with the MWP. But it seems a shame for you to give up something that makes you so happy."

Then he crossed to the door and shut it behind him.

CHAPTER 9

"NOTHING," MAL SAID a few hours later, stepping back in disgust. The MWP's rogues gallery was divided into familiars and non-familiars; the familiars section had photos of both human and animal form. And not a damned one of them matched either of the men who had followed him from the saloon yesterday.

Bertie frowned. "Are you certain about the breed? We can look at the canid shifters again." He put one hand to the wooden frame.

"Of course I'm sure," Mal snapped. "Don't you think I know a bloody foxhound when I see one?"

Bertie held up both hands. "Sorry; didn't mean to imply otherwise. It's just in the heat of the moment, sometimes things get confused. But you're right."

Mal winced. Bertie was just doing his job, after all. "I shouldn't have barked at you. Things are just getting to me, I guess."

"Understandable." Bertie paused, then glanced around. The rogues gallery was held in a smaller room a floor above the detective's area. The room used to photograph suspects was adjacent to it, as was the dark room to develop the film. At the moment, they were the only two people present. "Are things going well with Dr. Yates?"

Now wasn't that a knot to untangle. "Well enough," he said neutrally.

"I don't mean to pry," Bertie said hastily. "It's just that I've heard things. That in high society, familiars aren't supposed to be out of animal form except in the servants' quarters. Is that true?"

"Not so far," Mal replied cautiously. "Not with just the two of us in the apartment, anyway."

"Ah." Bertie nodded. "I expect things will change after the wedding, when you move into one of the big houses on Fifth Avenue. Though I suppose it's a small price to pay to live in a mansion, eh?"

Was it? He'd be warm and well fed, if nothing else. Exiled from Owen's bed and spending most of his day as a fox, but so what? Some familiars preferred animal form anyway.

Nick wouldn't agree with the exchange. But Nick was a stubborn fool whose pride would have him starve in the streets before taking anything from a witch.

Voices drifted through the open door, coming their way. "…good to see you again," said one. Tom Halloran, that was the witch's name. The hexbreaker. "We ought to get drinks one night. Cicero will complain about going to an ordinary, working man's saloon, but he'll survive."

"Aye, I'd like that," replied a voice Mal would have preferred never to hear again. The two men stepped inside, Patrolman Bill Quigley dressed in his blue uniform just as he had been the night of the Jacobs murder.

Mal took a hasty step back, in case Quigley decided to take out the handcuffs. "What's he doing here?"

Quigley glared at him. "If it were up to me, I'd be here to arrest you for burglary. But as the charge has conveniently gone away, I'm here to liaise with the MWP. The ordinary police needed someone to coordinate the investigation into the Jacobs murder, and I volunteered. Which unfortunately means talking to you."

Mal put a hand to his chest. "Patrolman, you wound me. I'm a reformed man, I am."

Quigley snorted. "I'll believe it when I see it."

"Now, Bill, don't be so hard on the fellow," Halloran interjected. He was a big man, with a thatch of blond hair and an easy smile. "You stood by me, when everyone else thought they ought to lock me up in Sing Sing and throw away the key."

"Aye, but I knew you for years beforehand," Quigley objected. When Halloran arched a brow, he sighed. "Fine, have it your way. Malachi, you have your chance to prove you're a reformed character."

"How very generous of you," Mal said, giving Quigley his toothiest grin.

"Any luck with the gallery?" Halloran asked, nodding at the photos.

Mal shook his head. "Nay. Not a foxhound in the bunch."

"Of course. That would make things too easy," Quigley said. "All right, let's go see your witch, so I don't have to repeat myself."

"Cicero and I have a case of our own," Halloran said. He clapped Quigley on the shoulder. "But it was good to see you. Don't forget that drink." He glanced at Mal. "And don't let them be too hard on you, just because of your past. I believe you're going to make the most of your new opportunity."

Mal blinked. "I...thank you?"

Halloran left, and Quigley gestured to Mal. "Lead the way then."

"So what did Halloran do, that they would have thrown him in Sing Sing?" he asked as they walked.

"That's his business, not yours," Quigley replied. "If he wants you to know, he'll tell you."

"All right, all right, just making small talk," Mal said, lifting his hands quickly. Owen would probably know, anyway.

Owen looked up from the device when they stepped into the lab. He'd made progress while Mal was staring at photographs. The device was starting to look like something more than just a pile of parts. "Patrolman Quigley," Owen said, straightening his spectacles. "Can I be of assistance?"

"Can we," Mal corrected, though he wasn't entirely sure why.

Owen nodded. "Of course. Can we be of assistance?"

"The regular police sent me to liaise with the MWP," Quigley explained. He eyed the device curiously. "Any idea what this thing does, then? Your report said it ain't a clock."

"It isn't, and not yet." Owen frowned at the device as though it had personally offended him. "I'll know more once I'm further along in restoring it."

Mal perched on his stool near Owen. "So, regular police out of leads, eh?" he asked with a grin. "Come to see if we can solve the case for you?"

Quigley glowered. "None of the usual informants have anything useful," he admitted. "We've chased down every clue, but come up with nothing. And of course the blasted newspapers can't wait to make us look bad, and everyone from the mayor on down is demanding the murder be solved yesterday." He nodded at Mal. "You'd best be glad you've got Dr. Yates's protection, that's all I can say."

A shiver ran up Mal's spine. If Owen hadn't been his witch, he'd either be dead or sitting in the Tombs right now. Or in an interrogation room at police headquarters, while the coppers beat a confession out of him.

Owen touched his hand beneath the table. Startled, Mal glanced at him, and got a reassuring smile. "A good thing he's safe with me, then," Owen said.

Unexpected tightness gripped Mal's throat. Which was stupid, really. Owen was just doing what he felt to be his duty, that was all. No sense in getting choked up about it.

Quigley folded his arms over his chest. "So, Mr. Malachi, I've got to ask. You're a second-story man—reformed, of course. You sorts know each other, and if you didn't recognize the murderer, there's surely someone who would. Is there anyone we ought to be talking to?"

Mal hesitated. He couldn't lead the coppers back to his friends. Back to Sophie, who'd always stood by him, or Madam Galpern, who had saved him from the orphanage and taught him the skills to get by. Madam Galpern might not have known who else was working the Jacobs mansion when he'd talked to her before, but surely she'd made it her business to find out by now. And she did work with the police from time to time—mostly by the way of bribes to captains and judges, of course. She might be willing to help him, especially if it meant removing some of the competition.

"I might," he said carefully. "But we have to do this my way. On my terms. So listen up."

"You shouldn't have come with me," Mal complained an hour later. "If someone sees me with a copper, it'll ruin my reputation."

Owen snorted. They'd taken the El to Grand Street, then set off on foot. As usual, the sidewalks were crowded with pushcart vendors, the street choked with pedestrians, carts, and the occasional cab. "You're mad if you think I'm going to let you out of my sight after yesterday."

"And I ain't forgotten the chewing the captain gave my arse after you pulled your vanishing act the night of the murder," Quigley growled. "You're lucky I don't handcuff you to my wrist."

Mal rolled his eyes. "Although I appreciate your concern," he said, aiming the words at Owen, "it ain't possible. My friend don't know either of you. She ain't going to talk openly with you there." He halted in front of a saloon halfway down the block from the haberdashery. "Wait here. I promise I'll call for you through the bond if there's even the slightest bit of trouble. Then you and the patrolman can break down the door and come dashing to my rescue."

Owen looked uncertain. Quigley scanned the street, and his mouth pursed beneath his mustache. "Going to see Madam Galpern, are you?"

Mal blinked. "Nay, of course not. She makes women's hats. I've got no need for one of those."

Quigley snorted. "Aye, a hat maker. A hat maker whose got enough officials in her pocket to avoid the inside of the cell where she belongs." He sighed and glanced at the saloon. "Go on with you, then. Dr. Yates and I will have a drink, and you'd best be back before we're done. Or we'll come get you."

Mal wanted to argue, but one look at the determination in Owen's eyes told him he wouldn't get far. "Fine. Drink slowly, though."

He set off through the crowd, not glancing back at Owen or Quigley. In truth, it was probably a good thing they were there. Someone knew his haunts, well enough to have men looking for him at the saloon where he regularly met Sophie. They'd surely have someone watching for him outside the haberdashery. The thought made the skin between his shoulders itch, and he hastened his steps.

The bell rang cheerily over the door as he stepped inside. Madam Galpern stood at one end of the shop, supervising a hexwoman marking the inside brim of a hat. She glanced up—and the welcoming smile on her face drained away.

Mal held up his hands. "I know you asked me to stay away, but I need help, and lots of it."

Madam Galpern considered him a moment, then nodded. "Of course, dear. Let's go upstairs, shall we?"

He gratefully followed her to the second floor. Taking off his hat, he held it in his hands, while she poured a measure of brandy into a single tumbler. Seating herself on a brocaded divan, she looked up at him coolly. "Now, tell me, how can I be of assistance?"

No sense in beating around the bush. "I need to find out who murdered Mr. Jacobs," he said. "The fellow tried to kill me himself two days ago. Yesterday, two others followed me. One was a familiar—a foxhound, which I don't think was a coincidence." He swallowed. "Fellow was a thief, wasn't he? Part of a gang, it seems like. You know every pickpocket and second-story man in this city, or at least know someone who does. Ordinarily I wouldn't ask you to turn anyone over to the coppers, but this is my life we're talking about. It's him or me."

"Oh, you poor thing." She sat forward, full lips pursed sympathetically. "Of course I'll help you."

Relief flooded through him. "Thank you. I knew I could count on you."

"Naturally, I'll expect some help from you in return."

The relief drained away. "Maybe you didn't hear the news," he said hesitantly. "But I'm bonded to a witch now. A copper, in fact. I ain't told him nothing about you—I wouldn't do that," he added hastily. "But I can't be doing any second-story work again."

Madam Galpern's smile sent a little chill through him. "Oh, Sophie came by and told me all about your unexpected rise in society. You haven't just bonded with a witch policeman, but with Owen Yates. I have it on good authority that the Yates family isn't as wealthy as they used to be, but their fortunes are going to reverse very soon."

Mal's heart beat against his ribs. "With the wedding. Aye."

Her smile grew wider. "Allow me to congratulate you on your good fortune. As it happens, it's my good fortune as well." She leaned back against the brocade pillows. "Mrs. Yates—of course I mean your witch's mother, not his future wife—is the owner of a necklace set with a spectacular gem. A twelve-pointed star sapphire called the Star of Winter. She doesn't wear it often now, but when she was young and at the height of her beauty, she was never seen without it around her neck."

Mal's mouth went dry. "And?" he asked, though he could guess well enough.

"I have a buyer who is *very* motivated to acquire the gem, and soon." Her smile showed teeth now. "I propose a deal. I give you the name of the murderer, and in exchange, you give me the necklace."

Fur and feathers, this was turning into a disaster. "I can't!" he objected. "Owen knows I'm—I mean, I was—a thief. They'll suspect me in an instant!"

"Then I suggest you fabricate an excellent alibi," she replied. "But you're in luck. This has been planned for some time. My buyer already commissioned a replica to be left in its place. All we lacked was access to swap it with the original. As I said, Mrs. Yates no longer wears the jewel often. With luck, no one will discover the loss for years to come."

Mal's fingers had gone cold. If he did this, and Owen found out… what would happen? Would he have Mal thrown in jail? Have Halloran sever their bond and find another familiar?

That seemed likely. Even if Owen didn't want to cause a scandal, he'd probably toss Mal right back to the gutter. Find another familiar eager for the good life, and pretend they'd been bonded all along.

But if Mal didn't agree to the deal, he'd have to rely on the police to find the murderer before he became the next victim. And given what

Quigley said, that didn't sound like a bet he wanted to make.

Owen wouldn't find out. Mal would be careful.

"All right," he said aloud. "You've got yourself a deal."

Though Owen had been grateful Mal returned from the haberdashery unharmed, his familiar was unusually quiet all the way back to the Coven.

"She'll help me," was all Mal had said. "It'll take her some time to find who's responsible. Once she does, she'll let me know right quick. A murder like Jacobs's is bad for her business, after all. The sooner the killer gets put away, the sooner things will get back to normal."

Quigley seemed less than pleased to be working with the criminal element. But he appeared to recognize they had little other choice; certainly the regular police force had made no headway in the murder. "I'd best go report in to my captain, then," he said heavily when they reached the steps leading up to the Coven. He scanned the steps and door briefly, as if looking for someone, then sighed. "Send word if you come across anything new, and I'll do the same."

"Bye!" Mal called cheerily after him. When Quigley was gone, he shook his bright head. "I'll never get used to working with coppers. At least it's only temporary."

The reminder sat heavily in Owen's belly, and its weight only increased when he found a note waiting in the lab for him. "Mother requests my presence for a small dinner," he said sourly. "Nathan must have told her about you."

Mal cocked his head. "You don't sound pleased."

"We're already to see her tomorrow night. And…I'd hoped to spend the evening with you," Owen said. Heat crept up his cheeks as he realized what he'd said. "That is…"

"You don't want to waste the time we've got?" Mal stepped closer and ran a hand down Owen's side, across his thigh.

Owen's mouth went dry, and his cock swelled in response. "Something like that."

Mal gave his prick a firm squeeze, drawing an involuntary gasp from him. "I'll wait up for you."

"Th-thank you." Owen swallowed hard. Mal let go of him and moved away; Owen wasn't certain if he was glad for the distance or not. "Really, I don't mean to sound selfish. About the invitation, that is. It's only that family can be…complicated."

"Aye," Mal said ruefully.

Owen flushed again. "I'm sorry. It must sound like a bunch of whining to you. How old were you when you went to the orphanage?"

"Eight or nine." Mal shrugged. "I don't rightly know how old I am, to be honest."

The bronze gears of the device gleamed as Owen settled himself back at the table. "Were either of your parents familiars? It runs in families, they say, the same as witch blood."

"Not as far as I know." Mal straddled the stool beside him. His amber eyes had gone distant. "Though I don't know much, truth be told. I was too young to have even been certain I was a familiar, when they threw me out."

Owen's hand froze, half-way to one of the gears. "They threw you out?" He'd assumed Mal's family had been carried off by some plague or tragedy.

"Aye." Mal hunched his shoulders. "They had too many mouths to feed already. Had to earn my keep, didn't I?"

"At nine years old?"

"Old enough to sell newspapers." Mal shrugged, as though it didn't matter. "The last day, I'd managed to scrape almost five dollars together, if you can believe it. *Five* dollars! Ended up robbed by some older boys, though. When I showed up with nothing in my pockets that evening, Ma told me to get out. I'd never amount to nothing. I tried to tell her what happened, but Da wanted results, not excuses. He fetched me a good one across the face and threw me into the hall. I spent a few nights sleeping wherever I could find a spot, then made my way to the orphanage."

"I see." Owen's parents didn't believe in excuses either, it was true. When he'd been nine, he'd been expected to answer his tutor's questions without hesitation or error. A Yates must excel at all things; that was the lesson he'd learned.

But even if he *had* failed, even if he'd disappointed his parents, they wouldn't have thrown him out on the street and left him to make his own way through the world. They expected him to know his duty to them, but they in turn stood by their duty to raise him to manhood. Oh, there had been more than a few moments when he'd believed they might disown Nathan, that was true.

But by then Owen had been the heir. Had the influence to put his foot down…so long as he complied in other ways. "And then you met Madam Galpern?"

Mal's eyes widened in faux innocence. "I'm sure I don't know who you're talking about." Owen gave him a look, and he relented. "Quigley needs to keep his big mouth shut. Aye, I met her, a year or two later. She saw something in me—the first time anyone ever did."

No wonder Mal was loyal to her, and to this other friend he'd met at the saloon yesterday. Owen touched his hand gently. "I'm sorry."

When they first met, he'd assumed Mal chose to be a thief because of some moral failing. Perhaps he'd merely done what he had to, and in the process fallen in with the wrong people, never knowing anything else.

Things would be different now, though. Even though they couldn't stay lovers for much longer, Owen would see that Mal could count on him.

Mal squeezed his hand. "Nothing to be sorry about. So, should I come with you tonight, instead of tomorrow? Meet the family?"

"Not tonight." Owen winced. "I suspect…well. You'll get a formal introduction to Mother tomorrow."

"And you want to prepare her for what she's in for?" Mal asked with a sly grin.

Owen snorted. "The other way around—I wish to spare you for as long as I can. Once we're done here, go back to The Folly for dinner. There's a restaurant on the first floor, near the entrance. Order what you like, and have it sent up to the apartment. You're fond of chicken, aren't you?"

Mal licked his lips. "Well, I am a fox."

"I suggest the coq au vin. It's quite good." Owen hesitated, but it had to be said. "And *please*, Malachi, have Bertie accompany you. You should be safe inside The Folly, but I'd prefer it if you didn't take the El alone."

He expected an argument, but Mal only nodded. "Aye. I've no desire to get myself killed, believe me. I've learned my lesson."

"Thank you." Owen had the sudden urge to lean over and kiss Mal. But that was foolish. They had sex, but they weren't lovers in any other sense of the word. And even that would end soon.

Instead, he gestured to the gears on the table. "I'm guessing a thief needs a good eye, and I could use a second set of hands. Would you care to assist? I'll explain some of the principles behind the mechanical movement, if you'd like."

Mal's worried look eased into a smile. A real smile, not the sharp grin he usually offered Owen. "Aye. I would indeed."

Chapter 10

When Owen arrived for dinner, it was to discover Edith and Kirk Vandersee there as well. He restrained his annoyance—this had seemed an excellent opportunity to question Mother about where Mrs. Jacobs might have been the night of her husband's murder. But he couldn't ask such delicate questions in front of anyone else without appearing horribly gauche.

Instead, he kissed his mother on the cheek, then bent over Edith's hand. She was a plain woman, her mousy brown hair swept into some complicated arrangement a fleet of hairdressers had no doubt labored over for hours. A delicate string of pearls circled her neck, and she wore an evening dress of blue silk. He tried to imagine stripping the silk from her body, kissing her neck tenderly, and cupping her breasts. The images left him utterly unmoved.

Still, he would manage. There were plenty of hexes meant to ensure a man's performance. He could even draw up his own, once he learned the correct pattern. He would identify her preferences and ensure her pleasure. At least one of them should gain satisfaction from the experience.

"Miss Vandersee," he said, and tried to sound happy to see her.

"Dr. Yates, it's lovely to see you," she replied woodenly. "I was so pleased when your mother told us you were coming."

"Quite; quite," Kirk enthused, shaking Owen's hand. "Any progress on the Jacobs murder?"

"None I can comment on," Owen replied, which wasn't entirely false.

"How ghastly," Mother exclaimed. Her hair was swept into a coiffure even more elaborate than Edith's, and pearls trimmed her gown of bronze silk. "If you men insist on speaking of such matters, I must ask you to withdraw."

Kirk immediately bowed over her hand. "Please, do forgive my terrible manners, Mrs. Yates. I let my concern for you and Edith get the best of me."

Owen barely kept from rolling his eyes. Still, Kirk's lie worked, as Mother beamed at him. "Of course, Mr. Vandersee. You're always so thoughtful."

The dinner gong rang, and Kirk offered his elbow to her. "May I have the privilege of escorting you?"

That left Edith for Owen. She kept the touch of her gloved hand so light on his arm, he could barely feel it. As they walked, he tried to recall the last time he'd seen her. It had been shortly after his proposal, which, if not ardent, had been extremely proper. Her acceptance had been as serene as his offer.

Well, they both knew the arrangement wasn't one of passion. It hadn't bothered him then; why should it now?

They took their seats. "Is Father not joining us?" Owen asked, as the servants brought the first course of green turtle soup.

"He's at a dinner meeting with the mayor and other important people. The elder Mr. Vandersee is there as well, which was why I invited Edith and Kirk to join us tonight." She shivered delicately. "Safety in numbers and all that."

"We appreciate your thoughtfulness," Edith said. Owen suspected she would have much preferred spending the evening in, but hadn't felt able to deny her soon-to-be mother-in-law.

"The men are encouraging the mayor to take action to protect us all against this horrid maniac," Mother went on. "Really, it's a disgrace the fiend is still running loose. He might strike at any of us!"

"That isn't likely," Owen reassured her. "He was after a very specific artifact in Mr. Jacobs's possession."

"Enough—we shan't speak of such things any further," she said. "Owen, I believe you have an announcement to make?"

So Nathan had told her. Kirk and Edith both looked at him, brows arched in curiosity. Owen cleared his throat. "Yes. I've bonded with a familiar."

"Congratulations, old boy," Kirk said, raising his glass. "As high as you scored on the witch tests, we all expected this sooner or later. What sort of animal is he?"

"A fox," Owen said.

Mother sniffed. No doubt she'd wanted something a bit more regal. Her own mother had a cheetah familiar; a portrait of the two of them hung in the drawing room, the cheetah sitting at her feet, a jeweled collar around its throat. Owen tried to recall its name, or even gender, and failed.

"How lovely," Edith said with a genuine smile. "What's his name?"

It was probably too much to hope they'd get along. "Malachi."

Mother carefully set her spoon aside and signaled for the servants to bring the next course. "Dreadful. I certainly hope you intend to change it."

Something seemed to constrict Owen's chest, making it difficult to breathe. "No," he said, as the saddle of lamb was laid out in front of him. "I rather imagine he's accustomed to it, after all."

"It sounds Irish." Mother frowned as if she'd smelled something unpleasant.

Blast. Owen should have expected this. "Probably because he is Irish."

Mother's eyes widened. "And you…well." She sat back. "What's done is done. Has he already converted?"

The memory of Mal's many blasphemies came back full force. "I haven't brought it up," he said, as neutrally as possible.

"So long as he understands he'll have to give up his papist ways by the wedding," Mother said.

Edith took up her own wineglass. "Well, I for one look forward to meeting Mr. Malachi," she said. "I assume you'll bring him to the dinner party tomorrow night?"

"I had planned on it," he admitted, a bit surprised she'd asked.

"He can meet the rest of the family then," Kirk agreed.

Mother looked shocked. And, to be honest, Owen was rather taken aback as well. Kirk had never struck him as being particularly unconventional in his thinking about familiars.

"Yes," Mother said frostily. "And then perhaps you can introduce us to your hunting dogs, Mr. Vandersee."

"Mal is a person," Owen said, more sharply than he intended. "Not a pet."

Mother sniffed. "Have that attitude, and soon he'll be ruling you, rather than the other way around."

Heat crept up Owen's face, and he hastily took a sip of wine.

"Mrs. Yates, you said the flowers you chose for the wedding would be pink and white?" Edith asked.

Ordinarily, Edith's mother would be the one to make the wedding arrangements. As Mrs. Vandersee had passed many years ago, and Mr. Vandersee never remarried, Mother had eagerly seized on the opportunity to order what was sure to be the wedding of the year, if not the decade.

"Lily of the valley and pink chrysanthemums," Mother replied. "I approved the final design for your bouquet last week…"

Owen supposed he should be grateful at least someone was excited for the wedding, even if it wasn't either the bride or groom. The rest of the dinner passed in uncomfortable harmony, while he and Edith nodded and made approving sounds as Mother waxed rhapsodic over the guest list.

At last it was time for Edith and Kirk to leave. As they bundled into their coats and hats, the housewitch moved quietly through the foyer, charging and igniting the hexlights. His familiar, a spaniel, followed on his heels. As he watched, Owen realized he'd never seen the familiar in human form. He didn't even know her name.

"Mother, may I have a word with you in private?" he asked.

As soon as they were alone, she said, "I'm disappointed in you, Owen. I expected better when it came to your familiar."

Owen wanted to object. Point out that she was hardly being fair. After all, it wasn't as if either he or Mal had chosen one another—it was simply that their magic was the most compatible. Shouldn't she be glad he was exercising his talents to the fullest?

But she'd see his words as ones of complaint—or, even worse, an excuse. Neither of which had ever been tolerated in the Yates household. So he only said, "Yes, Mother."

"When your father hears…" she sighed and shook her head.

"I know you find it a distasteful topic, but I wished to speak to you about the murder," he said.

She frowned. "I'm certain I wouldn't know about anything connected with such a sordid affair."

"Actually, the question I had was about Mrs. Jacobs." Owen paused, wondering if there was any delicate way to put it. "Specifically, about her whereabouts the night of the murder."

Mother took it as he'd expected her to: poorly. Her eyes flashed fire, and she let out an affronted gasp. "Surely you don't mean to suggest Mrs. Jacobs had anything to do with her husband's death!"

"Not directly—clearly she didn't kill him with her own hand—but if she was perhaps involved with, say, another man—"

"Owen Reynard Yates!" Mother drew herself up to her full height, which was still a head shorter than his own. "I can't believe you would even make such a suggestion."

He held up his hands in an attempt to pacify her. "Mother, I know it's shocking, but it's something we must consider. If you've heard any sort of rumor connecting her with someone, a close friend or a widower, perhaps—"

"I refuse to listen to another word of this." She folded her arms across her chest and leveled an icy glare at him. "Why are you wasting time asking such questions, when you know very well none of *us* would be involved in murder?"

Owen arched a brow. "Us?"

"People of quality. The Four Hundred." She turned away from him. "This crime was committed by one of the lower classes. To even suggest Mrs. Jacobs had the slightest involvement is simply beyond the pale."

"Mother—"

"No. I will speak no more of it."

Blast. She'd been his best hope. But once she made up her mind, neither heaven nor earth would move her to change it. The only person who had ever gotten the better of her was Mrs. Vandersee. Her determined campaign for acceptance in society, coupled with the willingness to spend lavishly on balls and costume parties, had broken Mother's resistance and won the Vandersees a place among the elite, despite the newness of the family's fortune.

"Good night then, Mother," he said. "I'll see you tomorrow evening."

He was glad to escape to the sidewalk. A carriage waited a few feet away, but to his surprise, both Kirk and Edith still stood not far from the steps leading up to the house.

Both of them faced a man whose name Owen struggled to remember. Creswell, that was it—Davis Creswell. His family wasn't badly off, but their fortune was too small and too new to earn admittance into the Four Hundred.

Kirk stood with his shoulders squared and his hands drawn into fists. But all of Creswell's attention was fixed on Edith. A look of pleading distorted his handsome face, and his blond curls were mussed.

Dark circles ringed his brown eyes, as though he hadn't slept in days. "Edith, please," he said.

Edith stood before him, her shoulders sagging, her gaze averted. Her face in the electric street lights was astonishingly pale.

"How dare you address my sister in so intimate a fashion?" Kirk snapped. "How dare you address her at all?"

Owen's fingers tingled, and he was suddenly aware of the warm place behind his heart. He had hexes in his wallet, and magic to charge them now, should Creswell mean them ill. "What seems to be the trouble?" he asked.

Creswell's gaze shifted to Owen, and his expression changed to one of loathing. "You," he said.

"Mr. Creswell, please." Edith spoke at last, lifting her gaze to him. "Dr. Yates and I will be wed soon. There is nothing more to be said. Please leave us, and don't try to contact me again."

A look of pain flashed across Creswell's features.

"You heard my sister," Kirk growled. "Leave now."

For a moment, Owen thought Creswell would refuse. Then the man looked back to him once again. "I hope you appreciate the treasure you've been given, sir," he said coldly. "Good night to you all."

He turned on his heel and stalked away down the sidewalk. Edith stood very still, but she watched him depart with wetness clinging to her lashes.

The devil? Owen stepped closer. "Miss Vandersee? Is everything all right? Did he offer you some insult?"

Edith drew in a long breath. "Thank you for your concern, Dr. Yates. I am quite well. Kirk, please take me home."

"Forget Creswell," Kirk said. He led her to the carriage, and the footman hastily jumped down and opened the door for them. "He's not worthy of you."

"So I am told," she replied.

The door closed. Owen caught a glimpse of her pale face through the window, before the driver snapped the reins. The carriage pulled away, leaving him standing alone on the sidewalk.

Mal sat on the edge of his bed, sipping a cup of tea. *His* bed—it seemed like such a luxury, still. Almost as much as the tea set, painted with hexes to keep the contents hot.

The apartment was surprisingly lonely without Owen to keep him company. He'd grown used to having his witch around.

Once Owen got married, though, he probably wouldn't have much time for Mal. Not with a wife, and eventually children.

No sense brooding over it. Mal had known what he was getting into when he agreed to bond with Owen. Besides, a little bit of loneliness was a small price to pay for his own bed, and fancy clothes, and not having to wonder where his next meal was coming from.

Still, it would be nice to spend some time together now. Take advantage of their arrangement. Mal had made a detour between the Coven and the Folly that evening. Bertie had seemed dubious when Mal asked him to wait outside the pharmacy, but the last thing Mal wanted was half the MWP gossiping about his private life.

The pharmacist hadn't so much as blinked, of course. The contents of the box were sold as medical devices, and hell, maybe someone even used them that way. A second stop at a hardware store had secured a length of rope.

Owen was in for a treat. If he ever came home.

It had been just as well Owen wasn't with him this evening, though. He'd caught sight of Sophie, loitering just outside The Folly when he and Bertie arrived. After saying goodnight to Bertie, he'd waited a few minutes, then slipped back out into the street himself.

He hadn't gone out of shouting distance of the guard, of course, or down an alley where he might be cornered. Sophie had just winked at him and passed a small package, before going her own way. He'd sauntered back into The Folly less than five minutes after leaving, and had a leisurely dinner of coq au vin in the restaurant before returning to the apartment.

Only then had he taken out and unwrapped the package she'd given him. Inside was a replica of the necklace he was meant to steal, glittering with glass diamonds. He couldn't even imagine how much the real thing must be worth. Even if the necklace was broken up into its component gems and sold off, it would represent a small fortune. Whole, it would be worth a large one.

There was a note with it, too, telling him where to meet Sophie once he had the necklace. That he burned in the fireplace, all the while trying not to think too hard about what he was planning to do. Of course, Owen would be furious if he found out…but he wouldn't. No one would learn what had happened for years to come.

Everything would be fine. He'd give Madam Galpern what she wanted, and she'd give him what he needed. He was trying to save his own life and bring a killer to justice. There was no reason to feel guilty.

No reason at all.

At last, the sound of the door opening and shutting echoed through the apartment. The walls were thick, so Mal had left the door to his bedroom open in order to hear Owen's return. He finished his tea, giving Owen a few minutes to settle in, before padding out to find him.

Owen stood before one of the windows in the parlor, staring out over the dark bulk of Central Park. He'd taken off his coat, but otherwise remained dressed. In one hand he held a violin, its wooden body gleaming golden-red in the soft light. The bow dangled loosely from the fingers of his other hand, but he made no motion to set it to the strings.

"I didn't know you played," Mal said.

Owen started and glanced guiltily over his shoulder. "I ought to give it up. It's silly, really."

Mal cocked his head to one side. "What do you mean?"

"There isn't much point to it." Owen lifted the bow sadly. "It isn't a very practical use of my time."

Fur and feathers, no wonder Owen so seldom smiled. Someone had filled his head with nonsense, and after their conversation earlier, Mal suspected the blame lay at the feet of Owen's parents. "Well, I ain't saying a fellow like you is going to be busking on Broadway," he said. "But not everything needs a point, does it? Not past making you happy. Ain't that enough of a reason by itself?"

Owen smiled a little, but it was tinged with sadness. "That would be selfish."

"Nay, it wouldn't. Not if it don't hurt anyone else." Mal resisted the urge to yank at his own hair. Or march over to Fifth Avenue and tell the Yates family just what he thought of them. "And if that ain't enough for you, then what about making me happy?" He gestured at the violin. "Play for me."

"It's after ten o'clock," Owen said. "I've lived here for years without a single complaint from the neighbors. I don't want to start now."

Mal's gaze went past Owen, to the darkness beyond. "Then put your coat back on, and let me find my shoes."

Chapter 11

"**You're completely mad!**" Owen exclaimed. The bitter cold stung his cheeks and nibbled at the tips of his ears. His gloved hands cradled his violin case, which Mal had insisted he bring with them.

Mal went ahead of him, the lantern in his hand one of the few spots of light within the vastness of Central Park. His red hair matched the color of the flames, and when he cast a crafty smile over his shoulder, Owen could almost believe he was being led astray by some pixie.

"It's freezing cold," Owen went on. "And dark. What if there are squatters in the park? There used to be an entire shantytown, before the police cleared them out. This is absurd."

"Aye, that it is," Mal agreed cheerfully.

"Not to mention we shouldn't be wandering around when there are dangerous people looking for you."

"Which is why we slipped out the servants' entrance," Mal replied with a wink. "Who would expect a Yates to use anything but the front door?"

Owen wasn't entirely convinced, but several minutes of waiting in the dark and cold a short distance from The Folly hadn't revealed any pursuers. Likely Mal was right, assuming the killer and his cohorts hadn't fled New York altogether by now.

They penetrated farther into the heart of the park. The world lay silent and still around them, the sounds of the city cut off by trees and rises. Clouds hid both stars and moon, threatening either rain or snow. A brisk wind shook the branches of the trees, and they groaned like something alive as they rubbed together.

"Ah, here we are." Mal strolled onto the plaza in front of Bethesda Terrace. The fountain lay silent, its water turned off for the winter. A few gaslights illuminated the carved balustrades and the hexwork mosaic laid out around the fountain.

Mal put the lantern on the fountain, pausing just a moment to look up into the face of the bronze angel. "All right, then," he said, turning to Owen. "There's no one here to complain about the noise. So play."

Owen looked around at the deserted park. "It's freezing," he repeated. "The violin is hexed to keep it in tune, but my fingers are numb."

Mal snorted. "It's a good thing you ain't performing at Madison Square Garden, then." He leaned against the side of the fountain. "I ain't expecting the singing of angels, Owen. I just want to hear you play."

Owen shook his head, but placed the violin case on one of the terrace steps and opened it. "I must be insane to be agreeing to this," he muttered as he took out the instrument.

Hexes worked into the wood kept it in tune, but he ran through a set of exercises to warm up his fingers. "What would you like to hear?" he asked.

Mal shrugged. "Whatever you feel like playing."

Owen paused, searching through his memory. Mal's red hair was the brightest thing in the winter park, and the hazy recollection of a jig he'd played only in private came back to him. No doubt he'd miss some of the notes, but Mal seemed willing to forgive any failings.

His tutor never had, of course. Or his parents. He might have been the second son, but perfection was still the only option. Early on, it had become clear he would never be a master, so there was no point in wasting time on lessons that would lead nowhere. It had become a furtive exercise, something to be done only when no one else could hear.

But Mal wanted to hear. Mal didn't expect perfection. He expected…joy.

Owen brought the bow down across the strings.

A look of delight lit up Mal's face, and he tossed his head back with a whoop. Flinging his arms out, he started to dance.

God, he was graceful. And fast; every movement quick and certain. His amber eyes glowed, and his grin showed off sharp, white teeth. Mal's whoops and hollers urged Owen on, and he found himself improvising the notes he couldn't remember.

He led Mal, or perhaps Mal led him, as though the music was a dance shared between them. Owen swayed, then bent, letting the stiffness fall from his shoulders. The violin responded, its sound richer somehow; wilder.

Mal laughed, skipping and jumping, clicking his heels together before spinning like a madman. He circled around Owen, flashing in and out of animal form: one moment a gleeful young man, the next a prancing fox, both with the same red hair and amber eyes, both utterly unselfconscious. Splashes of joy washed through the bond, infecting Owen's own nerves, and he found his feet moving in response.

Time ceased to have meaning. The cold faded away; the city might as well not have existed. There was nothing but the two of them, locked together by the music, by a flashing bow and flashing feet, and an expanding bubble of delight.

When it ended, Owen found himself panting, winded as if they'd fucked. Mal ran to him, face pink with cold and exertion, and they embraced. Both of them were laughing like a pair of fools, but there was no one to see them but the trees and the wind, and the silent bronze angel.

Mal drew back a little and ran his gloved fingers over Owen's jaw. "See? Ain't you glad I dragged you out here?"

Owen's cheeks ached from his grin, as though the muscles weren't used to such exertion. "Yes, you maniac," he laughed. "I am."

"Good." Mal kissed him. "And you're going to be even gladder when I drag you into bed next."

They stumbled into the apartment, laughing and wild. The guard at the entrance must have thought them both drunk, leaning on one another, their cheeks flushed pink from the cold. The sight of Owen's smile made Mal's heart soar; it transformed his face, wiping away care. It reminded him of the look Owen got in bed, when he let go of everything and allowed himself to have a good time.

And a good time was exactly what Mal was going to show him.

Owen left the violin case on the table in the ante room, and let Mal drag him down the hall to the bedrooms. Mal swatted him on the arse. "Get in there and take off your clothes. I've got a surprise I need to bring from my room."

"A surprise?"

"Aye. Did a bit of shopping earlier." Mal smacked his arse again, harder. "Now, do as you're told. No backtalk."

"Yes, sir," Owen said. He was already stripping off his vest when Mal turned away.

Mal retrieved the packages from the pharmacy and hardware. When he returned it was to find Owen waiting naked by his bed, prick stiff from excitement. "Good boy," Mal said, putting the packages aside. He ran a hand down Owen's bare torso, from the base of his throat to his cock. Owen let out a little gasp, lips parting with desire.

"How are your wrists?" Mal asked. He reached past Owen and pulled out the rope he'd bought. "Feeling up to this?"

Owen nodded eagerly. "Yes, please. They're fine—no pain at all."

"Then get on the bed. Hands and knees. I want access to your mouth and your arse."

A moan of longing escaped Owen, and he hurried to obey. Mal secured the ropes to the bedposts, then bound Owen's wrists together in front of him. It forced Owen to rest on his elbows, rump nicely in the air and legs spread.

"Now I've got you right where I want you." Mal began to strip off his own clothes—he should have had Owen do it for him. Next time, he would. When he was naked, he ran his hand down Owen's spine—then gave him a sharp smack on the bottom. Owen let out a little cry of surprise, body jerking.

"Such a lovely arse." Mal dropped his hand lower, gave Owen's balls a squeeze. "I'm going to fuck you soon, don't you worry. But tonight, I think I'd rather have you stuffed fore and aft."

Owen gave him a puzzled look. Mal winked and fetched the box from the dresser. "They sell these dilators for 'medical purposes,'" he said, opening it and showing the contents to Owen. There were four inside, in different sizes. Made from hard rubber, each had a flared base at one end and what looked unmistakably like the head of a cock at the other. "But I'm guessing you can figure out what most people use them for."

Owen's lips parted, his eyes going wide. "What are you going to do?" he asked hoarsely.

"What do you think?" Mal selected one of the medium sizes. "I'm going to stuff your arse with this, then fuck your mouth."

A shiver of desire ran visibly through Owen. Mal snagged the jar of oil he'd bought along with the dilators. He coated his fingers, then reached for Owen.

"Ask me to do it," he ordered, slipping one finger in.

Owen lowered his head to the comforter, a groan escaping him.

"Please do it."

"Do what?" Mal added another finger. "What do you want me to do?"

"P-Put that in my ass and fuck my mouth."

Mal nipped Owen's buttock with his teeth, making him jump. "Good."

Owen groaned again when Mal worked the dilator in. His body shook, goose flesh pebbling his skin, though from excitement rather than cold. "There you go," Mal said, sitting back to admire the view. "You like that, don't you? Like having something nice and thick in you."

"Y-Yes."

Mal gave Owen's hard prick a stroke, dragging a sound of startled pleasure out of him. Then he moved to the head of the bed and grasped Owen's hair, pulling his head back far enough for easy access. "Now take it," he said, and shoved his cock into Owen's eagerly open mouth.

Owen moaned, his eyes closed. And Saint Mary, did he look a sight: arse in the air, lips around Mal's prick, eyes screwed closed, his skin rosy with arousal. The ropes creaked as he pulled on them, as if he needed to reinforce his own sense of helplessness. Surrender.

"Look at me," Mal ordered breathlessly.

Owen's eyes flew open, the argentine irises mere rings around pupils black with lust. Mal met his gaze and held it, even as he tightened his grip on Owen's ashen hair. "Watch me watching you," Mal said. "You should see yourself, tied down, helpless, while I do whatever filthy thing I want to you."

Owen made a muffled, wanton noise around Mal's prick. Begging, needing, pared down to nothing but sensation. Mal's balls drew tight, and he let out a short, barking noise as he spent into Owen's mouth.

"Saint Mary," he swore as his softening cock slipped free from Owen's swollen lips. Then he slid down the bed, took hold of Owen's cock, and tugged.

It didn't take long. Owen shuddered when he came, then collapsed onto the bed, face-down. Mal flung a leg over him and cuddled in, kissing Owen's shoulder. "Good?"

"God, yes." Owen lifted his head slightly. "Could you remove…?"

Mal did so, then untied him. He leaned back in the bed, floating in a contented haze, while Owen stumbled into the bathroom.

Owen glanced at the clock when he returned. "It's later than I thought," he said, sounding surprised.

Mal peeled open eyes that wanted to slip shut. "Worth staying up for?"

Owen sat beside him, a tender smile curving his lips. "Yes. All of it. Thank you, Mal. For going to the park with me."

Mal grinned. "A shame the pond ain't frozen yet. We could've gone skating."

"I'll take you skating later in the season," Owen promised.

Later. Except later wouldn't—couldn't—be like this.

"I imagine you'll want to take your wife, instead," Mal said.

The closeness they'd shared seemed to evaporate. "We'll still be friends," Owen said, but he sounded as though he meant to reassure himself as much as Mal. "We'll make it an outing. All of us together, as a family."

"Aye," said Mal, but the words tasted like ash in his mouth. He slipped out of the bed and made for the door. "Get some sleep. Like you said, it's late, and tomorrow's coming whether we want it to or not."

Mal trailed after Owen into the Coven the next morning, desperate for another cup of coffee. Of course, he had no one to blame for his exhaustion but himself.

But it had all been worth it, just to see Owen happy.

Saint Mary, he hoped this Edith would be good for Owen. Mal liked women in bed just as much as men, but he didn't think Owen felt the same. But even if they weren't compatible beyond what it took to get a few children, maybe she'd at least be Owen's friend.

Let him take her skating, maybe.

Right. While Mal trotted behind them in fox shape, a silent presence.

"Malachi?" the witch on duty at the desk called as they passed by. "A feral by the name of Nick is here, looking for you. He's up in the detectives' area now."

Owen and Mal exchanged a look. "Maybe he has some information," Mal said.

"Let's hope so," Owen replied, lips tightening. He'd told Mal of his failure to get anything useful out of dear old mum over breakfast. Mal hadn't been too surprised to hear it, though. Of course the nobs closed ranks, refused to believe any of them could be involved, and got angry when anyone suggested otherwise.

Owen wasn't like that, though. Which begged the question of why he spent so much damned time trying to keep them happy, no matter the cost to himself.

They found Nick standing at Rook and Dominic's desk, muscular arms folded over his chest, feet set apart in a belligerent stance.

"A *name*, Nick," Rook squawked, flinging his arms up in exasperation. "Give us a name, if you've got one."

"Oh no. I agreed not to take matters into my own hands, and bring the problem to you." Nick glared down at his much smaller brother. "But I'm not letting your lot run roughshod in my colony. Not among my people."

Mal perked up. "You know who sold me out?"

Nick glanced at Mal, then at Owen. His expression turned sour, as though he'd smelled something foul. "I did. Another familiar, who was at the bar the night you came in. Must've overheard our conversation—damned owls, they have the best hearing even in human form."

Owen frowned. "Then give us his name."

"Not until we're back at the tenement." Nick turned his stubborn gaze on Owen. "As I told my fool brother, I'm not letting a bunch of *witches* and their tame familiars into the colony without me there to supervise. So be patient and come with me, or throw me in jail for refusing to cooperate. Choice is yours."

"Oh for God's sake, Nick." Rook rolled his eyes. "No one is talking about throwing you in jail, or beating the name out of you, or anything like it. Do you have to be so overly dramatic all the time?"

Mal glanced at Owen. He could only communicate directly through the bond while in animal form, but he hoped Owen understood the question in his gaze all the same. He must have, because Owen nodded ever so slightly.

"We'll go with you," Mal said soothingly. "Owen and I."

Nick's dark gaze shifted from him to Owen, then back again. "This is your case?"

"Saint Mary, I ain't a copper!" Mal exclaimed, offended. "But, aye, Owen is working on it."

"We should send word to Patrolman Quigley," Owen put in. "He'll want to be a part of this."

Nick's lower lip jutted out. "He's regular police then? Witch potential?"

Owen blinked. "I'm certain I've no idea what his potential might be."

"Damned witches." Nick stomped one foot in frustrated anger. "It's a dark day I have to turn on another familiar."

"Your cooperation may help put a murderer behind bars," Owen said.

"If this fellow hadn't betrayed Malachi, I wouldn't care," Nick replied bluntly. "The rich bastards can damned well look after themselves, and the witches too. But Mal was under my protection, and if I turn a blind eye to ferals betraying each other, then we've got nothing left. So send your note to your fucking policeman, and let's get this over with."

Chapter 12

They took the Sixth Avenue El to the Tenderloin district, the train jerking and clattering its way along the track. Quigley and Mal had found seats next to one another, and were soon arguing over the relative merits of various baseball players. Owen watched them converse, unable to hear most of what was said over the sounds of the train, and tried to ignore Nick's looming presence beside him.

What had birthed Nick's hostility toward witches and police, Owen couldn't imagine. Certainly Rook had never shown any such tendencies. Rook's witch Dominic was an excellent hexman, and Owen had relied on Dominic's expertise many times. Rook had never been anything other than pleasant. A bit frivolous and silly at times, joking at inappropriate moments—though going by Malachi, perhaps that was simply a trait of familiars in general.

He couldn't imagine Nick cracking a smile, let alone a joke. The feral towered over him even seated, smelling of sweat and grime, as though he hadn't bathed in days. Then again, Mal had smelled much the same, their first night together.

As though he'd heard Owen's thought, Nick said, "You'd best be treating Malachi right."

Owen drew himself up, offended. Who the devil was this fellow, to suggest he'd mistreat a lover?

No. He couldn't think of Mal as a lover. But even if they hadn't been friends, had been barely civil, it was still beyond the pale to suggest Owen would renege on his responsibility to his own familiar.

"Mal seems quite content, thank you," Owen replied frostily.

Nick was clearly unmoved by Owen's warning tone. "I've heard how you rich bastards are. Forcing your familiars to stay in animal shape, except in front of the servants. At least you let him keep his name."

A deaf man could hardly miss the heavy note of sarcasm in Nick's last sentence. Owen narrowed his eyes and tried not to recall his mother's words of the night before. Her shock he would tolerate a familiar with an Irish name and Irish beliefs, and what Mal might have wanted never crossing her mind.

He couldn't speak of such private matters to Nick, of course, so he only said, "Mal made his choice, and he chose me. How we conduct our business is none of yours."

To his surprise, Nick let out a bitter laugh. "Oh, yes, his *choice*."

"And what the devil do you mean by that?"

Dark eyes fixed on him. "Are you really that stupid?" Nick wondered. "Fine, witch. Let me lay it out for you. The MWP wasn't going to protect Mal if he didn't bond with you, were they? So his *choice* was being turned over to the regular police, and either rotting in jail or possibly having a confession to the murder beaten out of him. Or if that didn't happen, he could take his chances on the street, and hope the killer was caught before he succeeded in murdering Mal." Nick shook his head, long hair rustling over his shoulders. "Jail or death. Some *choice*."

Owen's chest tightened; he couldn't seem to get enough breath. "We all do things we would prefer not to," he said. Certainly he didn't wish to marry Edith—nor she him, if last night had been anything to go by. Duty to their families compelled them; they were without real choice in the matter.

Although, to be fair, neither of them were facing jail or death if they refused that duty.

Nick snorted, a harsh explosion of air, like an irritated horse. Fortunately, the train reached their stop before he could go on. They descended from the El, and went west on 28th Street. The streets were choked with all manner of humanity: laborers, peddlers, pushcart vendors, beggars, newsboys, rag pickers, and more. Grocers shouted at one another in Russian, only to be abused in Italian by a drunk woman passing by. Lines of washing hung between and in front of buildings, the cloth flapping in the brisk breeze. Music halls rubbed shoulders with what could only be brothels, judging by the women on the stoop or watching out the windows.

Owen had read the newspaper stories declaring the district a cesspool of vice, with more gambling halls and bordellos than anywhere else in the nation, let alone the city. It was the first time he'd actually walked the streets, though. Strange to think they were only a few blocks from the mansion where he'd grown up. It almost seemed a different world.

Nick stopped outside a building, the lowest floor of which was a saloon. A placard in the window proclaimed FAMILIARS ONLY. *Caballus* was stenciled in faded letters on the glass, and a sign featuring a rearing horse hung above the door. Broken chains flew from the horse's forelegs.

"Subtle," Owen remarked.

Nick ignored him. "All right. I've some rules for you lot. I'll lead, you follow. When I need your fancy badges, I'll let you know."

"Now see here," Quigley started.

"Sure thing, Nick," Mal said. "But will you at least tell me who it was as sold me out?"

Nick's lips tightened. "Ulysses."

Mal let out a sigh. "At least it wasn't one of my fucking roommates," he muttered.

Here was a chance for Owen to show Nick that he wasn't mistreating Mal. "You knew him?" he asked, putting a sympathetic hand to Mal's shoulder.

Mal shrugged. "A bit. Know most of the ferals in this part of town a bit, though, don't I? Owl. Drank with him once or twice. Didn't seem like a bad sort."

"I'm sorry."

Mal cast him a grateful smile. "Thanks."

Nick sighed loudly. "Let's just have this done with."

They followed Nick as he clomped up the narrow stair. Owen had been in a tenement before, in a different part of town, when they'd had to visit Tom Halloran and Cicero on the sly. The interior had looked nothing like this building, however. That tenement had been clearly made with human use in mind, whereas someone—Nick, or the inhabitants themselves—had altered this one for the convenience of animals. The windows on the landings opening onto the central airshaft had platforms outside, where bird familiars could land and safely transform before opening the window and climbing inside. Perches jutted out of the walls at regular intervals, some of them occupied by sleeping owls or ravens, who stirred and glared when they passed underneath. Many of the doors had smaller flaps cut into them; Owen glimpsed a rat going through one, and wondered if it was a familiar or just an ordinary animal taking advantage.

There had once been wallpaper on the walls, but it was now peeling and stained. Broken windows were either boarded over or stuffed with rags. The air of the hall was frigid, unwarmed even by the light of the sun. A man lay unconscious on one of the landings, clutching an empty whiskey bottle to his chest. From the smell, he'd soiled himself, but Nick, Mal, and Quigley just stepped over him as though the scene were perfectly ordinary.

Dear God. Mal had *lived* here? In this cold and filth?

Nick finally came to a halt in front of one of the doors. "This is Ulysses's apartment. I don't know if he's here, but you can take a look around and wait for him if he's not," he said, pulling a key from his pocket.

Quigley stepped to the door and drew out his nightstick. "Police!" he called, pounding on the door with his fist. "Open up!"

There came the sound of a window scraping shut, barely muted by the thin wood of the door. Nick's eyes widened. "The fire escape!"

Quigley swore and struck the door with his shoulder. It shuddered in the frame, but failed to give.

Nick thrust the key into the lock. "Locking hex—it won't open!"

"Out of the way!" Owen ordered. He stepped up to the door, removing the wallet with his hexman's tools from the inside of his coat. "Let me try a counter-hex."

"Counter-hex?" Quigley asked.

Owen sketched rapidly on the door. "It's of my own devising."

"Hurry, then—he's getting away!"

"I'm quite aware of that," Owen replied tightly. When he was done, he slapped his palm onto the hex. Magic rushed into him from Mal, a hot flood pouring through the bond, through Owen, and into the hex. "Undo the locking hex," he said.

The door swung open, and the smell of blood rolled out to greet them.

Quigley rushed in past Owen, then stumbled to a halt. "Saint Mary, preserve us!"

The room was tiny, smaller than Owen's ante room at The Folly. Every inch was packed with belongings: a stove, a bed made from a plank laid across two barrels, a rickety table, old crates packed with clothes or rags, pots and pans hanging from the ceiling, and two more makeshift beds on the floor.

Blood painted the walls, ceiling, and stove. A man lay motionless on the plank bed, his throat torn out.

Nick charged across to the window opening onto the fire escape. He grabbed it, then swore. "The killer jammed it!"

Quigley joined him, and together they forced it open. Quigley climbed out the escape; his footsteps rang on the iron ladder as he hastened down, accompanied by the shrill blowing of his police whistle to summon help.

The color had drained from Mal's face. He took a step toward the bloody bed, then stopped. "Ulysses was a bastard for giving me over, but he didn't deserve to die. Who could've done something like this?"

Owen bent to examine the body, trying not to breathe too deeply. "Not the same man as the one who killed Jacobs and tried to kill you."

Nick came back from the window. "How do you know?"

"Jacobs's murderer could take a form small enough to use the electrical wires for his escape. A squirrel, most likely." Owen took a deep breath and instantly regretted it. "Ulysses was killed with a single blow, powerful enough to remove most of his throat. That suggests a tiger, or a lion—something far too large. We should look for hairs."

Mal shook his head. "That wouldn't do us any good. This ain't a Fifth Avenue mansion with just one housewitch and familiar wandering about. Most of us here sleep in animal form, because it takes less room than a bed." He nodded at Ulysses. "Unless you're one of those who hate being an owl, or whatever. Neighbors visit each other in all sorts of shapes, and who knows how many familiars have rented this flat before Ulysses moved in. There's probably hairs in here from every type of animal you can name and then some."

"Better hope Quigley has luck chasing him down," Nick said. He glanced at Ulysses's body, then shook his head. "Bad way to go. I'll leave you to your investigation."

"What should we do?" Mal asked, once Nick had left.

Owen settled his spectacles more firmly on his nose. "Look around the room for anything that might give us some clue."

There wasn't much to see. They picked through the clothes, and Mal peered under the bed, which turned out to be where Ulysses stored his shoes. A newspaper lay on the only rickety table. Owen moved it aside, then stopped.

Beneath the newspaper was a thin, cheaply printed pamphlet. A lurid illustration showed a gleefully evil man looming over a cowering dog. WITCHES—OR VAMPIRES? screamed the title. And at the bottom, in smaller print: *Only theriarchy can keep witches from draining our lives.*

"Theriarchy," Owen said numbly. "Dear God, not these lunatics again."

Mal sat in the chair in Owen's lab, his feet propped on the desk. They'd spent the last several hours giving their report to Ferguson. Bill Quigley hadn't caught the fleeing murderer, though one or two witnesses offered vague descriptions of a dark haired man running from the building.

Ulysses's body had gone to the coroner, in the hopes of narrowing down the type of animal that had killed him. "Though, since the coroner is drunk half the time, he's as likely to say Ulysses was trampled by an elephant," Owen had said glumly.

Now Owen sat at his table again, slowly assembling the pieces of the device, while Mal thumbed through the pamphlet they'd found in Ulysses's apartment. "So you've tangled with these fellows before?" he asked. "Theriarchists, I mean."

"Unfortunately." Owen peered at the plates he was currently mounting to the connecting rod. "You recall the attack on the consolidation ceremony on New Year's?"

"Who could forget!" Mal exclaimed. "Anarchists, wasn't it? I spent the night getting drunk at Caballus, but the papers were full of nothing else for the next month."

"I was in the midst of it," Owen said with a wry twitch of his lips. "It was…terrifying."

"I imagine it was." From what the papers had said, Owen was damned lucky to have escaped unharmed. And thank Saint Mary he had. "So what are you saying? That these theriarchists had something to do with it?"

"The case wasn't mine, but I was tangentially involved." Owen carefully placed another plate onto the device. "The anarchists were partially guilty, but my understanding is they were being used the entire time. The theriarchists masterminded and carried out the attack. Some of them were killed in the mayhem, but there were hints they were only part of a much larger conspiracy. If they're involved, we could be in for a great deal of trouble."

"Just because Ulysses has a pamphlet don't mean there's a connection with his death," Mal pointed out.

"No. But it's worrisome." Owen peered at the device through a magnifying glass, then set it aside. "I've seen what the theriarchists are capable of. How far they're willing to go." He paused, considering. "One of the MWP familiars, Isaac, was held captive by them for a time. We might ask him for insight."

Mal went through the pamphlet again, more slowly this time. The writer hadn't held back their opinion, that was for certain. The text, accompanied by lurid illustrations of witches abusing familiars, claimed draining magic for hexes was no different than a vampire draining the blood of its victims. Familiars, it said, had more to offer society than their magic—but their magic was the only thing society cared about, and so suppressed their other natural talents. The pamphlet concluded by calling for an end to all bonding and the destruction of all hexes.

It sounded like just the sort of thing Nick would love, to be honest. Ulysses having one pamphlet was less surprising than the whole tenement not being awash with them.

Not that he thought Nick had anything to do with Ulysses's murder, or any of the rest of it. Nick had a bit of a temper, true, but killing a fellow feral? Not a chance.

Owen's stool creaked as he sat back. "Oh."

"Oh what?" Mal asked, tossing the pamphlet onto Owen's desk. "Have you found something?"

"Yes." Owen's silver eyes gleamed with excitement behind the lenses of his spectacles, and a smile of genuine delight curved his mouth. "I want to consult with Dominic before I say anything, but…I think I know what the device does."

Owen stood behind the table the partially constructed device sat on, surveying his small audience. Mal perched on the edge of the desk, while Dominic, Rook, Chief Ferguson, Quigley, and Athene all crowded in front of the table. The unbonded familiar, Isaac, had also joined them, though he stood well away from everyone else. Mal hadn't met him before—not that he could claim to know most of the MWP familiars by any stretch. Overlong brown hair tumbled into his face, hiding his eyes. Thin fingers plucked nervously at the silver charm he wore around his neck, as if the habit in some way soothed him. Quigley cast him a concerned look or two, but Isaac never raised his head to see it.

"All right," Ferguson said, drawing Mal's attention back to the device. "What does this thing do that has the two of you so worked up?"

Owen exchanged a glance with Dominic. But Dominic gestured to him. "Go ahead. It's your case."

Owen straightened and clasped his hands behind him, as if preparing to deliver a lecture. The sight brought a grin to Mal's face. "The device is a remarkable feat of hexology and engineering," Owen said. "Today, we've uncovered one of the lost secrets of the ancient world."

Athene shot him an impatient look. "Get to the point, Dr. Yates."

"Yes, of course." He cleared his throat self-consciously. "One of the first things I noticed when examining the plates is that they're inscribed with what you might call the building blocks the ancient Greeks used to create their hexes. It seemed an odd choice, as most of them don't work as complete hexes themselves. However…"

He moved a small lever near the base of the device, then began to turn the crank. The gears rotated, swinging some plates out of the way while bringing others into alignment. "These plates now form a single, complete hex." He shifted the lever a second time, then turned the handle again. "And now we have a different one."

"It's very clever," Dominic interjected. "Though the potential hexes are limited due to the materials involved, you could use this device to create and use a wide number of different hexes without a hexman. A sleeping hex, for example, could be created once, then the device altered, recharged, and used to cast a locking hex instead.

Mal arched a brow. "Not very portable, though, is it? I mean, compared to a scrap of papyrus or whatever they used back then."

"It probably wasn't used for day to day sorts of hexes," Owen said. "But it doesn't just allow one to have access to hexes without a hexman. There are two other advantages. The first is that it seems built to cast hexes over a large area. So if I used it to create an unlocking hex, I might be able to unlock every door in the Coven at once." Owen glanced at Dominic. "This second part is a bit more speculative, but Dominic agrees the potential is there."

Ferguson crossed his arms. "Don't keep us in suspense, Dr. Yates."

"Yes, of course." Owen cleared his throat again. "We ordinarily use hexes separately from one another. That is, if I cut myself, I might take a pain hex and use bandages hexed to prevent infection, but the two have no effect on one another. Even in the case of the chained hexes, one is activated, then the other at some later time. But this device allows one to create multiple hexes simultaneously."

He moved the lever to another position and turned the handle again. The plates swung and shifted, creating a far more complicated pattern. "Here we have the two previous hexes, both displayed at the same time.

More, some of the idiosyncrasies of the hex signs used suggest they may be linked together in some sophisticated fashion. I'm not certain how it would affect the outcome of the hexes—once I finish putting the device entirely back together, I'll have a better idea."

"So why did someone just leave this in a tomb?" Mal asked, cocking his head. "I mean, I suppose the owner was some ancient nob, burying gold and Mary knows what in the ground with him. But this seems, I don't know, useful. You'd think his heirs would've kept it."

Owen bit his lip uncertainly. "I'm only speculating here," he stressed. "But do you see these clamps on the front? I imagine they were used to hold an object to lend even more power to the hexes cast by the device, by absorbing more magic. As I said before, the effects of the hex could be spread out over a larger area than usual. But doing so would be dangerous to the familiar whose magic was being used. It would certainly strip them. It might even kill them."

Isaac flinched and looked away.

Quigley picked up the pamphlet they'd found at the apartment. "And the theriarchists might be involved." His voice was tight, flat with anger.

"Any insights, Isaac?" Ferguson asked.

Isaac's arms were folded tight around him. Rook moved to stand by him. Not touching, but within the periphery of Isaac's vision.

"It's the sort of thing they would use," Isaac said with a shrug. His eyes remained fixed on the floor.

Mal frowned. "Even if it killed familiars?"

Isaac let out a rough laugh, which held no humor. "I'm sure there are those willing to give their lives to the glorious cause. But more likely, they would have used a 'traitor' like me. Some poor feral who didn't believe wholesale murder was the way to achieve anything."

"Thank Mary we have it instead, then," Quigley said fervently.

"I think you're forgetting who kept it out of their hands in the first place," Mal pointed out.

Quigley shot him an annoyed look…then shrugged. "Aye, fine. Thank goodness you picked that night of all nights to climb in through Jacobs's window. I have a question, though."

"Which is?" Owen asked.

"How did the theriarchists even know it was there to steal it? Let alone that it would be something they'd want to steal." Quigley spread his hands apart. "We didn't find any mention of it in the list of items Jacobs had bought at auction. And when we questioned Mrs. Jacobs, she said she hadn't even seen the thing. It must have still been in a crate, or newly unboxed. Only the auction house had a complete listing."

"The theriarchists must be keeping an eye on auctions of antiquities," Owen said. "Or have someone on staff in their employ, I suppose."

"First Vikings, and now ancient Greeks," Rook said with a shake of his head. "The theriarchists do love their history, don't they?"

"That's actually not a bad point." Dominic glanced from Rook to Ferguson. "If there really is theriarchist involvement, it suggests Owen isn't the only person in New York interested in recovering the lost secrets of ancient hexwork. And that they're better positioned to find such treasures."

"A collector?" Owen hazarded.

Ferguson's frown deepened. "Which would mean money, and lots of it. So let's all hope you're wrong." He let his arms fall. "Finish the device, Dr. Yates. Quigley, if your captain is amenable, I'd like you to take a look at the auction house."

"Aye," Quigley said. Within a few minutes, everyone else had herded out the door, leaving Mal alone with Owen.

"Good work," he said softly.

A startled smile passed over Owen's face. "Thank you. It's been… enjoyable. I'm glad I was able to finish it before the end of the week." The smile faded, and he picked up one of the remaining plates. "Speaking of which, I'd best get to work. We have only a few hours before we have to leave to get ready for dinner."

Chapter 13

Owen walked into the apartment parlor, unbuttoning his vest. Mal slumped in one of the chairs, his red hair fiery against the green upholstery. The last light of the setting sun reflected from the low clouds, illuminating the park beyond and outlining Mal in soft gold.

He looked different, in repose. Mal was movement: quick and fast, his voice lilting with a ready joke, his mouth stretched into a crafty grin. But now his lips were pensive, his eyes fixed on something distant only he could see. The sudden urge to kiss away the brooding expression seized Owen, so strong he could barely breathe through it.

But he couldn't. Put a hand to Mal's shoulder, perhaps, but to show that level of affection outside the bedroom would be to set a dangerous precedent. Bad enough they'd kissed in the park like a pair of fools. He couldn't fall into such a habit of intimacy, not with the wedding less than three days from now.

It didn't stop him from wanting to, though.

"Mal?" he called softly. "It's time to get changed for dinner."

Mal's expression shifted, moodiness vanishing behind a swift smile. "I don't see any reason to. I'll just be in fox form the whole time, won't I?" The lightness of his tone didn't quite reach his eyes. "In fact, maybe I should strip naked."

The memory of the conversation with Nick came back forcefully. And perhaps Owen had been right, and everyone did things they would rather not, for all sorts of reasons. But that didn't mean life had to be needlessly unpleasant, not when something could be done to make it less so.

Mother and Father would be disappointed. But Owen had a duty to Mal as well, too. Even if they couldn't be lovers, Mal was a part of his family now.

"You aren't going in fox form, unless you'd prefer it," he said. "You're my partner in magic, my…friend. Not my pet."

The cheeky smile fell away from Mal's face. "But I thought…won't that make your parents angry? And your bride-to-be as well?"

"They will simply have to adapt." Owen met Mal's amber gaze squarely. "I won't stand by and let them treat you like some lesser being, just because you can turn into an animal."

Mal's gaping mouth shut slowly. "Then…then aye. I'll change." He bit his lip, an uncertain flash of white teeth against pale pink. Then the uncertainty slipped away, replaced by the vulpine grin that never failed to send a rush of blood into Owen's groin. "But we need to get you ready first. Go to your bedroom."

Owen's breath caught. "We can't. We'll be late."

"Backtalk?" Mal rose to his feet and gave Owen a swat on the bottom. "Do as you're told, boyo."

Owen's breath caught and his heart stuttered. He nodded. "Yes, sir."

Owen hurried to the bedroom. Mal sauntered behind at a more leisurely pace, disappearing into his bedroom and returning with the oil…and one of the dilators he'd used on Owen last night.

They didn't have time…Owen would face enough censure tonight without being late…yet he couldn't bring himself to argue.

Mal cocked a brow at him. "Still dressed? Take off your trousers and drawers. Now."

Owen's cock sprang free when he pulled off his clothing. Mal caught it, gave a slow tug that drew a whimper from Owen. "Ready, ain't you? Too bad you're just going to have to wait. Hands on the footboard and legs spread."

He hurried to obey. Mal unbuttoned his own trousers and pulled his hard prick out. "Look," he said, holding the dilator beside his cock. "See how it's a bit thinner than me? That way you'll still be nice and tight when I fuck you tonight."

A whimper escaped Owen. His heart pounded, and his head swam.

Mal moved behind Owen, and a moment later, fingers slick with oil pushed into him. He gasped, closed his eyes, then opened them again. "But first," Mal went on, "I'm going to make sure you spend the whole evening thinking about what's...*coming.*"

The head of the dilator pressed insistently in. Mal worked it slowly, patiently, until resistance gave way suddenly and it slipped inside. Owen's hands tightened on the headboard until his knuckles were white; he felt opened, helpless, out of control. His prick ached, liquid dripping from the tip and onto the carpet.

Mal leaned in, cock pressed against Owen's hip, to growl directly into his ear. "Now you're going to dress for the evening. And every time you so much as move all night, you'll remember what I'm going to do to you when we get home."

Oh God. "I can't," Owen said, the words a humiliating plea. "I can't sit there at dinner, in front of everyone, like—like this!"

"Like what?" Mal teased. He pressed his fingers against the flared base of the dilator, rocking it just a bit. "Opened and ready for me? Seems like your prick don't mind the idea." He stepped back, giving Owen a stinging slap on the buttock. "Now, get dressed. We wouldn't want to be late, after all."

Trepidation tightened Mal's stomach as the carriage pulled to a halt in front of the enormous mansion. A footman in green livery stepped to the curb and opened the door, his expression impassive.

"Ready?" Owen asked.

Mal had never been one for fancy clothes, but he had to admit, Owen looked practically edible in his white tie and tails. Mal wasn't dressed quite as well, not having had time to be fitted for something so nice, though his suit would have put to shame anything seen in his old neighborhood.

He wouldn't have been wearing even that, if Owen hadn't decided to say to hell with tradition. Mal had the feeling it wasn't easy for a fellow who ordinarily followed the rules to the letter, but Owen was doing it anyway. For Mal.

And Mal was about to pay him back with betrayal.

"I ain't sure I'll ever be ready," Mal replied, as lightly as he could. "But we're late enough as it is."

"And whose fault is that?" Owen asked, shifting to climb out of the carriage. A light flush stained his cheeks, and Mal grinned.

"Just remember to walk normally."

Owen shot him an exasperated look, but he couldn't very well say anything in front of the footman. They climbed out onto the sidewalk, then up the stairs to the Italianate mansion, where another liveried footman opened the door for them.

Mal caught his breath at the sight that greeted them. The entrance hall was brightly lit by a huge chandelier blazing with hexlights. Two enormous stairwells descended from the second floor; on the wall in between them hung a life-sized portrait of a young woman. Diamonds dripped from her hair, arms, and dress, and around her neck was a diamond necklace set with a twelve-pointed star sapphire that had to be the Star of Winter.

The current version of the woman in the portrait awaited them in front of it: considerably older and thicker, though no less encrusted with jewelry. She wore a gown of royal purple, a tiara sparkling with diamonds, and a collar dripping with pearls. A stomacher of diamonds competed with the dozens of diamonds and pearls pinned to her bodice. She looked like someone had upended a jewelry case onto her. To her right was a gray-haired man who looked strikingly like Owen. They were talking to another older man, two younger men, and a woman, all of them just as ostentatiously dressed.

Servants quietly took Owen and Mal's overcoats. Another servant, dressed in a green velvet coat, white knee breeches, and black stockings offered a silver tray laden with canapés. "Just take one," Owen murmured to Mal.

Mal nodded and hastily stuffed it in his mouth. The glimpses he'd had of the Jacobs mansion had left him breathless, but this?

And Owen had grown up here?

"Owen," said a frigid voice.

If Mal had been in fox form, his tail would have bristled. As it was, he tried to keep his pulse under control as he turned to face the woman beneath the portrait. The one who had to be Owen's mother. "You're late," she said. "You should have been here to greet our guests."

"Even I managed that," said one of the younger men with a wink. "Does that mean I'm the favorite now?"

Mal suppressed a laugh. "You must be Nathan."

Nathan put a hand to his chest dramatically. "I see my reputation precedes me. Whatever you've heard, it's all true, I assure you."

Owen's mother didn't seem amused.

"Forgive me." Owen swallowed, but his voice remained calmly polite. "Mother, Father, Nathan, may I introduce my familiar, Malachi."

Oh hell—was he supposed to shake hands with them? Bow? Kiss Mrs. Yates's hand? Mal settled on a shaky smile. "Hello."

"Malachi, this is my mother, Mrs. Josephine Yates, my father, Mr.

Seymour Yates, and my brother, Mr. Nathan Yates." He turned to the others. "And it seems I also have the pleasure of introducing Mr. Adam Vandersee, his son Mr. Kirk Vandersee, and Miss Edith Vandersee."

Mal's heart sank. This was the woman meant to be Owen's wife. The one who would take his place in Owen's bed in just a few short nights. She and her brother were cut from the same cloth, both plain and dark haired. They seemed vaguely familiar, especially Kirk—probably from the society pages, since Mal certainly wouldn't have run into rich folk like them anywhere else.

A bright smile illuminated Edith's face, turning her from ordinary to more than a little pretty. "It's such a pleasure to meet you at last, Mr. Malachi," she said, extending her hand.

Taken aback by her warmth, Mal bowed over it. She smelled of honeysuckle perfume: a delicate, gentle scent that seemed to suit her. "Thank you, Miss Vandersee," he managed. "It's a real treat to meet you, too."

And hell, it would even have been true, if she hadn't been engaged to Owen. Other than Nathan, she was the only one with the balls and grace to actually say hello to him, while the rest just stood around looking like they thought Mal might piss on the floor.

With any luck, maybe they'd even get along. Not that it made Mal any happier about Owen marrying.

A servant dressed all in black livery approached Mrs. Yates carrying a box. "Madam? The jewelry you asked for."

The sense of relief at the distraction was palpable. Mrs. Yates took the box and opened it. "I thought you might like to wear this at your wedding, Edith dear," she said.

And took out the Star of Winter.

An involuntary gasp escaped Mal. Sure, he had the copy hidden deeply in his pocket even now. But the real thing *felt* different. Not the glittering diamonds or the silver setting, but the sapphire itself. It seemed charged, almost, a thing of astonishing power.

No one else seemed moved by it, though. Maybe they were just used to it. Or maybe it was the sort of thing only a familiar could sense, the potential in it crying out to be filled with magic.

Edith's expression grew fixed. Probably she'd already picked out her own jewelry, this close to the wedding. "Thank you, Mrs. Yates."

Mrs. Yates smiled and closed the box. "Jane, give this to Miss Vandersee's girl, to put with her other things," she instructed as she handed it to a maidservant. The maidservant whisked it away silently.

Mal watched her go. Damn it, if only he knew the layout of the house. This was his chance—possibly his only chance—to get the Star for Madam Galpern.

And here it was, just lying in a box, instead of behind layers of security hexes. Just waiting for him to take it.

Another man dressed in livery appeared in one of the doorways, followed by a second man and a familiar in the shape of a spaniel. The housewitch, Mal guessed.

"Shall I ring the gong for dinner, madam?" the first man asked.

"Yes, do." Mrs. Yates glanced at Owen, avoiding even looking at Mal. "James will see to your familiar."

Owen opened his mouth to protest. "Thanks," Mal said, cutting him off. Owen cast a quizzical glance, but Mal gave him a small shrug. "I ain't sure I'm up to a dinner that means using more than one fork, not in front of your parents," he whispered.

Disappointment flashed over Owen's face, but he nodded. "Of course. I'll see you soon, then."

As it turned out, the housewitch and his familiar lived and dined apart from the rest of the Yates servants. Which was just fine with Mal; it would be far easier to sneak away from two people than ten.

They ate in the housewitch's small garret room. The place was utilitarian compared to the rest of the mansion, but a sight better than Mal's old apartment. Not as fancy as his bedroom in The Folly, but at least it was warm.

Would Owen put Mal somewhere like this? Or would he get better treatment, since he was Owen's familiar, not just a hired servant? Maybe he'd have a little room off of Owen's, like a valet or some such. Maybe on nights when Owen wasn't visiting his wife, they could…

No. Owen had already put paid to such a notion. His blasted sense of honor wouldn't let him.

Just as it hadn't let him treat Mal like a pet instead of a person.

Once safely in the servant's area, the spaniel—Betsy—had shifted into her human form. She spoke little, but spent dinner glaring daggers at Mal. Her witch, James, clearly didn't think much of him either.

"If you would care for some pointers as to how things are done in a proper house, I would be pleased to give them," was James's opening volley. Without waiting for assent, he immediately launched into a droning lecture concerning deportment, when to assume human form, and a dozen other rules.

"And no tail wagging," he added severely. "I'm not certain if that's something foxes do, but if so, don't. It conveys the impression of frivolity."

"Oh aye, we wouldn't be wanting anyone to think we're having fun," Mal muttered. No wonder Betsy was so sour-faced.

"Additionally," James added, eyeing Mal as he enthusiastically tore apart a bite of chicken with his fingers, "your manners aren't fit even for the servants' table. Now…"

Mal ignored him, save to make certain his table manners became even more offensive. By the time dinner was over, it was clear neither James nor Betsy wanted to spend another moment in his company.

"We have other duties to attend to," James said, rising to his feet. "Wait here, and someone will fetch you when Dr. Yates is ready to leave. Please do not touch anything."

Mal waited several minutes after they left. When he was certain they were gone, he slipped to his feet and cracked open the door.

Silence. All the servants were busy with the dinner party, or their own evening duties. Which meant, so long as he could stay away from the dining room, he ought to be able to avoid almost everyone. And if anyone did find him, he'd claim to be looking for a bathroom. That ought to be indelicate enough to give James conniptions.

Even so, he slipped into fox form, which would make it easier to hide if he needed to. Hopefully Owen wouldn't suddenly take it into his head to try and look through Mal's eyes.

He skulked down the servants' hall. His sensitive hearing brought him snippets of conversation from a half-open door, where some of the staff were no doubt having their own meal.

There came a series of loud gasps. "It's true!" exclaimed a woman. "I swear it on my mother's grave. Mrs. Jacobs was right there, in the house—I saw her."

"And her a good thirty years older than Mr. Vandersee!" exclaimed a delightedly scandalized voice. "No wonder they've kept it so quiet!"

Judging by the age comment, they must be referring to Kirk Vandersee and not his father. So, old lady Jacobs was having an affair, and with a much younger fellow. No wonder she hadn't been in the house the night of the murder. Should Mal tell Owen?

Except he'd have to admit how he'd come by such information, which could lead to awkward questions. Ones he couldn't afford to have asked. At least Mrs. Jacobs had just been sleeping with the wrong fellow —and the man in question was about to become Owen's brother-in-law.

There wasn't any connection to the murder, and it could cause trouble between Owen and his new bride.

That in itself was tempting…but no. Neither of them deserved that. Bad enough Mal was betraying Owen's trust by stealing the necklace; there was no need to add spitefulness to his short comings.

It took Mal a good ten minutes to locate the suite where Miss Vandersee's things had been left for the duration of the visit. Fortunately, all the servants on duty seemed to be focused on the dinner party, and Mal didn't encounter anyone in the ladies' wing while he sniffed the doors, searching for traces of honeysuckle perfume.

As soon as he found her scent, he shifted back into human shape and slipped inside the room. Quickly shutting the door behind him, he was glad to see the hexlights had been left on for Miss Vandersee's convenience. The sitting room was plain by the standards of the mansion—the tables and chairs weren't even gilded, and there was only one vase laden with hothouse roses.

And on the small writing table, beside a reticule and coat that must belong to Edith, sat the box containing the Star of Winter.

Mal's heart beat in his throat as he approached. This was it. All he had to do was switch out the real necklace for the fake one. Take it to Sophie. And in turn, she'd give him the name of Jacobs's murderer.

He would find some way to slip out of the Coven tomorrow and send an anonymous message to Quigley. With any luck the man would be behind bars in days. Mal could stop looking over his shoulder. Stop having to be escorted everywhere. He could leave, when sharing space with Owen and Edith became too painful to bear, and not have to worry about ambush.

The replica felt oddly heavy as he pulled it from his pocket. This would be the biggest heist he'd ever thought to pull off, even if he wouldn't see any proceeds from the sale. But what did it matter? He looked around the sitting room, at the marble fireplace, the jewel-encrusted clock. The Yateses had money, and the Vandersees had even more. And hell, with any luck, no one would even realize the necklace had been substituted for a fake. They'd never know they'd lost anything.

Mal would know.

He'd sworn to Owen that he'd reformed.

Owen would never find out. What he didn't know wouldn't hurt him—or Mal. This was Mal's life on the line, after all.

Owen had stood up for Mal tonight. Even before tonight, he'd treated Mal like a person. And last night, in the park, laughing as he played the violin…he'd shown Mal a side of him that Mal didn't think he'd ever shown anyone else.

The bond burned inside him, a steady warmth tucked right against his heart. If he concentrated, he could sense Owen dimly through it. Sitting at dinner, never thinking for a moment Mal would stab him in the back.

Owen *trusted* him.

Mal's hand hovered above the box for a long minute. Then, with a muttered oath, he shoved the fake necklace back into his pocket and left.

Chapter 14

Owen sat at the dining table as the courses came and went, and tried not to give into despair.

The food was perfect, naturally. Salmon cutlets, terrapin, ribs of beef, canvasback duck, and partridge with truffles, all flawlessly prepared, all tasting like ashes to him.

He gazed up and down the table. Another small dinner party, this time with only fifty guests invited. A mere fraction of the number who would attend the wedding breakfast on Saturday.

This was what his life was to be from now on. An endless round of dinners, balls, and entertainments, both hosted and attended, so as to retain position in society. A part of him was beginning to understand why Mr. Astor had fled to his yacht and left his wife to do as she wished.

Not that he would—could—do the same. Not and live with himself, at any rate. It wouldn't be fair to Edith. His gaze found her, seated several chairs away, a blank expression on her face as she listened to an aged senator drone on. She seemed no fonder of entertainments than he.

But they would host them nonetheless, for the sake of whatever children they would have. Of maintaining a place in society for the next generation; and, in Owen's case, for the previous generation as well.

His mother beamed from her seat at one end of the table. This was what she loved most of all: to be at the center of society, an arbiter of taste and fashion. God and the accountants alone knew how much this dinner must have cost, but the pending influx of Vandersee cash meant she could once again be as extravagant as her heart desired. Or as society demanded.

He shifted slightly—and was immediately once again aware of the dilator's presence. Thanks to Mal, he'd spent half the night in a state of utterly inappropriate arousal.

Mal. The thought of his familiar lightened his heart and brought a smile to his lips. He'd thought them so unsuited at first, and yet Mal had never failed to make him smile. He could be himself with Mal, as he'd never been able to be with anyone else.

"You seem to be in a good mood," Kirk remarked.

Owen's cheeks heated; if Kirk knew what had put him in such a mood… "It's a lovely party," he said inanely.

"Our parents seem pleased, at least." Kirk glanced at the head of the table, then back to Owen. "Nathan is looking well."

"He's happy." Thank heavens. "Mother and Father less so, but they'll come around."

Kirk nodded and sipped his wine. "Will we see you at Delmonico's for Thanksgiving tomorrow?"

Owen hesitated. He knew his parents would prefer it if he joined them, but he was sick of socializing. "I rather thought I'd visit Peter instead."

A shadow fell over Kirk's face. He and Peter had been close as boys. Along with Kirk's younger brother, Robert, they'd spent endless hours together both in town and in Newport. Owen had been too young to join in their games, but he could recall watching them out the window as they clambered about on the rocks above the surf, or frolicked on the grassy lawn.

Then Robert died, and Peter had his accident, and now only Kirk remained.

"Give him my best," Kirk said, and finished the glass of wine.

"You could come see him, if you wished," Owen suggested hesitantly. Mother and Father wouldn't approve of anyone outside the family, the doctors, and the servants seeing Peter in his condition, but surely they'd make an exception for Kirk.

"Perhaps I will," Kirk said, though Owen wasn't certain how sincerely he meant it. His gaze drifted to Edith. "I suppose if things had gone differently, Peter would have been the one marrying my sister."

An unexpected thorn of regret snagged on Owen's heart. Would Peter have been any happier about it than he was? For that matter, would Edith have been?

Probably not, since it seemed she had feelings for Creswell. But Peter had been handsome and dashing; surely he would have been a better prize than Owen by any measure.

Owen took a deep drink from his own glass. There was no sense in might-have-beens. The past was locked into place, and the future just as immoveable. They all had to accept their lots and soldier on.

But for the first time, he would have given up almost anything to change it.

Sophie awaited Mal on the corner a block west of Fifth Avenue. The temperature had dropped, and snow began to sift down from the low clouds. The wires overhead swayed and hummed in the brisk wind.

"Mal," she said, hurrying to him. Her breath steamed in the cold air, and her nose was red and chapped. "You did it? You've got the Star of Winter?"

Mal let out a long, slow breath. He'd stolen a mackintosh left near the servants' entrance, which at least kept off the damp snow, but the cold still bit deep. "Nay," he said heavily. "And I ain't going to. Madam Galpern will have to find someone else."

Sophie stared at him for a long moment, lips parted, as though she wasn't sure she'd heard him aright. "What do you mean? Madam told me you don't get the murderer's name if you don't deliver the goods."

"I know." Mal shook his head. "But Owen…he's been good to me, Sophie. I couldn't bring myself to do it."

"You idiot." Her eyes narrowed into blue slits. "They're going to kill you. Are you really going to risk your life for some rich nob?"

"There are other ways of finding the murderer." Or at least, that's what he'd been telling himself since he'd left the Star of Winter behind. "If Madam Galpern figured out who killed Jacobs, so can the police. It might take them longer, but I've got protection until then."

Sophie took a step back from him. "So that's it? You think you're safe, so to hell with the rest of us?"

He reached out, but she avoided him. "Nay, of course not."

"Madam Galpern is relying on you!" Sophie clenched her fists. *"I'm* relying on you. I had part of the cut coming to me from this job! You're warm and have food in your belly, and fancy clothes to wear. You think you can just forget where you came from? Pretend you're a nob, choose these rich bastards over those who've looked out for you your entire life?"

"Saint Mary, that's not it at all!" Mal protested. "It ain't like that."

"It's exactly like that." Sophie retreated further, shaking her head in disgust, as if she couldn't stand the sight of him. "But you ain't one of them. They'll never see you as anything more than just a thief."

His throat constricted. "That ain't true."

"Remember tonight, Malachi. When the nobs turn on you; when you're lying there, bleeding out in the gutter somewhere, remember that you spit on the ones as tried to help you."

"Sophie, please," he said. But she turned her back on him, and stalked away down the street, until the shadows swallowed her up.

"At last," Owen said, when the elevator let them out in front of the apartment well after midnight.

He unlocked the door and gestured Mal to enter before him. His familiar had been unusually quiet the entire ride back, though Owen hadn't wanted to risk the possibility of being overheard by the footmen by asking what was wrong. Following him in, Owen locked the door behind them and shed his overcoat. "Is everything all right?"

Mal had already slipped out of overcoat and suit coat alike. "Aye. Just thinking."

Owen cocked his head uncertainly. "Thinking…?"

"That I'm glad we met." Mal's smile was uncharacteristically wistful. "Glad you're my witch."

Owen's throat tightened. "So am I. Mal…"

Mal shook himself, like a fox flinging water from his coat. "Speaking of thinking," he said, his tone deliberately lighter, "did you think of me often tonight?"

Heat scalded Owen's face—just as it had practically every time he moved at dinner, and was reminded of the intrusive object. And of Mal's plans for him after. "I had little choice otherwise," he said.

Mal let out a bark of laughter. "Just as I wanted. Get in the bedroom."

Owen hesitated, but whatever odd mood lay over Mal seemed to have vanished, at least for the moment. So when Mal arched a brow and growled, "Now," Owen hastened to comply.

As soon as they were in the bedroom, Mal kicked the door shut. "Take off those nice clothes," he said, and went to wrestle the standing mirror into a new position at the foot of the bed.

Owen's fingers shook on the buttons. Mal's gaze seemed to singe every inch of exposed flesh, until he stood naked, helpless, his cock jutting obscenely out in front of him. He clasped his hands behind his back and waited for orders.

"Good boy," Mal murmured. He held out his arms. "Now, undress me, then get on the bed. Hands and knees."

Every scrape of cloth against Owen's erection was exquisite torture. When he finally had Mal naked, he climbed eagerly onto the bed and waited. The feeling of being exposed, vulnerable, sent a thrill through his blood and made his breath come in short, excited gasps.

Mal's fingers trailed along Owen's back, then across one buttock, to dip in between his legs and give Owen's sack a quick, sharp tug. Owen whimpered.

The mattress sagged under Mal's weight. The familiar remained on his knees, prick stiff in front of him. "Suck me." His eyes lifted to the mirror he'd repositioned. "I'm going to watch while you do it."

Owen wrapped his lips around Mal's cock, tasting the tang of his excitement. He slid down hungrily, taking Mal to the root. Mal kept his hips still for once, letting Owen do all the work.

"Spread your legs wider," Mal ordered. "Aye, like that. I can see your arse in the mirror, spread open by the dilator. One day I'm going to use the biggest one on you, really open you up. You'd like that, wouldn't you? To suck me off, with that big heavy thing shoved up your arse."

Owen moaned helplessly around Mal's prick. Mal made a strangled sound, then pushed Owen away. "St-stop." He closed his eyes and gripped the base of his cock hard. "I ain't going to come yet."

Owen's own cock ached with need, but he already knew Mal wouldn't let him touch himself.

Mal reached out and ran a thumb over Owen's lips. "I'm going to fuck you now," he growled. "Beg for it. Beg me to fuck you with my big cock."

Lust tightened Owen's throat. "Please," he managed.

"Please what?"

"Please, sir. Please fuck me with your big cock."

Mal grinned, exposing his sharp teeth. "Turn around. I want you to see your face in the mirror while I bugger you."

Owen's arms shook so badly he wasn't certain he could support himself. His lack of spectacles meant the figures in the mirror were a blur of light and shadow. "I can't see."

Mal slid out of bed, plucked up Owen's spectacles, and gently settled them onto his nose. "There you go."

The sight of his own face red with lust, lips swollen, sent an odd shiver of humiliation and excitement through him. Mal climbed in behind him, then grabbed the oil and slicked his cock.

Owen whimpered again when Mal pulled out the dilator. For a moment, he felt empty, the sensation of fullness gone and leaving him aching.

Then Mal pressed the head of his cock in.

A cry escaped him as Mal's thicker prick stretched him open. Mal grabbed his hip with one hand, and the other tangled in Owen's hair, pulling his head back. "Watch," he said, and pushed in deeper.

And oh God, there was so much of him, so much longer than the squat dilators. Mal shoved in deeper, and deeper, and Owen's mouth gaped open, his cheeks scarlet, his prick hard and aching. It had been so long since he'd been fucked, and never like this, with a hand gripping his hair and the other man commanding him.

And Mal said *he* was glad Owen was his witch? Owen ought to be on his knees, thanking fate or God or the universe itself for bringing Mal to him. His fantasies had by necessity centered around the physical act alone, because he'd never dared imagine the fullness of what they had together. Never believed he'd find someone he could trust so implicitly, could surrender himself to so completely. Mal was everything he'd dreamed of and more: friend, lover, partner in every way.

"Fuck, this is good," Mal gasped. "Damn, you're so tight. Feel that, Owen? Feel me in you, all the way to my balls?"

"Y-Yes," Owen groaned. "Please, Mal, please."

He wasn't even sure what he begged for. He saw Mal's savage smile in the mirror, smelled the wildness of his scent. The warmth of their bond burned in his chest, the connection even deeper than their physical joining.

"I'm going to give you the ride of your life," Mal promised. He drew out, almost too far, but before Owen could object over the loss, he shoved back in.

Then he was moving, thrusting hard. His hand tugged hard on Owen's hair, and his fingers dug into Owen's hip. Pleasure shocked through Owen, Mal's prick pressing against the spot deep inside. He cried out with every thrust, an unrestrained sound he was powerless to suppress. His skin burned, and his length ached to be touched.

"Please, let me touch myself," he begged. "Please, I can't stand it."

"You'll stand what I tell you to stand," Mal said between clenched teeth. "Fur and feathers, I can't last much longer. Do it, then—stroke yourself off while I come up your arse."

Owen grasped his prick and tugged frantically. Mal drove into him, again and again, so deep—then froze with a hoarse shout, spilling inside Owen's body. It shoved Owen over the edge, and he shook as he spent onto the bedding.

Mal's cock slipped free. Owen found himself almost face-down, on his elbows and knees, head bowed and his heart thudding in his chest. He felt raw, all the trappings of life scraped away, leaving behind only the core of himself exposed like a nerve.

Mal's touch turned tender. "Come here," he coaxed, and slid his arms around Owen. "That's it." A soft kiss pressed against Owen's temple. "Such a good boy, aren't you? So good."

Owen curled into him, content to breathe Mal's scent. He felt as though he drifted on a warm cloud, protected and cherished, every worry gone. Lassitude gripped his limbs, and he wasn't entirely certain he'd be able to move for the rest of the night.

After a while, Mal dropped a kiss on his shoulder. "I'm going to get a cloth to clean us up. Just stay here."

Owen nodded. A few minutes later, Mal returned. The washcloth was warm, and Mal's touch gentle.

"There." Mal lifted the blankets. "Now, let's get you tucked in."

"Stay with me," Owen said.

It was a terrible idea, of course. Sex was one thing, but sleeping together, when Mal had his own, perfectly good bed...

It should have felt too intimate. But instead it only felt right.

As soon as he was beneath the covers, Mal slipped in as well. "All right," he said, his arms going around Owen. "I'll stay."

The next afternoon, Owen took a step back from the device and eyed it critically. It had taken on the shape of a sort of box when viewed from the outside, its inner workings exposed or hidden by the lever and the turning of the crank.

"Finished," he said.

"Well done!" Mal sat perched on another stool, where he'd been helping Owen off and on. And asking questions throughout—intelligent ones, Owen had to admit. His fox was clever, even if uneducated.

What hexes they might have made together, if only they could stay. With his expertise and Mal's magic, they might have revolutionized forensic hexology.

"Are we going to test it?" Mal asked.

"That might not be wise," Owen admitted, though in truth he badly wanted to do so. "Remember what I said about it possibly being dangerous to the familiar used to charge it? And besides, some of the hex signs are obscure, their meaning lost. It might not be entirely safe to test them."

"We'll be careful," Mal said. "And we'll take it someplace away from any buildings. If we're out in the middle of a field, at least we won't have to worry about anything exploding, right?"

Owen laughed at Mal's eagerness. "I doubt any of the hexes cause explosions. Although some of them…"

"What?" Mal prompted.

"I'm not sure," Owen confessed. "Some of the symbols seem related to the sky, the wind. Combined with another hex, I wonder if they could be used to create weather magic?"

"That's illegal, ain't it?" Mal asked.

"Highly. And for good reason—causing rain in one place can easily result in a drought elsewhere. Some of the earliest laws against certain types of hexes were enacted in Ancient Egypt, to keep anyone from trying to disturb the yearly flooding of the Nile."

"So no explosions, and we avoid the weather magic." Mal winked at him. "What do we have to worry about?"

"You, silly fox." Owen leaned over and kissed Mal's forehead. The gesture seemed natural, even though he knew it was foolish to risk such a habit. "I'm worried about you."

They'd waked this morning in each other's arms, bodies tangled together in the sheets. They hadn't made love—had sex, that is—again, but there had been tender kisses and soft touches aplenty. Owen wasn't entirely certain what had changed, but Mal seemed less guarded, somehow.

He cleared his throat, telling himself to concentrate. "It might be safe, if I was careful not to draw too much magic from you. But I'd want Halloran and some familiars about, just to make sure nothing went wrong."

"Smart," Mal said with a nod. "You're a genius, to have put this back together. I'm proud of you."

Owen flushed with a mixture of pleasure and embarrassment. "It was nothing. I just rebuilt something someone else made. All my contributions have been small. Perhaps if I'd been able to invent the poison-identifying hex…"

"You talk like you're an old man." Mal put his hand on Owen's. "You're just getting started. Some day—"

There came a sharp knock on the door. Mal snatched his hand away, as if Owen's skin had become red hot.

"Come in," Owen called.

The door opened, and Kirk Vandersee stuck his head inside. "Kirk?" Owen said blankly. "Is something wrong?"

Kirk shook his head as he came inside. "Everyone is healthy and safe," he said, which was an odd way of answering. He gave Mal a nod, then turned his attention fully on Owen. "I need to talk to you."

"You've never been here before this week, and now you visit twice?" Owen asked. "Is this about the Jacobs murder? If I knew anything further about the investigation that I could share, I assure you I would have told you last night."

Kirk cast another glance at Mal. "It isn't that. May I speak with you privately?"

Mal shrugged and hopped off the stool. "I'll just go see what Bertie is up to, then," he said.

Kirk flinched—then nodded. "Yes. You should do that."

Once Mal was gone, Owen folded his arms over his chest. "That was very rude," he told Kirk. "If this is a personal matter, you should have waited to call on me at home. And if it isn't—"

"I'm sorry," Kirk interrupted. He ran his hand through his hair. "I didn't mean to offend Mr. Malachi. But I've come because…well. There's no easy way to say this. The Star of Winter has been stolen."

Chapter 15

"I...what?" Owen asked. His head spun—the Star of Winter alone was nearly priceless. Along with the diamonds and silver setting, the loss was astronomical. "How could such a thing happen?"

Kirk slumped into one of the chairs. No wonder he looked so harried. "We don't know yet," he said. "We wouldn't even know it was missing, except the woman putting the final touches on Edith's wedding dress had an appointment this morning. Edith offered to show it to her, so she could match some bows to the blue sapphire. The box was empty."

Owen let his arms fall to his sides. "I assume you've questioned the servants?"

"Obviously. We've started within the household, but if that doesn't turn up anything, the investigation will move to your parents' house. Edith never looked at the box again after receiving it last night, so it's possible the necklace was stolen during dinner." Kirk hesitated visibly. "Owen...we've been friends for a long time, so please don't take this the wrong way. But I follow the papers, and I talk to your family. I know how you and Malachi first met."

Owen's heart stumbled. Could what Kirk insinuated possibly be true?

Mal was a thief, and had been most of his life, according to his own words.

Was a thief. Was, but no more. He'd promised Owen he would reform.

"You're wrong, Kirk," Owen said. "Mal had nothing to do with this."

Kirk hastily held up his hands. "I'm certain you're right, old boy. I didn't mean to cause offense. Just…suggest you check his possessions. To make sure."

Owen's fingers clenched. Mal had given Owen his word. After everything else, after everything they'd shared, going through his room would be an insult of the deepest order. It would imply Owen didn't trust Mal. That he thought Mal didn't actually care about him.

Mal had held him with such tenderness last night. It would take a hard heart indeed to go from stealing from Owen's family, his bride-to-be, to those gentle kisses this morning.

Wouldn't it?

"I trust Malachi," he told Kirk, struggling to keep his emotions from his face. "As his witch, I will personally vouch for him. Does that satisfy you?"

"Of course it does." Kirk rose to his feet. "Say no more. If you don't mind, I'd prefer you not repeat this to anyone. Including your familiar."

Owen nodded. "Very well."

"Thank you." Kirk put his hat back on. "And now, if you will excuse me, I should return home and assist Father and the police."

"So what did your friend Kirk want?" Mal asked. He'd eaten lunch with Bertie, Isaac, and the wolverine Greta in their small office. Bertie had fetched sandwiches for them all from the nearby deli—fish for himself, chicken for Mal, and roast beef for Isaac and Greta. They'd loitered a bit, gossiping about the other familiars. Life in the barracks sounded far different from life in a feral colony. Here, the familiars were all united by their job with the MWP. Until they met their witches, they lived, slept, and worked together.

Some members of the colony had been close. But Mal had already had a family with Sophie and Madam Galpern, and he'd come to the colony more for the protection Nick offered than from any fellow feeling. For the first time, he wondered if he shouldn't have spent more time getting to know the other ferals.

When he returned to the lab after lunch, it was to find Owen looking as though he'd received some unpleasant news.

"Nothing important," Owen replied when Mal asked him about it.

"Just a detail concerning the wedding. I don't know why he didn't just send a note, honestly."

"Oh." Mal nodded. Maybe Owen was in a bad mood after being reminded of the wedding. He'd certainly been…well, not loving, that would be absurd. *Friendly* this morning. Maybe he didn't want to think about his upcoming nuptials, when he'd have to give up all they'd done last night.

Although there might be a way around that. Did Owen know they made devices for women to wear? Edith might like to try it that way.

"Edith seemed nice," he said, uncertain if he ought to bring her up or not. "I liked her."

A little to his surprise, Owen seemed grateful for the topic. "She is. I don't claim to know her well, but I've never heard anyone speak a bad word about her. Certainly she has always been unfailingly kind to me. As unlike her own mother as it's possible to be, or so they say."

Mal cocked his head. This sounded like a story he ought to know, if he was to be living with them. "Tell me about Mrs. Vandersee."

"Edith and I were quite young when all this happened," Owen cautioned him. "But the story is something of a legend in society. Rose Vandersee clawed her way into high society by force of will alone. Well, that and a great deal of money to enforce her will, naturally."

"Aye, I imagine that would help," Mal agreed. He leaned forward and put his elbows on his knees. "So how did she do it?"

"The Vandersee family were swells—rich, but they didn't meet the criteria for admission into the Four Hundred. The fortune was made by Adam Vandersee's father, you see, who invented a hex back in Holland and then sold it in New York. It could ensure sanitation of canning lines in factories. He took the initial investment and built the company to greatness. But the money was too new—to be worthy of entering into society, one must be at least three generations removed from the source of the fortune."

Mal shook his head. "I swear, the things you worry about when you've got the money, eh?"

"Quite." Owen wiped down the work area around the device. "Mrs. Vandersee was determined not to let that stop her. She threw an enormous costume ball. Rumor has it the final cost was over $250,000."

"Holy Familiar of Christ," Mal breathed. That was more money than most people could hope to earn in several lifetimes. "One party cost that much?"

"It did." Owen smiled ruefully. "Of course the newspapers were beside each other when the scope of it was discovered. Invitations flooded out from the Vandersees' newly built chateau, which was rumored to rival the wealth and glory of Versailles itself. Who could resist the chance to see it for themselves?" His smile turned sly. "But there was one society lady who hadn't received an invitation. My mother."

"Oh, I'm betting she didn't like that," Mal cackled. "I'm surprised her hair didn't catch fire."

"Ah, but you see, by the rules of etiquette Mother herself adhered to, Mrs. Vandersee *couldn't* send an invitation. Mother had never invited her to call, so *surely* an invitation from an inferior wouldn't be welcome. Mother tried to stick it out, but when she realized literally everyone was going except for her, she gave in and had Mrs. Vandersee over for tea. Her invitation to the ball arrived the next day. The affair was an immense success, and the Vandersees were ensured their place among the Four Hundred."

Mal shook his head. "She's seems like quite the woman."

"She was, I'm sure." Owen's expression sobered. "She didn't get to enjoy her triumph for long. Almost immediately after the ball, her youngest son died. He was only ten months younger than Kirk; the two of them were as close as twins, I'm told. Once the period of mourning ended, Mrs. Vandersee returned to society, but people reported a new hardness about her. A bitterness, even. She passed just a few years later."

Owen pushed his stool back from the work table, but his gaze remained distant, fixed on something Mal couldn't see. "Kirk once told me she died from guilt over his brother's death. Which made no sense—Robert was lost in a boating accident, his body never found. The only member of the family on board at the time was Mr. Vandersee."

"That must have been hard on Kirk. On all of them," Mal said.

"Yes. It was. Kirk was the elder, and so had always felt himself responsible for his little brother, or so I suspect. And Edith as well, of course, but she was several years younger, and she and Kirk were never as close." Owen seemed to return from his thoughts, and glanced at Mal. "There's something I'd like to show you tonight."

"It's Thanksgiving, ain't it?" he asked. "I thought we'd go to dinner at the restaurant in The Folly." He waggled his brows. "Or are you offering to show me something else tonight, eh?"

Owen laughed. "Not that. Well, perhaps later." He glanced at the clock. "We can get dinner at the restaurant after, though. Will you come?"

"All right," Mal said puzzled. "You know me. I'm game for anything."

They met Bertie on their way out of the Coven. To Mal's surprise, the bear insisted on accompanying them.

"Just a feeling," he said, as they stepped out onto the marble steps. He tipped his head back and sniffed the cold air. Snow flurries had left a dusting of white on the roofs and a thin layer of slush in the streets. "Besides, it's Thanksgiving, which means they're serving turkey in the barracks tonight. And I hate turkey." At Mal's skeptical look, he shrugged. "Honestly? My family threw me out at Thanksgiving, so I'd rather work than sit around and brood."

Mal winced. "That's hard. I'm sorry."

Bertie shrugged. "It was a long time ago. But I'm not much for celebrating."

"Understandable," said Owen. "Then come along, and safeguard us both."

Sometime later, a cab let them out in front of what probably passed as a modest house to people like Owen. Trees lined the street; bare now in the winter, but in the summer it would be a beautiful, shady thoroughfare.

"So whose place is this?" Mal asked, looking up at the stately townhouse.

"The family owns it, actually." Owen turned to the cab. "Wait here, if you will, driver. Bertie, would you like to come inside?"

Bertie waved a hand. "I'll stay here with the driver," he said. "Though maybe you could send something out to warm the blood?"

Owen smiled. "Gladly."

A man in somber clothing opened the door. No livery here, Mal noted. Was this some sort of secret hideaway, and the Yateses didn't want anyone to know they owned it? Maybe they installed mistresses here.

"Dr. Yates," the footman said, stepping smartly aside. "Let me take your coats, and then I'll summon Mrs. Lewis."

"Thank you," Owen said. They entered a small foyer and waited, while the footman vanished with their coats. Though less lavish than the Yates mansion, or even The Folly, the room showed off the wealth of its owners in the form of gilded mirrors, a marble floor inlaid with a hex meant to promote the health and luck of those inside, and a statue of a half-man, half-goat, like a familiar caught halfway into transformation.

"This belonged to my maternal grandmother, before her marriage, then again after her husband's death," Owen said, looking about. "She lived here with her familiar for many years. Of course, most of the rooms are closed off now. The staff is too small to keep it up, otherwise."

This was getting stranger and stranger. "Does someone live here?" Mal asked.

"Yes." Owen's shoulders slumped. "My brother, Peter."

Before Mal could reply, a cheerful, plump woman dressed like a nurse bustled into the foyer. "Dr. Yates! Oh, it's so good to see you again. Mr. Yates will be just thrilled you could join us for Thanksgiving."

"How is Peter doing?" Owen asked.

"Today's been a good day," she said, beckoning them to follow her. "He's in the library right now—he likes to watch the birds in the trees through the window, don't you know. And of course I read to him, when he seems bored."

She led them into a room lined with books. Though smaller than the library at the Jacobs manor, it felt far more lived in. The air smelled of old paper and wood polish, and the gaslights gleamed from the golden titles stamped on the books' spines. A single chair occupied the room, its upholstery worn. A basket of yarn sat beside it, which no doubt belonged to Mrs. Lewis.

A wheelchair sat in front of one of the large windows, through which Mal could see the electric lights of the street outside beginning to come to life. The figure in the wheelchair made no motion to indicate he knew they were there.

Mrs. Lewis bustled over to him. "You've visitors, Mr. Yates! Your brother has come to see you for Thanksgiving, just as I mentioned earlier. And there's another gentleman with him." Well, that was the first time anyone had ever called Mal a gentleman. She turned to Owen. "I'll leave you to visit, but if you need anything, just ring the bell and I'll be right here."

The door shut behind her, leaving them in the silent library. Owen walked around the front of the wheelchair, then crouched down to look its occupant in the eye. "Good evening, Peter," he said. "I've brought someone I'd like you to meet."

Mal approached hesitantly. The man in the wheelchair resembled Mrs. Yates in coloring, though he had the same silvery eyes as Owen. His head was oddly misshapen, as though parts of the skull no longer fit as they once had. Withered hands lay on the blanket in his lap, and his clothing looked as though it had been made for a more robust frame. His mouth was parted, the breath raspy, but his eyes tracked Owen's face, and his features twitched into something like a smile.

Owen took one limp hand. "I'm sorry it's been a few weeks since my last visit," he said. "Things have been busy at work. But I wanted to make certain to wish you a Happy Thanksgiving."

Peter made a sound that might have been an attempt at speech in reply. Poor devil.

But Mal wouldn't have wanted someone pitying him, were their places reversed. So he put the thought aside, as best he could.

"I have some news," Owen continued. "This is my familiar, Malachi. Mal, this is my older brother, Peter Yates."

Mal bobbed his head. "Hello. It's a pleasure to meet you, sir."

Peter made a small sound, and one hand jerked in Mal's direction. Mal wasn't sure if he should take it, so he held his own hand out uncertainly. Peter's fingers tapped his, then fell to his lap again.

"Mal, why don't you ring the footman to bring in another chair, so we can all sit?" Owen suggested. It seemed like it would have been easier to move Peter, since his chair had wheels, but maybe Owen didn't want to disturb his view.

"Did Nathan come to see you?" Owen asked, once they were all settled. "He's to be my best man at the wedding, you know."

They sat together, while Owen had a mostly one-sided conversation with his brother. He told Peter about the case, what the families they knew were up to, and the general news of the world. He responded to Peter's jerky movement and sounds with the ease of old practice.

It was almost peaceful. Until in the midst of a story about some business deal of their father's, Peter's eyes suddenly widened.

His whole body jerked, and for a moment, Mal thought he might be having some sort of fit. But Peter's eyes remained locked on the window as he flailed and moaned.

"Peter!" Owen went to his knees by the chair, grasping Peter's arms to hold them still. "It's all right! It's all right."

Peter struggled against his grasp, groaning frantically. His eyes flicked from Owen to the window, again and again.

"He sees something outside," Mal said, and peered out.

Full night had fallen, and there was little to see except for the occasional flakes of snow and the pools of light cast by the street lamps. Bertie had climbed out of the cab and stood by it, talking idly with the driver. Otherwise, the street appeared deserted.

Mal frowned. "Nothing," he said with a shrug.

Owen sighed. "Ring for Mrs. Lewis, if you please."

She came as quickly as she'd promised. "I'm afraid he's grown agitated," Owen said helplessly.

"There, there, that's all right," she said. "Likely it's just frustration. Still, the doctor said not to do anything to agitate him, and to make sure we keep on a regular schedule."

"Of course," Owen said. "We'll just be on our way. Peter, I'll be back after the wedding. Before we leave for Europe, even if I have to stop in on the way to the docks."

Soon enough, they were back on the street. Owen tucked his hands deep into the pockets of his coat, and his shoulders hunched. "What say we go home?" Mal suggested.

Bertie overheard. "Do you need me to keep an eye on your backs?"

Mal considered, but they'd be in a cab. No one could exactly accost them on the street that way. And so long as they were let off within the safety of The Folly's courtyard, everything should be fine. "Not needed, but thanks for the offer."

"Should we take you anywhere first, Bertie?" Owen asked.

Bertie shook his head. "No, don't worry about me. I'd rather walk for a bit, clear my head. Some of the theaters on Broadway are open tonight, despite the holiday. Maybe I'll take advantage and watch a show."

Once they were safely ensconced in the cab, Mal took Owen's hand in his. "Thank you," he said quietly. "For introducing me to your brother."

The light of a passing street lamp reflected from Owen's glasses. "I worshipped the ground Peter walked on," he said. "He set the example for us all. First in everything—sport, school, whatever he turned his hand to. He would have gone into business and found some way to save the family fortune."

"Or be the one marrying Edith," Mal guessed.

"Yes. He would have done it without an instant of complaint." Owen swallowed. "May I tell you something? Something which must never go beyond the confines of this cab?"

Mal nodded. "Of course. You can tell me anything."

"Peter wasn't injured cleaning a gun. He shot himself deliberately."

"Oh hell." Poor bastard. "I'm sorry, Owen."

"Peter always had his moods, of course." Owen stared out the window, thin lipped. "But I always thought him happy enough. I was already at the MWP when it happened. In fact, I was supposed to meet him for lunch, but I grew involved in my work and missed the appointment. And that night, Peter shot himself. I can't help but think, if I'd met him as intended, I would have seen the signs. Or he might have confessed his plans to me, or…"

Saint Mary, no wonder Owen acted the way he did. He felt he had to sacrifice himself to take the place of the brother he'd adored.

"Or nothing," Mal said. He squeezed Owen's fingers, hard. "If he'd never told you he was—was sad, or hopeless, or whatever he was feeling—before, why would he then? You can't blame yourself. It wasn't your fault. Maybe it wasn't anyone's fault."

"That's very kind of you to say," Owen replied.

"It's just the truth." Mal brought Owen's hand to his mouth, pressed it against his lips. "You didn't cause this to happen. You have to stop feeling as though—"

He stopped. There was something large and dark, coming fast from a cross-street. A pair of horns gleamed in the street lamps, an instant before a heavy weight slammed into the side of the cab.

Chapter 16

The cab tipped violently up onto two wheels. Owen fell heavily against Mal, and they both smashed into the door on Mal's side.

The shift in weight was enough; with a groan, the whole cab crashed down onto its side. The top of Mal's head clipped Owen's chin, and the taste of blood filled Owen's mouth.

"What the hell happened?" Mal exclaimed. Outside, the driver was yelling, the horse shrieking in fear and pain.

"I don't know," Owen said. "Are you all right?"

A huge pair of bull horns ripped through the cab's thin roof, barely missing Mal's face.

"Sweet Mary!" Mal shouted. Owen yanked him back, farther from the horns.

The horns tore free—then an instant later smashed back in, in a slightly different spot. Looking for them.

"It's a familiar!" Owen exclaimed. "Trying to kill us."

"I've noticed! Now help me." Mal shoved at the door now over their heads. "Damn it! The bloody bull twisted it half off its hinges. It won't open all the way."

The bull let out a bellow that turned Owen's knees to jelly. "Break the window! You can squeeze out through it in fox shape."

Mal didn't argue. He smashed his elbow into the glass, turning his face aside as it rained down. Shifting into his fox form, he scrambled out.

And let out a startled bark as a human hand grabbed him by the scruff and hoisted him away.

"Mal!" Owen shouted.

"Owen! It's him!"

Owen flung himself against the door, as hard as he could. It remained stuck.

He had to get out of here; had to get to Mal. Fear washed through the bond, his own and Mal's intermingling.

He shut his eyes, and got a confused glimpse of the world through Mal's. Mal was struggling, twisting and trying to bite. But the man kept an iron grip on his scruff, carrying him away from the cab.

There came the crack of a gun. The man jerked, and his hold loosened by a tiny bit.

It was enough. Mal went into a frenzy: snarling and flailing, until he was dropped. He raced back toward the cab. The driver stood beside the struggling horse, gun in hand.

The bull let out an ominous snort.

Owen opened his eyes and tore his hexman's wallet from his pocket. Inks and pens went flying everywhere, and he sorted through them frantically. An unlocking hex wouldn't work—the door was jammed, not locked. He knew a dozen hexes to strengthen the parts of the carriage, but he needed it to fall to pieces.

If he could reverse one of them…

Not giving himself time to doubt, he snatched up a stick of red chalk and began to sketch a hex around the door's hinges. Omitting certain symbols, adding others, and oh God let this work…

He slapped his palm onto the jury-rigged hex, and the magic flowed. "Let me out!"

The hinges fell into pieces, pins shooting half-way across the wrecked cab. The hardware of the latch came apart as well, brass fittings pelting his head. With a cry of triumph, Owen shoved the door aside and scrambled out of the carriage.

Just in time to hear a shriek of agony. The driver crashed into one of the trees where he'd been tossed, and the bull backed up, blood blackening its horns.

Then it turned on Mal.

"No!" Owen shouted, and leapt from the cab onto the bull's back.

A tremendous bellow of rage echoed down the street. Before Owen could even attempt to get a grip on the bull's broad back, it bucked. For a moment, he was airborne, the world spinning madly around him.

Then he thumped onto the street. All the wind was knocked from his lungs, and pain shot up his spine.

"*Owen!*"

The bull turned and lowered its head.

"Stop!" Bertie shouted, and charged the bull from the side. He slashed at it with a knife from his belt. "I'm warning you!"

The bull seemed unimpressed. It turned to him, lowering its head.

Bertie shifted; where there had been a relatively large man, now towered an enormous grizzly bear. He reared back on his hind legs, and his roar shook the windows around them.

That was enough for the bull. It transformed into a man and took off running down the street. The man who had attacked Mal followed on his heels.

Owen took a great, gasping breath and managed to roll to his side. "I'm fine!" he called to Mal, who dashed toward him. "Don't let them get away!"

Mal shifted and dropped to his knees by Owen. "Fuck them," he said, grabbing Owen by the shoulders. "You're more important. Christ, Owen, I thought—"

There came the sound of screams from the intersection with Broadway, two blocks down. Owen and Mal exchanged startled looks. Bertie swore and jogged past them.

Bertie. Thank heavens he'd decided to take the most direct route to Broadway. Without his presence, the bull would likely have finished them both off.

Mal helped Owen to his feet. Owen ached, but he limped alongside Mal as they made their slow way to the intersection. A cable car sat unmoving, and a crowd had gathered around it.

As they approached, Bertie turned to them. "The bull familiar got away," he said. "But the other didn't quite make it."

The dead man lay sprawled half beneath the car, his mouth open as if in surprise. Red hair the same shade as Mal's curled around his face, and Owen realized they were of the same height and build. From a distance, they might have been mistaken for one another.

"It's him," Mal said.

"Who?" Bertie asked.

"The man we're looking for. The one who killed Mr. Jacobs."

"Good work, you two." Ferguson leaned back in his chair, looking far more pleased than Mal had ever seen him. "You've solved a very important case, made the MWP look good, *and* saved the cost of a trial." His grin widened. "Plus, this whole thing has left the regular police looking like buffoons, so even better."

Mal glanced uncertainly up at Owen. To his relief, his witch seemed equally confused. It had been a long night. After summoning help for the cab driver—the doctors believed the man would survive, thank heavens—they'd spent hours answering the questions of the regular police plus other witch police detectives, and helping Bertie fill out the paperwork. After, Mal had drawn a hot bath for Owen to soak away his aching muscles in. He moved stiffly, but the hexes tattooed on his skin had already taken care of most of the bruises. Too tired to even make love, they'd curled up together in Owen's bed and fallen asleep until the alarm clock woke them.

The good news was, they finally had a name for the killer. One of the regular police had recognized his body, having arrested him for burglary and theft a few years previously. Gilbert, a feral who turned into a red squirrel, just as Owen had suspected.

Owen removed his spectacles and cleaned them with his handkerchief. "Sir," he said carefully. "We should have had Gilbert's image in our rogues gallery, as he was a familiar with a criminal record. Why wasn't he in there?"

Ferguson snorted. "He was always booked by the regular police. They probably didn't bother sending over the photographs they took. I think I'll mention that, just in passing, to the Police Board when I meet with them this afternoon."

"I suppose." Owen put his spectacles back on. "But, though he murdered Jacobs, he wasn't the one who killed Ulysses."

Athene glided from her perch, shifting so her boots thumped lightly on the floor. "He hired a larger, more powerful familiar to do his dirty work, just as he did with the bull."

"But he killed Jacobs by himself, and tried to kill Mal," Owen protested.

Ferguson sighed and rubbed his eyes. "What are you saying, Yates?"

"That Gilbert wasn't working alone!" Mal exclaimed, unable to restrain himself any longer. "Someone hired him to steal the device." And if Mal had given the Star of Winter to Madam Galpern, they might even know who. He shoved the thought aside. "Gilbert tried to kill me, but then I was followed by two others from the saloon the next day."

"If they're all in a criminal gang together, it makes sense," Ferguson pointed out.

"A gang of ferals, watching each other's backs," Mal said slowly. It was possible.

"Like Molly's gang," Owen said.

"Molly?"

"One of the theriarchists." Owen locked eyes with Ferguson. "She's dead, but someone else might have taken her place easily enough. What if they wanted the device for some…some new scheme?"

"Then it failed." Ferguson sat back. "I appreciate your fire, Yates, but this is no longer your concern. Today is your last day with the MWP, remember?"

Owen stilled, and the expression drained away from his face. "I haven't forgotten."

"Then take the victory. Your name is all over the newspapers as the man who brought Jacobs's killer to justice. Your fiancée will have reporters knocking on her door from noon to night, wanting to know how she feels about marrying a hero."

Owen flushed. "That isn't how it was," he said. "And you know it."

"Then just smile and pretend to be humble when the reporters talk to you," Ferguson said. "Now, if you'll excuse me, I have other cases that need my attention."

Dismissed, they retreated back through the detectives' area. Mal remained silent until they reached Owen's lab. "You all right?" he asked.

"Yes," Owen said, automatically.

Mal shoved his hands deep into his pockets. Fur and feathers, he'd been counting the days until they were out of the Coven and away from the coppers. But Owen *loved* this. And Mal…

Loved Owen.

"Don't lie," he said quietly. "Not to me."

Owen stopped, just outside the door to the laboratory. Their eyes met, and something softened in Owen's gaze, the sleet gray darkening to pewter. "I should have bargained to stay on to the end of the year. I wish…" A sigh escaped him. "Well. If wishes were horses, as they say." He hesitated, then touched Mal's face tenderly. "I'm glad you'll be with me, after today. Is that terribly selfish of me?"

"I'm glad, too," Mal said. Even though they wouldn't be together the same way. "You'll keep playing the violin, won't you? You don't mean to give that up?"

Owen laughed. "No. I don't. I'll play for you again, as often as you'd like."

Turning from Mal, he reached for the door. It swung open at his touch.

"That's odd," Owen said. "I'm certain I locked it last night."

"Perhaps someone came in to clean?" Mal suggested.

Owen stepped inside. "No. Oh no."

He ran across the room, as if physical proximity to the work table would make it less empty. Mal stayed at the doorway, feeling all the blood drain from his extremities.

The device was gone.

"I can't believe this," Owen said, clutching at his hair. "Gone. Stolen."

All of his hard work, lost. His notes, burned to ash over his own Bunsen burner.

Gone. And the device was in the hands of the very people who had murdered Jacobs and tried to kill Mal and him.

He'd done their work for them, by rebuilding the device. He should have left it in pieces.

"Stolen right in the middle of the MWP," Mal agreed.

The Coven had been in an uproar since the theft was discovered. Ferguson had shouted himself hoarse at the witches, and Athene had personally interrogated every familiar on the premises. A bloodhound familiar had even come to the lab, trying to catch some faded scent, but found only those expected.

"Hexed shoes," Mal had suggested. "They don't leave any scent behind for the coppers to track." He'd gotten a glare from several of the detectives. Owen had glared back; perhaps Mal had been a thief, but he wasn't any more, and his knowledge could be of use.

In the end, there had been no clues of any kind. No one had seen anything suspicious. The device might has well have disappeared into thin air.

It was a black eye for the MWP, no doubt.

Now, only Mal, Dominic, Rook, and Owen remained in the lab. Dominic came to stand by Owen, putting a comforting hand to his shoulder. "I'm sorry. I'm sure this isn't how you wanted to spend your last day here."

"Not exactly," Owen agreed.

"We were going to have a party," Rook said. "Cicero had it all planned. There's this little resort on—"

Owen held up his hand. "I appreciate the thought," he said. "But Ferguson has everyone going over the Coven from top to bottom, looking for evidence. I understand."

"Maybe later," said Dominic. "Once you get back from your honeymoon and settled in your new life."

The thought hurt. Could he stand to see them again, knowing they were still working with the MWP? To ask if any new forensic hexman had been hired, or if Dominic was doing his best to fill the position? "I'd like that," Owen said.

He held out his hand, and Dominic clasped it solemnly. "It's been a pleasure working with you, Owen," he said. "I wish you much happiness. And congratulations on your marriage tomorrow."

None of Owen's friends would be there. Not his real friends, anyway. None of them had enough money, enough influence, to have made the guest list.

"Thank you, Dominic," he said.

Dominic looked down at him—then hauled him into an embrace. They clapped one another on the back, and tears unexpectedly stung Owen's eyes.

Dominic released him and stepped away. Without speaking again, he made for the door. Rook glanced after him, then back and Owen. "Good luck," he said. "You, too, Mal."

Then he flashed into crow form and glided after his witch.

Mal came over to Owen. Their hands touched, then curled together. "I'm sorry about your party," Mal said.

Owen snorted. "Considering that Cicero planned it, it might be just as well. Whatever resort he had in mind is probably full of exotic dancing and half-naked men."

Mal laughed. "And you suddenly don't appreciate half-naked men?"

"I do, but...I'd rather spend tonight with you." Owen met Mal's amber gaze. "One last time."

Something like grief seemed to shadow Mal's eyes. It couldn't be, of course—unlike Owen, Mal would remain free to do whatever he wished with whomever he wished.

"Aye," he said quietly. "One last time. Let's go home and make it memorable then, shall we?"

As soon as they reached the ante chamber of the apartment, Mal flung himself on Owen, kissing him ravenously. Owen held him close, feeling the press of Mal's erection through their trousers. Tried to memorize the taste of his mouth, the scent of his arousal.

Tomorrow morning, Owen would walk into the cathedral. Stand

before his parents, before every important person in New York City, and before God. Speak the vows that would bind Edith and him together for the rest of their lives.

So few hours left. He could feel the life he'd built falling away, one piece at a time. His job at the MWP was already gone. Next was his affair with Mal.

"I want you," Owen whispered. "Body and soul, and everything in between."

"Do you now?" Mal's ocher eyes narrowed slightly, and he grabbed Owen through his trousers. "Oh, I have plans for you," he murmured, squeezing. "You'll get everything you can take, and more."

Owen's breath came short. "Yes. Please."

Mal let go. "I'll get the ropes ready. You go fetch the dilators from my room. And think about all the nasty things I'm going to do to you with them."

Owen nodded, trembling. "Yes."

"Yes?"

"Yes, sir."

"Good boy." Mal swatted him on the backside. "Don't make me wait."

Owen scurried to Mal's room. He'd seldom set foot in here—no point in making a habit out of something that couldn't continue, after all. It smelled of Mal—a faint musk, underlain with something earthy and wild. Owen hesitated a moment; he'd forgotten to ask where the box was kept. Somewhere the servants wouldn't pry when they came in to clean, no doubt.

The wardrobe seemed most likely, so he went to it and opened the doors. Hunkering down, he shifted aside Mal's shoes. As he did so, he knocked over a small pouch shoved behind them. It toppled over with a heavy *thunk*, and the end of a silver chain fell out.

A chain that looked very familiar.

Owen's heart beat in his ears. His hand wavered over it. It couldn't be. He was mistaken.

Mal wouldn't do that to him.

He picked up the pouch and upended it. The Star of Winter tumbled out into his hand.

Mal stripped back the thick comforter and top sheet. The fireplace would help warm the air, and he'd keep Owen's blood too high to notice any chill. Humming to himself, he took the rope from where he'd stowed it in Owen's dresser. And a few silk handkerchiefs. One would do as a blindfold, but perhaps a gag was in order as well? Owen would like that—it would mean a total surrender of control.

He heard Owen step into the room behind him. "Good boy," he started as he turned, but the words died away on his lips.

Owen stood in the door, his face ashen. In his hand wasn't the box Mal had sent him to fetch, but the replica of the Star of Winter.

For a long moment, silence hung between them, broken only by the soft crackle of the fire, the moan of the wind past the window.

"I can explain," Mal said at last, mind scrambling for some way *to* explain.

"Don't bother." Owen's voice was hoarse, his eyes gone gray as sleet. "I defended you to Kirk. I told him you couldn't possibly have stolen it."

"Stolen…" Oh hell. He had to have misheard. "Someone stole it?" Owen's expression of shock shifted toward outrage, and Mal hastily added, "The real one, I mean? Because that ain't. It's just paste and glass. You can break one of the diamonds with your shoe."

Owen hurled the necklace to the floor with such suddenness it caused Mal to jump. Glass turned to powder under his heel.

"S-See?" Mal said, because Owen's expression hadn't changed. "Just glass and paste, like I said." Saint Mary, let him find some way through this. "So what's this about the real thing being stolen?"

"Stop pretending to be surprised." Owen's voice was cold, flat, but his hands trembled at his sides. "What happened? Did you forget to take the replica with you that night? Or did you not have time to replace the necklace after you pocketed it?"

"I know this looks bad," Mal said, holding his hands up. Fear coursed through his veins—even if he told Owen everything this very moment, would Owen forgive him? "But I can explain."

"I can explain it, too." Owen's frigid tone seemed to leach all the heat from the room. "You're a thief and a liar. I must have been out of my mind to have ever trusted you. But don't worry. I see you now for what you truly are."

Mal couldn't get enough breath. His heart labored in his chest, as if his blood had turned thick. Frozen, maybe, gone to slush before Owen's icy glare.

"Owen," he tried, though what he could say, he didn't know.

"Did you steal the device as well?"

"Nay!" Mal took a step toward him, but Owen moved back, and he stopped. "I swear, I didn't."

Owen shook his head slowly. "As if your word means anything. Get out."

Mal's lips had gone numb. "Wh-what?"

"Get out." Owen stepped aside and pointed at the door.

No, this wasn't happening. Owen wasn't throwing him out on the street.

This wasn't happening again.

"You can't," Mal said. "Our bond. You're my witch."

A look of disgust tightened Owen's features. "A mistake from the beginning. I'll call upon Tom Halloran at my first opportunity and ask him to break it. Now. Get. Out."

Mal's walk through the apartment to the door felt like something out of a nightmare. He had to wake up.

"Wait," Owen said.

Thank God. Mal turned, and found Owen behind him. He'd picked up the violin case from where it still remained on the ante room table.

"I don't know how much your cut of the theft was," Owen snarled, thrusting the violin into Mal's arms so hard it staggered him. "But this should be enough to get you out of the city. Take this to your precious fence and use the money to leave New York. I don't ever want to set eyes on you again."

Chapter 17

The next morning, Mal carried the violin down the street toward Madam Galpern's, his steps sluggish. He'd spent the night at a 24-hour restaurant, drinking cup after cup of coffee until the sun came up. His head ached and his throat hurt, and the cold, clear wind did nothing to make him feel better. Even the sunny sky seemed to mock him.

It was a beautiful day for a wedding. Was Owen already at the cathedral on Fifth Avenue?

Their bond was still intact, its soft warmth a mockery of the comfort it had so briefly offered. Mal could find out where Owen was. Could shift shape and beg Owen to just *listen* to him.

But what would be the point? Owen had made it clear enough he thought Mal was nothing but a liar and a thief.

And he was right. Maybe Mal didn't steal the Star of Winter himself, but he also hadn't told Owen that Madam Galpern had an interested buyer.

How could he have, though? She'd been the one to take him out of the orphanage and start training him up. He couldn't betray her by telling the coppers she was planning a theft. She was the only one who'd ever seen anything of worth in him.

At least until Owen.

He'd tried to belong to two worlds at once. To Owen's glittering, warm, safe world where money flowed like water, all the while staying loyal to Sophie and Madam Galpern, and keeping his mouth shut about the proposed job. Hell, he would have kept his mouth shut even if he'd known she had someone else ready to steal it at the Vandersee household. Though how the devil she'd found out Mrs. Yates had lent the necklace to Edith, he didn't know. Someone on staff, no doubt.

His time with Owen had been like something out of a fantasy. A dream of fine food, of soft sheets and hot water and new clothes. And like any dream, he had to wake up eventually. Go back to the gutter where he belonged.

If Owen would have just *listened* to him. Given him half a minute to explain. But of course he'd been willing to think Mal a thief at the drop of a hat.

They'd been too different from the start. And to think, Mal had actually believed that Owen *cared* about him. What an idiot he'd been.

No one else was in the shop, thank Mary. A frown creased Madam Galpern's brown face when Mal stepped inside. "What on earth are you doing here, Malachi?"

He hefted the violin in its case. "I've got something for you."

One perfect eyebrow arched. "Oh really? I thought you were *reformed*."

His head ached. More than anything, he wanted to curl up and drift off to sleep. Preferably to wake up in Owen's arms and find it had all been a terrible dream. "The violin ain't stolen. And I'm sorry I let you down," he said. "Though it sounds like you had someone on the Vandersee staff who came through anyway."

A tiny hint of surprise flickered over her face, there and gone so quickly he wasn't certain he'd actually seen it. "That's none of your concern, Malachi. And I still don't know why you're here. Surely in your new life, you have no need to sell a violin to make ends meet."

He didn't want to say the words…but he had no choice. She wouldn't do business with him if she thought he was with the coppers. "Owen—Dr. Yates—threw me out. Thanks to *your* plot. I didn't inform on you, but he found the fake necklace where I'd hidden it. He thinks I'm a thief."

"You are a thief, my dear."

"Right." He swallowed thickly. "Owen ordered me to leave town, and gave me the violin to raise funds. So that's what I'm doing."

"How generous of him," she murmured. "And he didn't turn you over to the police?"

Mal had plenty of time at the restaurant last night to think it over. "Didn't want the scandal. His own familiar, stealing from his bride-to-be?

Better I disappear all quiet-like than it reach the papers. They've got enough money that the loss of the Star won't impact more than their pride."

"I see." She looked at him for a long moment, as if considering.

"Please." He'd beg if he had to. "I'm selling the violin no matter what, and I hoped you'd give me a fair price. For old time's sake. And I…I wanted to say goodbye. To you and Sophie." He swallowed. "I know I let you down."

Just like he'd let Owen down. Just like he'd let his parents down, all those years ago. He'd never be good enough for anyone, it seemed.

Madam Galpern sighed. "Turn the sign to *closed* and come upstairs."

Mal did so, then followed her to the lavish sitting room. "Why don't you sit down and let me pour us drinks," she suggested.

Mal sank into the chair, holding the violin case across his knees. Now that the moment was here, he found he didn't want to sell it. He had to—he'd left Owen's apartment with nothing else but the clothes on his back. Most of the coin in his pocket had gone to coffee throughout the long night. There was no choice but to turn the instrument over to Madam Galpern and take whatever money she gave him for it. He had no practical use for it, certainly.

But it was the last thing he had of Owen. The only thing. Well, except for the warm place the bond made behind his heart. Soon, even that would be gone thanks to the damned hexbreaker, and he'd have nothing.

He ran his fingers over the case, remembering how Owen had laughed that night in the park. How he'd come alive while playing, just as he'd come alive beneath Mal's hands in bed. Forgotten his accursed duty, his responsibilities, for a few seconds and just been…happy.

Mal blinked rapidly. He'd been beaten for crying too many times as a child; he couldn't break down in front of Madam Galpern now.

"So Dr. Yates believes you stole the Star of Winter," she said from the sideboard. "That you are, in fact, a hardened criminal."

"Aye," Mal agreed miserably.

"So he wouldn't be surprised—disappointed, no doubt, but hardly surprised—if you broke in here, intending to steal from me. I confronted you, and then…"

She turned from the sideboard, a pistol in her hand.

"Sadly, I was forced to defend myself," she said, and leveled the gun at him.

~ * ~

Mal surged to his feet, but the bore of the gun followed him.

"I wouldn't, my dear," Madam Galpern warned.

Mal's fingers were like ice where they still clutched the violin case. The black mouth of the gun seemed to swallow the morning light coming through the windows, and he couldn't look away. "What's going on?" There had to be some mistake. She wouldn't threaten him like this. "I know I let you down, but I'm still one of yours."

Madam Galpern sighed. "Don't be stupid, my dear. You've done nothing *but* let me down for years."

Ice water seeped down his spine, and his gut tensed. "Wh-what do you mean?"

"Why do you think I plucked you from the orphanage, so long ago?" she asked. "Because you had quick fingers? Don't be ridiculous. This city is swarming with pickpockets, and second-story men can be found on any street corner. But familiars are far more rare."

His pulse pounded at the base of his throat. "You only wanted me because I'm a familiar."

"Certainly. It's not as if there's a shortage of red-haired Irish brats." Her full mouth flexed into a scowl. "You were to work for me until you were ready to bond with one of my witches. *Then* you'd become really useful. But you refused."

He shouldn't give her any ideas, but he had no desire to be shot, either. "Then why not force me? If that's all I was to you."

She snorted. "I prefer that those in my employ work willingly. I've built my fortune on *loyalty*. Having someone who hated and resented me in the ranks seemed a risk. I hoped for a while you'd change your mind, but you were so horribly ungrateful. So when someone approached me, looking for a small, red-haired man to be the scapegoat for the Jacobs murder, you were the perfect choice."

Mal's head spun; it was all he could to do remain standing. He couldn't believe this. She'd betrayed him. The entire job at the Jacobs mansion had been nothing but a ploy to get him on the property at the right time. Gilbert was meant to kill Jacobs, leave behind a red hair to incriminate Mal, set off the alarm, and abscond with the device while the servants chased Mal. And since the ledger page describing the device had been lost, no one would ever have even known anything had been stolen. Never imagined anyone had been there except for Mal.

There would have been no need for the police to look any further. Case closed.

Mal would have gone to the electric chair, no doubt about it. And the whole time, he would have maintained his silence about who had given him the job in the first place, because he couldn't take his old friend Madam Galpern down with him. Couldn't hurt the only person who had ever seen any value in him.

His mouth tasted like metal and ash.

"And Sophie?" he managed to ask. "What if she'd been caught? Would you have let her rot in prison?"

"Again, you're being foolish." Madam Galpern smiled. "Sophie is useful. Unlike you."

Mal swung his violin case as hard as he could. There came the crack of the pistol firing, at the same instant as the case smashed into Madam Galpern's arm.

The gunshot set Mal's ears to ringing. She dropped the pistol, her lips parted in what might have been a cry of pain. Without hesitation, he swung again, this time directly into her beautiful face.

Blood gushed from her broken nose, and she fell heavily to the floor. He flung the shattered violin at her and ran for the door.

It burst open before he could touch it. The foxhound familiar stood on the other side in his human form.

Owen sat in the carriage taking him to the cathedral, staring out the window. Thank God only Nathan rode with him; he couldn't have stood any more company. As it was, at least he had a little while to collect himself.

Not that it would do much good. Nathan hadn't said anything, but he'd winced at Owen's appearance. Owen had done his best to look presentable, of course, but it was difficult to counteract a sleepless night peppered with bouts of drinking and crying.

He'd trusted Mal. Against all logic, against everyone warning him not to, he'd opened himself up to a thief. Allowed himself to be exposed, vulnerable, because he stupidly thought Mal was a decent man despite his history. And the whole time, Mal had just been cynically manipulating him. Pretended Owen's weakness made no difference; pretended to still respect Owen, while Owen panted and begged.

Owen closed his eyes against a wave of nausea.

"Are you all right?" Nathan asked. "I'm sure I could find some paper for you to draw an anti-hangover hex once we reach the cathedral, if you need it."

Owen opened his eyes and shook his head. "Not necessary." Out of habit, he'd tucked his hexman's wallet into his pocket. At the reminder, he half wished to throw it out of the moving carriage.

He didn't want to look at anything related to hexing ever again. Never wanted to think about magic, or familiars. About the moments of connection, something in Mal recognizing something in him. The splashes of joy through the bond, the night in the park.

Nathan frowned, not bothering to disguise his worry. "I thought Mal would be with you. Is he joining us later?"

It was a story he'd no doubt have to tell again and again for the next few weeks, but Owen had hoped to put it off for just a little bit longer. Until after the wedding breakfast, at least.

But as in so much else, he wasn't going to get his wish.

"Mal is gone," he said, and tried to keep his voice as neutral as possible. "It turns out he stole the Star of Winter."

Everyone would want to know why he'd thrown Mal out instead of turning him over to the police. And in all honestly, Owen himself didn't have a good answer. The thought of sitting through a trial, looking at the face of the man he'd loved…

Oh God.

Nathan's eyes widened. "Dear heavens! Are you certain? Did he sneak over to the Vandersee house after you fell asleep that night? How on earth did he get in?"

Owen frowned. "No, of course not. He took it while we were all at dinner, before it even had the chance to leave our house."

"I don't see how that could be," Nathan said with a frown of his own. "I visited with Edith yesterday, and she told me the last time she saw it was just before she turned in to bed. She gave it to the butler to put into the safe, but couldn't help showing it off first to the maid who dresses her hair, with whom she's on friendly terms. It was definitely stolen from the Vandersee mansion—from the safe, no less, so naturally the police are focusing on the butler. But if you're saying Malachi somehow snuck in during the early hours…"

Except Mal couldn't have. He'd stayed in Owen's bed for the first time that night, slept with him until it was time to rise and go to the Coven. "No." Owen's head swam. "Kirk must have been mistaken when he said…never mind. It wouldn't have been possible for Mal to sneak away without my knowing."

"Then it seems to me your familiar has been unjustly accused." Nathan put a hand to his arm. "Did you give him over to the police? Do I need to send someone to free him?"

"No. I let him go, because…" Owen took a deep ragged breath. "It doesn't matter. He's gone."

"Can't you find him somehow? Through the bond? That is how it works, isn't it?"

If Mal was still in the city…

But he wouldn't be for long. The expression on his face, when Owen had thrown him out, came back forcefully. Crushed. Broken. Tears gleaming in his wild eyes, hands clutching the violin.

"I can explain."

But Owen hadn't wanted an explanation. He'd been too hurt and betrayed to even listen. So he'd thrown Mal away. Just as Mal's parents had.

Mal must surely hate him now.

The carriage came to a halt in front of the cathedral steps. In a short hour or so, he'd say his wedding vows to bind himself forever to a woman he didn't love.

Maybe it was for the best. At least he wouldn't have to see Mal every day and be tempted to break the oaths he made before God. And Mal could surely find a better witch than Owen. Mal deserved someone free to love him.

"No," Owen said quietly. "It's too late now."

Mal hurled himself violently to the side. A gun fired, and his abused ears protested at the sound. Dropping to the floor, he rolled behind the couch. Instinct screamed at him to hide, and he transformed into fox shape and squirmed his way beneath a china cabinet with a low skirt.

The smell of blood came to his fox senses, accompanied by labored, wet breathing. Had the foxhound shot Madam Galpern?

The floorboards creaked beneath the feet of the gunman. "Come out, come out," he called in a singsong voice. "I can smell you even in this shape, vermin."

His shoes appeared beyond the cabinet's skirt. Mal scrambled back, pressing himself against the wall, his ears pinned to the sides of his head and his tail tucked against him. He was cornered—any minute now, the man would lean down, point the gun beneath the cabinet, and pull the trigger.

There came yet another shot. Mal jumped, his narrow skull impacting with the underside of the cabinet.

The gun struck the floor, gouging a strip of varnish from the wood. A moment later, the man followed, body limp as a sack of flour. His head ended up turned to the side, sightless eyes seeming to stare directly at

Mal, while blood trickled from the gaping hole in his forehead.

Mal scrabbled out from under the cabinet, his nails scoring the wood flooring. Madam Galpern leaned heavily against her favorite chair, her own gun in her hand. Her fashionable shirt and jacket were soaked in blood, and her breath rasped loudly. Their eyes met…and she slowly slumped to the floor.

Mal took back his human form and ran to crouch beside her. Her brown skin had gone gray, and the blood on her shirt was bright red—a lung had been hit, if not worse.

He snatched a pillow from the couch and pressed it against the hole in her shirt. "Who was he?" Mal asked urgently. "He was working with them, wasn't he? The folks who killed Jacobs and stole the device?"

Her eyelids fluttered, and she made a sound of pain that ripped at his heart, despite everything. "Tell me. Please," he said. "At least a name, something I can use to bring them down."

She drew in a deep breath, but it rattled in her lungs. He leaned close to her bloodied lips.

"Didn't know him," she rasped. "But there was another. Bertie."

Then the rattle in her chest ceased, and she slowly went limp beneath his hands.

Mal released the pillow and sat back on his heels. The place reeked of blood and piss, and the expensive carpet was wrecked. He felt lightheaded, as though the entire world had slipped to one side.

Bertie. Did she mean Bertie from the MWP?

But that wasn't possible. Bertie had watched over Mal from the start. He'd saved Owen on Thanksgiving. Kept the bull familiar from goring them to death.

In his mind's eye, Mal saw again the library, and Peter looking out the window. Frantically gesturing, wild with distress. And they'd put it down to some kind of fit, because there was nothing out there but good old Bertie.

That didn't make any sense, though. What could Peter, who had been an invalid for years, know about a MWP familiar that would disturb him so?

Mal hesitated. He could take fox form and speak to Owen through their bond. Warn him…

Except Owen already thought him a liar. He wouldn't believe a word Mal said. He'd probably just think Mal was trying to smear Bertie's reputation, especially since Mal had no proof Madam Galpern had even been referring to him. There had to be a hundred Berties in lower

Manhattan alone.

The clock chimed softly from the mantle. Owen had probably reached the church by now. For all Mal knew, he was in the midst of speaking his vows to his new bride.

Fur and feathers.

Mal rose to his feet. His trousers and vest were soaked in blood, but Madam Galpern had always kept spares on hand in case one of her thieves returned with incriminatingly stained clothing. He'd change as fast as possible, just to keep any coppers from looking twice.

Then it was time to pay Peter a visit, and pray the staff let him in.

Chapter 18

Owen looked out over the crowd gathering for the wedding. He'd spent the last hour by the door, woodenly accepting the congratulations of guest after guest after guest. Governor-elect Roosevelt, Mayor Van Wyck, senators and congressmen, railroad tycoons and steel magnates: in short, everyone of any importance in the entire state of New York was now packed into the cathedral to watch the nuptials.

Even poor Davis Creswell had come, with his family. Owen had a dire moment when he'd blinked out of his fog to find Creswell standing before him, red-eyed and unhappy.

Would Edith's eyes be red from tears as well? God knew Owen's probably were. Not that anyone would notice, or care. They were doing what was expected, what was best for both families. Ensuring their place in society. It was the only thing that mattered. The only thing that had ever mattered.

At least no one from the MWP was there. None of them were rich enough to have made the guest list his mother had compiled. At first he'd been disappointed, but now he was glad. It meant he didn't have to explain Mal's absence.

The door to the cathedral's great tower opened, and Kirk slipped out of the tower and into the side aisle. Owen frowned slightly—what business could Kirk possibly have had there? Perhaps he'd been making certain the bell ringers were ready to signal the end of the wedding, though that hardly seemed a job for the bride's brother.

It didn't matter. Perhaps Kirk had wished a few moments of privacy before the wedding. No one else had noticed; it would be an ill way to start his new life by pointlessly questioning his brother-in-law over his movements. Owen turned his attention back to greeting the guests.

At least the flood of arrivals had slowed to a trickle. Soon even that dwindled, as the hour approached noon.

Nathan touched Owen's elbow. "It's time to take our places," he murmured.

Owen glanced out the open doors. A procession of carriages which must contain Edith, her father, and her bridesmaids made its way through the crowds gathered outside. The sky had darkened, and snow was beginning to fall.

He walked up the center of the nave, feeling as though he were in a nightmare. He could sense every eye fixed on him, and concentrated on keeping his back straight. On representing the Yates family as best he knew how. Organ music filled the air, the lowest notes thrumming in his empty stomach, and he thought he might be ill.

The bishop and various priests emerged from the vestry. Owen took his place on the steps, Nathan at his side. Within minutes, the first bridesmaids proceeded into the church, escorted by a string of groomsmen Owen barely knew. In the front pew, his father beamed proudly, while his mother dabbed at her eyes.

She had outdone herself with the church. Ordinarily, Mrs. Vandersee would have planned the wedding, but as Adam Vandersee had never remarried, he'd been quite happy to let Mother handle the details while he paid the bill. An army of florists had transformed the stone and wood into a fairyland of pink chrysanthemums and white roses. Massive garlands hung from the dome, and ropes of flowers entwined the stone columns. Trellises of chrysanthemums and lily of the valley hid the chancel rail and lined the side aisles. Even more flowers dripped from every candelabrum.

Beyond the stained glass windows, the sky had darkened even more. The light which had streamed through them when he'd arrived at the church was utterly gone, as if night had fallen. The gloom seemed more fitting, somehow.

At last Mr. Vandersee entered, with Edith on his arm. A fifteen-foot train trailed after her, flecked with snow. The doors of the cathedral boomed shut, sealing away the worsening weather.

Adam led Edith down the aisle. When they reached the steps, he gently lifted the veil from her face, kissed her cheek, and went to sit beside Kirk. Edith handed her enormous bouquet to her maid of honor and turned to Owen.

Her face was utterly white, but composed. Had she seen Creswell in the audience? Or had she been so fixed on the waiting altar that she'd missed him?

Owen tried to give her an encouraging smile. She'd been so kind to Mal, the night of the dinner…

God. Mal. Why hadn't he let Mal explain? If only he had listened.

Then what? Mal would be in the audience, and he'd still be standing here. Nothing would truly have changed.

If only they'd parted on better terms, then. That at least Owen could have been done. But he'd been angry, humiliated…the idea he might have misjudged something so important, made such a mistake, had been too much to bear. So he'd acted to save himself any further pain, and in doing so wrecked everything.

The bishop began the sermon, but his voice faded to a background drone in Owen's ears. A storm must have set in; the wind howled outside, loudly enough to be heard in between rounds of organ music. Thousands of candles lit the cathedral, though, bathing it in golden light. The multitude of flowers perfumed the air, alongside the beeswax candles, and it almost seemed as if they stood amidst a spring time garden.

If only this had been the joyous new beginning the setting promised.

"Edith Alva Vandersee," the bishop said, "will you have this man to be your husband; to live together in the covenant of marriage? Will you love him, comfort him, honor and keep him, in sickness and in health; and, forsaking all others, be faithful to him as long as you both shall live?"

Tears gathered on Edith's lashes, and she visibly struggled to hold them back. "I do," she said.

Owen's heart knocked against his ribs. She was marrying him for the same reason he was marrying her: duty. They had a duty to their families. The Yates name would bring her family, including any children she bore, far more prestige than Creswell's could ever have done. It would open doors to all her relatives, including Adam and Kirk, which would have remained otherwise closed.

And with the Vandersee fortune available through regular payments to Edith, his own family's status would be assured. They wouldn't have to sell the Newport mansion, or Father's yacht. They could continue to live on Millionaires' Row; Peter could be maintained in a separate, discreet house. Everything could go on as it had; parties and fashion and the setting of taste.

The bishop turned to him. "Owen Reynard Yates, will you have this woman to be your wife; to live together in the covenant of marriage? Will you love her, comfort her, honor and keep her, in sickness and in health; and, forsaking all others, be faithful to her as long as you both shall live?"

He took a deep breath. "No," he said. "I will not."

Mal stumbled onto the stoop of Peter's house, his lashes crusted with snow, his teeth chattering. Taking a deep breath of icy air, he hung on the bell and prayed they would let him in without Owen's presence.

Clouds had already gathered to the northeast when he left Madam Galpern's, but they'd thickened rapidly into a dark line advancing over the city. In stark contrast to the blue of the clear sky, the clouds had been a horrible black-green, like a ripening bruise. Wind spread out before them, slamming the canvas awnings up and down, flinging discarded newspapers through the air, and tearing off hats.

The storm front reached him as he rode the cable car up Broadway. The air smelled of snow and something else, like ozone, maybe, even though he didn't see any lightning. Another passenger gave a startled cry, and Mal looked out the window just in time to see a wall of snow heading for them. It struck the car with shuddering force—the temperature plunged, and snow fell so thickly past the windows he couldn't even make out the sidewalk.

"This ain't natural," one of the other passengers cried, clutching at a rosary. "Holy Familiar of Christ, preserve us."

Still, the car strained on, into the blizzard. Mal tried to peer out the window, which was rapidly covered with ice and snow. By the time he climbed from the cable car at his stop, the snow had already accumulated to his ankles, and was coming down ever faster. Thank Mary he'd at least had the presence of mind to steal an overcoat from Madam Galpern's.

Even so, he was shivering hard on the stoop. The door swung open, and he found himself face to face with the footman from Thanksgiving. The man's eyes widened in surprise. "Mr. Malachi? We weren't expecting you. Did Dr. Yates send you?"

Well, Owen thought him a liar anyway. Might as well put it to use. "Aye. I need to speak with Mrs. Lewis right away."

The man stepped back. "She's in the library with Mr. Yates."

"Wonderful—this concerns him as well."

The footman frowned, but led the way. Mrs. Lewis looked up in surprise when Mal stepped into the library. "Dear heavens, Mr. Malachi! You must be chilled to the bone. Come in front of the fire—I'll make some hot chocolate up for you right away."

Saint Mary, that sounded heavenly. Unfortunately, there was no time for the niceties. "Mrs. Lewis, I need your help. Yours and Mr. Yates's."

Peter sat in his chair in front of the window. The trees outside bore a thick coat of snow, and the street rapidly disappeared under a white blanket.

The nurse frowned. "I'm sure we'll be glad to help in any way we can, sir," she said uncertainly.

Mal went to crouch by Peter's wheelchair. The pale gray eyes watching him were so like Owen's it brought a lump to this throat. Swallowing against it, he said, "You recognized the man outside the window on Thanksgiving, didn't you?"

Peter's eyes widened, and he made a noise of distress.

"Now, sir, you shouldn't go upsetting Mr. Yates," Mrs. Lewis said with a scowl. "Did Dr. Yates send you? He would have surely told you that."

Mal took a deep breath, feeling as though he'd unraveled inside. It was all too much: Owen throwing him out, spending the night in the restaurant with only coffee and the violin, Madam Galpern's betrayal and death… He wanted to collapse to the floor and cry, or sleep, not convince this woman he needed her patient's help.

"This is very important," he said, struggling to keep his voice calm. He'd thought hard on his way over, trying to come up with any way to communicate with a man who could no longer speak or write. "Peter, blink once for no, twice for yes. Did you recognize the man outside on Thanksgiving?"

Peter blinked twice in rapid succession. *Yes.*

"Well I'll be!" exclaimed Mrs. Lewis.

"And you wanted to let us know?"

Two blinks. *Yes.*

"Perhaps Mr. Yates recognized him as a friend of his brother's?" Mrs. Lewis suggested tentatively.

No.

Mal hesitated, trying to think of more yes-or-no questions. "Do you know his name?"

Yes.

"All right." Mal rubbed at his eyes. "Think, Malachi, you stupid fox.

Think! There has to be some way of communicating more efficiently."

"Sir," Mrs. Lewis said uncertainly, "I might have an idea. We have a talking board—just for fun, you understand. The cook's cousin is one of them spiritualists, you see. Had a bit of a laugh with it, nothing more. And only in our free time; that's without saying."

Probably she was afraid Mrs. Yates would have her fired for daring to enjoy herself. "Of course, Mrs. Lewis." He laid a finger alongside his nose. "No one will hear a word from me. Now what's your idea?"

"We use the planchette to point to the different letters. When we reach the right one, Mr. Yates blinks twice, and we spell out the words. Would that work?"

Mal glanced at Peter. "Peter?"

Yes.

"Get it," Mal ordered.

She obeyed with alacrity. As she returned, she said, "Sir…if this works…do you think we might be permitted to use it with Mr. Yates otherwise? To learn his wishes directly, I mean?"

He glanced up at Peter and met his gaze. Hard to say what sort of thoughts went on in that damaged brain, and it might all come to nothing, but in his place Mal would surely have been desperate for some way to talk to people.

"That's up to Mr. Yates here," Mal said. "It ain't anyone else's place to tell you what he wants or don't want. Now, we need to arrange the board where he can see it clearly while you move the planchette. I'll watch for his blinks and record the letters."

The nurse slowly moved the planchette across the letters. Peter's pale gaze remained fixed on its movements. For a long moment, Mal thought it wasn't going to work after all.

Then he blinked twice.

"Letter?" Mal barked.

"R," she said excitedly.

"Now go back to the beginning and start again."

It was frustratingly slow, but gradually the letters added up. R-O-B-E-R-T.

"Robert?" Mal asked.

Yes.

"That must be what Bertie is short for." Mal frowned. This wasn't proving to be nearly as helpful as he'd hoped.

"Shall we ask for a last name?" the nurse suggested.

Mal shook his head. "Nay. He's a familiar. He'll have given it up."

Peter let out a frantic moan. One arm jerked in distress, wrist striking against the armrest of his chair.

"I'd say Mr. Yates has more to tell us," the nurse said. "And I mean, surely this Bertie wasn't born with no last name, was he? He had one to start with."

Yes.

"All right," Mal conceded. "Then let's have it."

Painfully, letter by letter, Peter slowly spelled out Bertie's lost surname.

V-A-N-D-E-R-S-E-E.

"Vandersee," Mal whispered. "Robert Vandersee. But…wasn't that the name of the son who died?" Owen had mentioned Peter had been close with both Robert and Kirk; did Bertie just remind him of his old playmate?

The nurse sighed in disappointment. "It must be a mistake," she said, and patted Peter's hand. "As you said, Robert died years ago. And of course the Vandersees couldn't have familiar blood in their family."

Mal glanced at her. Behind her, snow was piling up against the window. The wind howled down the chimney, scattering sparks, and the clouds had cut off the sun, plunging the noontime street into twilight. "How can you be certain of that?"

She flushed. "Well, sir, you know how it is. It's all well and good for the higher ups to be witches and the like, but familiars…it would be a scandal, it would."

Mal's heart stuttered in his chest. What was it Owen had told him about the Vandersee family? "The sort of scandal that would have kept them from taking their place in society?" he asked. "Especially if, say, their younger son turned out to be a familiar just as Mrs. Vandersee was hosting her famous ball?"

The nurse went pale. "I-I suppose, but surely…no, it's not possible."

But it was. Hadn't Mal thought Kirk Vandersee looked familiar? Of course the man did; Mal had worked with Bertie half a dozen times already by then. He'd seen the family resemblance and not even realized it.

No wonder they couldn't find any photos of the killer or the men who had chased Mal—Bertie must have removed them from the rogues gallery. He'd volunteered to protect Mal, with the hopes of getting him alone and doing him in…except the opportunity had never arisen, until after Mal had already agreed to make himself useful by stealing the Star of Winter. When Mal failed to comply, they'd attacked outside with the hopes of killing him. And it would have worked, if Owen hadn't been there. Bertie hadn't intervened until Owen's life was in danger from the enraged bull familiar.

Bertie knew Nick had identified Ulysses—Nick had certainly been vocal at the Coven, even before Mal and Owen had arrived. Bertie would have had time to get to the tenement before them, shift into bear form and kill Ulysses with a single blow, and escape just as they arrived.

And he would have had plenty of opportunity to steal the device, once it was finished. Possibly the Star of Winter as well, depending on his relationship with the rest of his family.

Did Kirk know he was alive? Did Edith?

Kirk had been having an affair with Mrs. Jacobs, according to the servants Mal had overheard. But what if they had been plotting together instead? Jacobs ill-treated the servants; if he did the same to his wife, she would have been happy to see him dead. Not to mention the fact that she was in the perfect position to remove any papers listing the device among Jacobs's treasures.

And Edith. Bertie had saved Owen—or pretended to—when they were attacked by the bull and Gilbert. Mal had become a liability, but he'd wanted to keep Owen alive. For his sister's sake?

Or because every important person in New York state was currently at Owen's wedding right this moment? They would have arrived before the blizzard started.

They'd be trapped.

Fur and feathers, the rider on the cable car had been right. This blizzard wasn't natural.

Mal surged to his feet. "Peter, you're a damned hero. You might have saved a lot of lives today." If Mal wasn't already too late.

He started for the door. The nurse hurried after him. "Sir? You can't mean to leave."

"I have to warn Owen," he said. "Do you have a telephone? Call the MWP and the regular police right away, tell them there's trouble at the Yates-Vandersee wedding."

"I will, but the lines usually go down in storms like this. It's snowing something awful—you'll freeze to death if you try to cross town now!"

He flung open the door. Snow streamed down in a thick curtain, and mounds drifted across a street that had become impassable to any sort vehicle. "Nay, I won't," he said. "I'm a fox. I was made for this."

Then he shifted form and plunged out into the storm.

Chapter 19

A long moment of stunned silence hung over the cathedral—then a murmur ran through the crowd, growing louder and louder. Owen's father rose to his feet, his face as dark as the storm raging outside. "This is not funny, Owen," he said. "Now give the bishop your answer."

Owen swallowed. All his life, his father had made Owen's duties clear. To be first in everything; to obey without question; to surrender all for the good of the family. He wasn't Nathan; defiance was unthinkable. He owed his parents everything.

But surely he owed something to himself and Edith as well.

He straightened his shoulders. "I've already given the only answer my honor will allow."

"Well done," Nathan said, putting a hand to Owen's shoulder.

Owen turned to Edith, who looked as shocked as everyone else. "This is a travesty," he said. "You're a good woman, and you deserve better than this. You deserve to be happy." He smiled at her sadly. "You deserve love."

He held out his hand to her. Dazed, she put her hand in his, and he led her down the stairs.

His mother came to her feet and blocked their path. Adam Vandersee joined her.

"How dare you!" Mother hissed, her face white.

Adam's was scarlet in contrast. "Get back up those stairs, the both of you."

"No," Edith said. Her voice trembled, and Owen gave her hand a reassuring squeeze.

"You're just going to have to sell the house in Newport, Mother," he said. Then he aimed a glare at Vandersee. "And if society disapproves of selling a house to raise funds more than it disapproves selling your own children, then to hell with it. To hell with all of you."

Gasps rang out at his language. Owen stepped forward with Edith, and Mother gave way. "You'll be disinherited!" she shouted behind him. "As will you!" Adam added. "Get back here, Edith!"

Creswell rose from his seat at the end of one of the pews and stepped into the aisle. Owen glanced at Edith; her gaze was fixed on Creswell, tears streaming down her cheeks.

"Is this really happening?" she asked, when they reached him. "Am I going to wake up and find it a dream?"

Creswell blinked, beaming with happiness. "It's no dream, my darling," he said, taking her hand from Owen's. "I love you, Edith. I've asked for your hand before, but may I again? Will you be my bride, my love, my life?"

"Yes!" Joy transformed her face for Creswell, as it had not for Owen. "Oh, yes." Then she seemed to remember herself, and turned to Owen. "Will you be all right, my friend?" she asked.

He looked down on her. Outside, the storm raged. Surely it would have delayed anyone seeking to travel. He focused on the bond, on the warm spot behind his heart. Mal was somewhere to the north and west; how far, he wasn't certain, only that his familiar hadn't yet left the city.

There was still time to go to Mal. To apologize; to beg for forgiveness. He'd grovel in public, run an ad in the papers admitting he was an idiot, anything to convince Mal to give him another chance.

"Don't worry about me, Edith," he said. "And now, if you'll excuse me, there's somewhere I need to be."

He turned from the happy couple and began to walk toward the great doors. The howl of the storm penetrated the thick oak, but he didn't falter. He'd fight his way through a blizzard if that was what it took, so long as he could be at Mal's side again.

A figure stepped from the side of the narthex and blocked Owen's path to the door.

"Bertie?" Owen asked in surprise. How on earth had the familiar gotten admittance? There had been patrolmen from the regular police outside before the ceremony, making certain only those on the guest list were allowed inside, but of course they had been dismissed when the ceremony began. "What's going on? Is something wrong? Did the MWP send you?"

"I'm terribly sorry, Owen," Kirk called from behind him. Startled, Owen glanced over his shoulder and found Kirk making his way up the aisle. Another murmur of voices washed over the scene as Kirk reached Bertie's side. "But since you were kind enough to gather everyone who's anyone here today for the wedding, we can't quite let you leave yet."

He cast a cold gaze over the crowd, his eyes hard as chips of flint. "In fact, none of you will be leaving. At least, not alive."

Owen's heart beat very loudly in his ears. As outraged cries sounded behind him, two men stepped out from where they'd lurked in the narthex, moving to flank Bertie and Kirk. One of them he recognized as the bull familiar. The tower door swung open, and a stream of both men and women poured out. Most of them were poorly dressed, and all of them looked angry. They lined up along the side aisles, silent and menacing.

Were they ferals as well?

"What is the meaning of this?" Adam Vandersee marched up the aisle, his face a study in rage. "Will all my children turn against me?"

Rage transformed Bertie's face. "Why not? You turned against me first, *Father*."

Father. Bertie.

"R-Robert?" Owen gasped.

"That isn't possible!" Edith cried from behind him. "Robert died when we were children."

"No." Kirk drew himself up to his full height, leveling a glare at Adam. "That's only what Father and Mother wished us to believe, Edith. Our grandfather, the one who developed the hex used in our factories, wasn't a mere hexman as we've been led to believe. He was a *familiar*, who fled to this country after killing his cruel witch."

"Lies!" Adam shouted. "I will not hear this slander, Kirk! You've been deceived by this—this impostor."

But his protest sounded weak, as if he already knew the damage was done, and no one would believe him.

"Witch blood runs in families," Bertie said, the growl of the bear underlying his words. "If I had come to you when I was twelve years old and told you I was a witch, you would have had me tested. Bragged to your friends, even, if I scored high enough." His mouth twisted in fury. "But instead I came and told you I was a familiar. Just like your father.

And just like him, the truth had to be hidden, or else you'd never get your precious entry into society. The damnable Yateses would have seen you shunned."

Owen wanted to protest. Wanted to stand up for his family. But it was true. Mother would never have allowed a family with familiar blood into society, no matter how much money they had.

"So you chose them over me," Bertie went on, eyes narrowed. "You said we were going on the boat together, just you and I. And I was so *fucking* excited to have your attention all to myself for a while." He laughed bitterly. "Such a naïve cub. And then you took me, and you *sold* me to a witch who promised no one would ever see me again."

"Robert." Adam's voice trembled as he held up his hand. "We can speak of these things in private—"

"Do you know what he did to me?" Bertie roared. "Caged me, starved me, beat me! And of course, the law makes wider allowances when it comes to 'dangerous' familiars like bears and tigers, doesn't it? We have to be controlled; have to keep everyone safe! Just say he's dangerous, and there you have it! Muzzle him; chain him; keep him in a cage! All perfectly *legal*."

All the blood seemed to have left Owen's extremities. He set his feet in a wide stance, praying the justified rage in front of him could yet be diverted. "Bertie," he said. "I'm sorry. What happened to you was inexcusable. But some of the people in this very crowd are the ones who can change the laws. I'm sure now that they've heard your story—"

"Shut up, Owen," Kirk said. "God, you're tiresome. I can't believe Father would so demean Edith as to hand her over to a prissy fussbudget like you."

"How rude," Owen said, fighting to keep his voice steady. At least their attention was on him now, and not the innocents in the crowd. "So how did you come to the MWP, Bertie?" If he could only keep them talking, perhaps some solution would present itself. What, he couldn't imagine, but something.

Bertie's smile was crooked. "He finally slipped up. The bastard who force bonded me. He made a mistake, and I killed him. Hid his body where no one will ever find it, and returned to New York. I made new friends once I came here."

Oh no. "The theriarchists."

The ferals murmured their approval. Bertie inclined his head. "Eventually I gathered the courage to find my brother again. I prayed he didn't know the truth, and that he'd remember what it was like, when we were young. How inseparable we had been."

Kirk's hand settled on Bertie's shoulder. "I spent years mourning my brother." His voice was raw and ragged. "I was the oldest. He was my responsibility. For years I prayed to God to undo what had happened, to change our places so I could be the one on the water that day. Only to find out it had all been a cruel lie. My whole life from age thirteen on. Nothing but a damned lie."

"I did it to protect you," Adam objected. Owen ground his teeth together—did the man have no sense of self preservation? "And your sister. I did it for our family!"

"Shut up!" Kirk screamed. His voice echoed in the rafters, but the shriek of the wind outside nearly drowned it out. "You did it for yourself! But I see it all now. I see the corruption at the very heart of society. Nothing will change unless we force it to."

"And you have the ear of all these people now," Owen said frantically. "What happened to Bertie is abominable. Just—"

"An ear isn't enough." Kirk's eyes gleamed with a mix of fury and despair. "They'll never listen to reason. Try to tame a viper, and it will only bite you. Better to cut off its head."

Oh God.

Last January, the theriarchists had aimed to kill the new government of Greater New York. They'd failed…but here, today, were gathered an even larger concentration of government officials. Of heads of business.

A slaughter here would change the landscape across politics, across business, send shockwaves through all of society both in America and elsewhere.

"Owen!"

Owen stiffened in shock. *"Mal?"*

"Owen, please, just listen. I know you think I'm a liar, but just believe me, just this once. Bertie—he's Robert Vandersee."

A part of Owen almost wanted to laugh. Of course his clever fox had figured it out, though how he couldn't imagine at the moment. *"I know."*

"You do?"

"Yes. Because he's about to kill us all."

Terror flashed through their bond, which was strange, because an odd sort of calm had settled over Owen himself. *"Saint Mary, no. Owen, I'm coming."*

"No. Don't. Run, Mal. Get as far away as you can."

"Like hell I am! Use my magic, damn you! I'm on my way."

Owen took a deep breath. Adam Vandersee was yelling, as were others, but it all seemed very far away. *"I'm sorry, Mal. I realized this morning just how badly I've wronged you. I hoped...well. It doesn't matter now. Just run. Leave New York and save yourself. And, please, if you can find it in your heart...try not to despise me too much.*

"I love you. Now go."

Mal raced through the blizzard, tongue lolling out with exertion. His wide paws carried him over the top of the snow, and his thick coat kept the cold at bay. If he'd been a cat or a bird, he'd never have made it.

The snow came down almost horizontally, driven by the screaming winds. The city had ground to a standstill. Broadway was buried in snow and transformed into a forest of abandoned carts and wagons. Even the cable cars had come to a halt.

There came a loud crack, and he dove for the cover of a pushcart as an electrical pole toppled into the street. Wires snapped and sparked, and another pole gave way.

Fur and feathers, that was all he needed. To step onto a wire, half-hidden by the snow, and get electrocuted before he could reach Owen.

Owen...

Pulses of fear came through the bond now. He wanted to reach out to Owen again, to make sure he was all right—but if Owen was in a fight for his life, distracting him would be the worst thing Mal could do. At least he knew Owen still lived.

Mal slithered out from beneath the pushcart and picked his way over and around the fallen wires. A group of uniformed police were trying to struggle through the storm, but he doubted they would get far.

Which meant there was no help coming for those trapped in the cathedral, even if Mrs. Lewis had managed to get a call through.

At last the cathedral's enormous tower appeared, though its peak was lost amidst the driving snow. Mal wanted to charge up the steps, throw open the doors, join Owen—

But that seemed a fast way to get killed. So he pushed on through the snow, to the walled garden butting up against one side of the cathedral. Ordinarily, there was no entrance save through the church itself, but he was slim enough in fox form to squeeze between the iron bars. The door leading into the nave was shut, but the sound of screams and smell of blood reached through it.

Mal shifted back into human form. Taking a deep breath, he threw open the door, slipped back into his fur, and darted inside before his courage could fail him.

The interior of the cathedral had transformed into a slaughterhouse. Nearly a dozen ferals were inside, all of them the big, dangerous types: at least one tiger, two grizzly bears, a bull, and a whole pack of wolves. Trellises decorated with pink chrysanthemums lay overturned, the flowers crushed and drowned in blood. Someone had flipped over a pew, and the men who had brought guns to the wedding fired from behind it, protecting the entrance to the choir loft where screaming masses of guests huddled in terror. A stag with bloody antlers kicked at the closed vestry door, where presumably more of the weddings guests had taken refuge.

The familiars of the witches among the guests were fighting back. An owl swooped at the face of one of the bears, and a greyhound rushed in to nip at the stag's back legs. But all of them were the smaller, more common sorts of animal, and Mal knew they fought a losing battle.

A group of men and women stood back to back in the chancel, brandishing candelabras like spears. Mal glimpsed Edith among them, her white dress spattered with red, a grim look on her face. Whatever Bertie's plans, she clearly hadn't been a part of them.

And there, on the other side of the nave, not far from the entrance to the tower, stood Owen.

His fine suit was torn and stained, but his silver eyes blazed with defiance. He clutched one of the candelabras, white ribbon and pink flowers still trailing from it.

In front of him, gun drawn, stood Kirk Vandersee.

Mal exploded into a run. A startled roar came from behind him, and he dodged beneath a pew as the tiger lunged. The big cat hit the pew, hard enough to send it crashing into another, but Mal was already out from beneath it.

"Mal!" Edith shouted. He glimpsed a blond man beside her, arm raised. An instant later, an incense burner struck the tiger on the side of the head. Ash and coals went everywhere, and the tiger turned its anger on them, its roar shaking the building. A raven familiar joined in, tweaking the tiger's tail, then soaring away.

Mal hoped they'd be all right, but he didn't have time to spare. Without so much as slowing, he cannoned out from between the pews and sank his teeth into Kirk's calf.

Kirk let out a cry, and the gun fired. Terror shot through Mal, but a moment later, Owen swung the candelabra, striking the weapon from Kirk's hand.

Kirk tore free, and Mal leapt back, his mouth full of blood. Kirk collapsed against one of the pews, swearing furiously as he clutched his wounded leg. Mal started for him again, but Owen said, "Never mind him! Come on!"

He ran for the tower door. Mal followed, transforming into human shape as they passed into the bell ringing chamber. The bell ropes hung down through the hollow center of the tower, bracketed on all sides by winding wooden steps.

"What are we doing?" Mal called as Owen started up the stairs.

Owen glanced down at him. Blood speckled his glasses, and he looked worn and afraid.

"The storm isn't natural," Owen said. "Those hexes I didn't recognize on the device seem to have been indeed associated with weather magic. If I'm right, Kirk placed the device at the top of the tower, which means we have to get up there, stop the storm, and use the device to cast a sleeping hex. With luck, it will be powerful enough to halt the carnage down here."

"I always said you were clever." After the long run, mounting the steps of the tower was torture. Mal's legs ached, put he pushed forward. He could do this, for Owen's sake.

Owen shook his head. "I thought I told you to run the other way."

Mal grinned. "Aye, but I knew a nob like you would be lost without me."

"That I would," Owen said, affection in his voice. Just as when he'd told Mal he loved him.

The tower door slammed open below. Mal leaned over the rail, and saw the golden-brown fur and enraged eyes of an enormous grizzly.

"Oh hell," he said. "It's Bertie."

Chapter 20

The wooden stairs shook beneath the massive bear's weight as Bertie climbed after them. Owen's heart pounded madly—God, they'd never be able to outrun him. Even if either of them had been up to a race to the top of the tower, he wouldn't have time to change the device to a sleeping hex before Bertie was on them.

So they had to slow him down.

"Keep going!" Owen ordered, and pulled his wallet from his breast pocket. Inside was the fire hex he'd drawn to seal the bond between himself and Mal.

Owen slapped it down onto the wooden stair. Bertie roared beneath them, close enough now for Owen to see the enormous fangs.

Owen leapt back. "Ignite!" he shouted.

The worn wood of the step burst into flame, answering Bertie's roar with one of its own. The bear cried out in pain, falling back as the flames seared his muzzle.

Owen didn't wait to see what happened next, just charged up the steps, past Mal. "Run; run!" he shouted.

Mal followed him, panting. Already, smoke began to rise past them. "You slowed him down, but setting the stairs on fire behind us means we'll be trapped up here!"

"The fire suppression hexes on the cathedral will keep it from spreading," Owen said. "The only reason it's burning as much as it is, is because the hex is so strong."

The smoke died away quickly. Owen panted, lungs heaving from exertion. Landing after landing fell away beneath them—they must be close to the belfry.

Mal stumbled to a halt, gasping for breath. "Just a moment," he wheezed. "I need—"

The stairs shook beneath Bertie's weight as the grizzly charged up behind them. The thick fur on one side of his face was seared away, and he let out a roar of fury upon seeing them.

Mal's eyes widened. "The bell ropes! Jump!"

Mal led the way, flinging himself into the open center of the tower. He grabbed one of the dangling ropes. The bell it was attached to started clanging wildly.

Owen hesitated. If he jumped and missed, he'd surely fall to his death.

Behind him, Bertie reared up on his hind legs.

"Owen!" Mal shouted. He swung back toward them, grabbing a rope as he passed it, and shoving it in Owen's direction. His boots struck the side of Bertie's head, and the bear swiped at him. But Mal had already pushed off, swinging back the other way, switching from one rope to the next as he passed it.

Owen caught the rope Mal had sent in his direction. Gripping it tightly, he squeezed his eyes shut and leapt.

The bells clanged madly overhead. Owen opened his eyes, and found himself swinging above the dizzying shaft of the tower. The floor of the bell ringing chamber had to be a good two-hundred feet below.

Bertie roared in frustration. His bear form might be useful on the stairs, but he couldn't reach them on the ropes. Of course, they didn't dare leave the ropes now with Bertie there to catch them.

Mal swung on his rope, the arc not quite wide enough to bring him within Bertie's reach again. "Bertie!" he called. "Good job, trying to kill your sister on her own wedding day. She never did anything to you. Is that the theriarchy idea of how to treat people? Because I don't think much of it."

Owen cast a wild glance at Mal. What on earth was he up to?

The bear growled.

"Yes," called Owen. His arms ached, and he couldn't think about what might be going on below. "Your quarrel was with your father, not Edith! She didn't even know you were alive."

Bertie shifted back to human form. The fire had blistered one side of his face, but rage reddened it even further. "My *quarrel* is with a society that feeds on familiars, yet treats us like livestock. It's all coming down, Yates. Starting with you."

"Big words, for someone who's just standing there doing nothing!" Mal challenged.

Bertie snarled and leapt for one of the bell ropes. Its clangs added to the cacophony Mal was already creating, the entire tower resounding with their peals. Mal changed ropes, a heart-stopping movement, just as he and Bertie swung past each other.

"Missed me!" Mal shouted.

Owen realized too late that Bertie's trajectory would bring the bear straight into him. He tried to swing his weight to the side as Mal had, but ended up spinning in place. Bertie crashed into him, and they swung locked together. "I'm going to eat your little fox up in one gulp," he snarled into Owen's face. Clinging to the rope with one hand, Bertie reached for the knife at his belt.

A look of surprise crossed his face, and he blinked.

"Looking for this?" Mal asked as he swung back toward them.

The blade flashed, and the rope supporting Bertie parted before its keen edge. He let out a maddened yell and grabbed for Owen—but it was already too late.

Owen didn't look down to see whether he survived the fall. It seemed unlikely, to say the least.

Mal swung past, grabbing Owen by the waist and sending them both hurtling for the landing. "Jump!" Mal cried.

Once both feet were safely on the landing, Owen wrapped his arms around Mal. "How did you do that?"

"I'm a thief, ain't I? I lifted it when he swung past me." Mal pulled away and held the knife up. "Some of my best work, if I do say so myself."

"Quite." Owen resisted the temptation to hug Mal close again. "Now come—we're almost at the top."

The stairs ended at the pinnacle of the tower. Owen heaved the trap door open with a grunt; blowing snow had made its way beneath the roof of the small, open-sided room, and drifted across the floor.

Shaking with exhaustion, Mal followed him out. The wind screamed around them, and in human form his skin went numb almost instantly. Shivering, he followed Owen across the floor.

The device sat near the center of the tower, just as Owen had suspected. And on it, held in place by the delicate clamps on the front, was the Star of Winter.

Someone—Kirk, no doubt—had pried the twelve-pointed star sapphire free from the rest of the necklace. Held in the device and charged with magic, it glowed with an almost unearthly light.

"Dear lord," Owen said, crouching in the snow in front of the device and running his hand over the sapphire. "I never thought…but of course star sapphires have affinity with the heavens. Exactly what you'd use in weather magic."

Mal snorted and came to kneel beside him. "You didn't even guess? What kind of hexman are you, anyway?"

"Hmph. Watch and learn, fox."

Owen opened the clamps and removed the Star of Winter, before handing it to Mal. A bit surprised, Mal tucked it into his pocket. "All right," Owen said, manipulating the levers and crank on the device. The plates shifted back and forth in a dizzying dance that meant nothing to Mal. "One sleeping hex. Add in another hex to increase the area of effect, and a third to limit it to familiars." He sat back on his heels and bit his lip.

"What are you waiting for?" Mal asked. "Charge it!"

Owen put his palm on the device…then hesitated. "You remember what we spoke of. That the device could be dangerous. This will take a great deal of magic," he cautioned. "Likely you'd lose consciousness even without the sleeping hex. It might even…even hurt you."

Mal had heard stories of stripped familiars, their magic drained until they died. Snow and pellets of ice stung his face, and his hands had gone numb with cold. "There are people dying down there," he said, and didn't care that his voice shook. "So if I don't make it…tell the survivors they owe their lives to a thief."

Owen's fingers closed over his wrist, pulling him near. "You're more than a thief, damn it." A glaze of tears showed in his silvery eyes. "I'm so sorry I said those things. I was a fool, and I wish I could undo it all."

"I know." Mal took in a deep, shuddering breath. "Do it."

The tug on that space behind his heart was sharp, but no different than any other time Owen had funneled his magic into a hex. But it kept going…and kept going, as if the device were thirsty for everything he had to give.

He sagged to the side, his strength pouring out like blood. The world turned ashen, but the cold seemed to fade. He was warm, now. Warm, but oh so very sleepy.

His eyes slid closed. Distantly, he heard Owen shout something in what might have been Greek.

Then everything dissolved into blackness.

"Mal!" Owen cried.

The hex had worked—that was all. It had sent Mal into a deep sleep, along with the other familiars. The storm's wind moaned around him, but weaker now that the magic binding it in place was gone. No sounds came from the church below, either because the slaughter had ended or because they were too high now to hear anything.

Owen opened his wallet, dumping out hexes in his haste. He found the counter-hex he needed and slapped it onto Mal's forehead. "Awaken!" he ordered.

Nothing happened. Mal didn't stir.

"No," Owen said. He tore at the scarf around Mal's neck, frantic to check his pulse. Mal's head lolled to the side as he pulled on the fabric, and oh God, his face was so white. Pale as the snow, and just as cold.

"No," Owen said again. The scarf fell away at last, and he pressed his fingers to Mal's flesh. But they were so numb from the icy air, he could barely feel anything.

"Mal!" he shook the smaller man's form. "Mal, wake up! Wake up." Blinking through tears, he caressed Mal's face with his hand. "Wake up."

"My only regret," Kirk said, "is that I don't get to kill you both."

Before Owen could react, hands seized his collar and wrenched him to his feet. He found himself staring into Kirk's face. His old friend's expression was utterly transformed by rage; lips taut against his teeth, eyes wild.

"You killed Bertie!" Kirk screamed. "I'd just found him again, and you've killed him!"

Owen twisted and fought against Kirk's hold, but fury seemed to have lent Kirk the strength of ten men. He hauled Owen across the floor, heels scraping over the stone—and thrust him half-over the railing.

The hard limestone dug into Owen's lower back, and the collar of his coat nearly strangled him. He got an upside-down glimpse of the city, half-hidden through the curtain of snow and sleet. The ground was far below—nearly three hundred feet, and he clutched wildly at Kirk's arms, while the wind screamed and threatened to pull them both from the tower.

Kirk leaned over him. Snow crusted his hair and eyebrows, making him look even more savage. "I thought you were just a symptom of the disease infecting society," he growled. "I almost pitied you as much as I pitied Edith!"

"Kirk, please!" Owen cried. "You don't have to do this. The familiars below are asleep—you've lost!"

"We haven't lost anything." Kirk's eyes burned with unholy fire. "We're just getting started. With the device to aid us, we're going to reshape the world."

"Are you, now?" Mal asked.

Kirk jerked back, pulling Owen in just far enough to see Mal. The familiar stood swaying, but on his feet. The wind blew strands of his red hair across his pale face, and his amber eyes blazed with fury. In his hands, he held the device.

"Well, then, Kirk," he went on, hefting the device. "I guess you'd better catch it!"

Mal heaved the device at them. Kirk let go of Owen and lunged for it. It brushed the edge of his fingertips—and past, flying over the edge of the tower and into the vast, empty space beyond.

Overbalanced, Kirk wavered for a moment, his body angled dangerously far over the railing. Then the icy slush beneath his shoe slipped, and with a shriek, he tipped over the edge.

Owen twisted about, just in time to see Kirk and the device impact the side of the cathedral, bounce, then strike again, before hitting the ground far below in a shower of blood and shattered gears.

"Owen!" Mal gasped.

They fell into each other's arms, safely away from the rail. Owen clutched Mal to him, breathing deep. "Oh God," he whispered. "I thought you were dead. I thought—"

"I'm fine." Mal pulled back to look up at him. "Well, that's a lie. I feel like I'm about to fall over, and I've no idea how I'll make it back down from here. But I'm alive."

"Thank God." Owen bent to kiss him, but Mal put a shaking finger to his lips.

"You're married now, remember?" Mal said with a wistful smile.

"No." Owen shook his head. "I couldn't go through with making both Edith and myself miserable for the rest of our lives. I declined the honor in front of all society. I'll be disowned, most likely, but I don't care." He offered Mal a wistful smile of his own. "Do you still want me, even if I'm penniless?"

The look of joy on Mal's face made Owen feel as if he stood in the midst of spring, rather than a winter storm. "All I ever wanted was you," Mal said. "Just as you are."

Then he pulled Owen close and kissed him, until the wind drove them inside.

Chapter 21

Several weeks later, Mal held open the door to the laboratory beneath the Coven, while Owen carried in the last of the boxes. "There," Owen said, putting it on the table with the others. "Now all we have to do is unpack, and it will be as if we never left."

Mal touched the silver familiar's badge pinned to his vest. "Not quite. I wasn't a copper before."

After the battle at the cathedral, the Police Board and Chief Ferguson couldn't really object when Owen asked for his old job back. Of course, returning had required quite a sacrifice on Mal's part. Joining the coppers instead of running from them was a new experience, that was for sure.

And probably some of them would still look askance at him, though he'd gotten a gruff apology from Ferguson, at least. Seeing the happiness on Owen's face, though, made it all worthwhile.

Mal hopped onto the table and watched while Owen took out his diplomas to return to the hooks still in the wall. "So, what did the letter from Nathan say?"

Thankfully, Owen's family had escaped the slaughter in the cathedral without harm, after taking refuge in the vestry with the bishop. In the aftermath, when the newspapers praised Owen's quick thinking in large headlines, his mother decided against disowning him after all. A week later, the Fifth Avenue mansion quietly went up for sale, and Mr. and Mrs. Yates retired to the house in Newport. Society, it seemed, would have to go on without them.

It would have to go on without a great many others, as well. Though the majority of the guests had survived, a congressman, the owners of several banks, and a coal baron had died at the teeth and claws of the theriarchists. Already, the papers ran angry opinions demanding the government do something to regulate and restrain ferals. No laws had been passed yet, but Mal feared what would happen to familiars like Nick when they finally were.

"You can read the letter, if you like," Owen said as he hung the diplomas carefully. "In short, Edith—or should I say, Mrs. Creswell—is enjoying her honeymoon in France. Given the conduct of her parents and brothers, Nathan doubts she'll ever return to New York, and instead will live as quietly as she can on the continent." A pensive look crossed his face as he stepped back and eyed his handiwork. "I hope she's well, and that she and Creswell have a good life together."

"So do I." Mal slipped off the desk and wrapped his arms around his lover from behind. "I always liked her. Not enough to want to see her married to you, mind you."

Owen's hands settled over Mal's. "Speaking of unhappy marriages, Quigley sent a note by this morning," Owen said. "Mrs. Jacobs finally confessed. Apparently Jacobs was as beastly to her as he was to the servants—and vindictive enough to ruin her utterly if she'd asked for a divorce. Kirk found out and approached her with a proposal. He'd get rid of Mr. Jacobs, and in return all she had to do was remove any paperwork listing the device among the things Jacobs had brought from Egypt."

A shiver went through Mal, and he hugged Owen tighter. "If you hadn't happened by that night, it would have worked. No one would have known anything had been stolen. I would have gone to the electric chair for killing Jacobs."

"And likely the rest of us would have died at the wedding, yes." Owen turned in Mal's arms and pulled him close. "How odd it is to think the both of us would be dead, if not for a whim on my part."

"Aye." Mal pressed his cheek against Owen's chest, enjoying the warmth. Owen smelled faintly of spruce—they'd gotten a small tree for the apartment, to mark the holiday season. "Are you going to try to replicate the device?"

Owen was silent for a long moment. "I don't think so," he said at last. "I've been asked, of course, by Ferguson and the Police Board. The original was smashed beyond all hope of repair this time, and Bertie burned my notes, but with enough time I might be able to reconstruct it.

And a part of me wonders if it couldn't be done safely...but no. It was too dangerous. Let the knowledge be lost for another two-thousand years."

"I certainly ain't going to disagree with that," Mal said fervently. He'd been laid flat for a week after charging the device. "That thing was a menace to familiars. You'd think the theriarchists of all people would realize that."

"Yes." Owen sighed again. "I only wish we'd been able to find out more, before the executions."

All of the theriarchists captured by the sleeping hex at the cathedral had been swiftly tried and put to death. Though Mal couldn't feel much sympathy for them, he had to agree, it would have been nice to know who else might still be out there.

"Someone knows history," he said quietly. "The Viking hex, this device...you said it yourself. But none of the ferals at the cathedral had that sort of knowledge. Except for Bertie, most of them didn't have much of anything in the way of an education. And even his ended when he turned, what, twelve?"

"With any luck, the mastermind, whoever they might be—assuming it is only one person—was smart enough to flee the country," Owen said. "And will give up their dreams of stirring up any more trouble."

Mal doubted it, but he didn't say so aloud. Instead, he tipped his head back and regarded Owen. "You're happy to be back here, ain't you?"

Owen's smile warmed him to his toes. "Yes. But I'm especially glad to be here with you."

"I've something for you," Mal said. "To mark the occasion. It's in that cabinet, there."

Looking puzzled, Owen crossed to one of the cabinets, where Mal had hidden his surprise earlier. He opened the door—then let out a gasp.

"A new violin!" Owen turned to Mal, a delighted smile transforming his face.

Mal shrugged awkwardly. "I owed you one, after breaking the other on Madam Galpern's face. Play it for me tonight?"

"I'll play it for you any time you wish." Owen drew Mal close and kissed him tenderly. "I love you, Malachi."

"And I love you, Owen Yates." Mal stepped back and removed Owen's hexman's tools from the box they'd been packed in. "Now, come on. Let's make some magic."

Share Your Experience

If you enjoyed this book, please consider leaving a review on the site where you purchased it, or on Goodreads.

Thank you for your support of independent authors!

End Note

Thank you for reading Hexmaker. I hope you enjoyed reading Owen and Mal's story as much as I enjoyed writing it. Whether this is your first book of mine, or you've read my entire backlist, I invite you to join my Facebook group Widdershins Knows Its Own.

Mrs. Vandersee's grand ball and admission into society is loosely based on the real life showdown between Alva Vanderbilt and Caroline Astor. Mrs. Astor set the rules of society, including the critical division between the "nobs" and "swells," with nobs being a genteel three generations removed from the founding of their fortunes. Mrs. Vanderbilt wasn't about to be shut out of society just because she didn't meet that arbitrary standard, and eventually triumphed by throwing a fancy dress ball in 1883, which was estimated to cost over $250,000—equivalent to an astonishing $5.6 million in today's dollars.

The blizzard of November 26, 1898, was a real storm, which pounded New York and brought the city to a standstill. As far as I am aware, however, it was an entirely natural event in our world, and not the product of dangerous magic.

Though we now think of Thanksgiving as a time to gather extended family in the kitchen of whatever poor family member gets stuck with feeding them all, in the late 1890s it was far more typical to eat out at a restaurant. Hence the fact the elder Yateses are planning to eat at Delmonico's rather than host a family gathering on Thanksgiving. Nor did the typical workman receive the day off; holidays from work were both unpaid and exceedingly rare.

Dr. Young's Rectal Dilators were sold as medical devices from the end of the century through 1940. If you do a quick image search, you'll note their rather suggestive shape. Though presumably some people did use them as prescribed, these forerunners of the modern butt plug were doubtless often put to the entertaining use Mal and Owen found for them.

About The Author

Jordan L. Hawk is a trans author from North Carolina. Childhood tales of mountain ghosts and mysterious creatures gave him a life-long love of things that go bump in the night. When he isn't writing, he brews his own beer and tries to keep the cats from destroying the house. His best-selling Whyborne & Griffin series (beginning with *Widdershins*) can be found in print, ebook, and audiobook.

If you're interested in receiving Jordan's newsletter and being the first to know when new books are released, please sign up at his website: http://www.jordanlhawk.com. Or join his Facebook reader group, Widdershins Knows Its Own.

Printed in Great Britain
by Amazon